CIRCLE OF LOVE

By

Dawn Elizabeth

© 2000, 2003 by Dawn Elizabeth. All rights reserved.

No part of this book may be reproduced, stored in a retrieval system, or transmitted by any means, electronic, mechanical, photocopying, recording, or otherwise, without written permission from the author.

ISBN: 1-4033-3331-9 (e-book)
ISBN: 1-4033-3332-7 (Paperback)

This book is printed on acid free paper.

1stBooks – rev. 03/28/03

Prologue

Michael stood in the beautiful heavens and looked down upon the Earth as the tiny baby girl was born. His heart was filled with an unspeakable joy as he listened to her newborn cries. She had been one of His most precious creations; her heart and soul would be joined with a baby boy who had been born months earlier. These two souls would share a love that would last throughout all of time. They would both endure a long, hard road on their path of life until the day that they were destined to be united.

As if they were one soul occupying two bodies, they would feel each other's emotions and know each other's thoughts. They alone would know the meaning of true love. They were His chosen souls to live and love in the way He had meant for it to be. Very few on Earth are granted His gift of true undying love.

The guardian angel smiled as he turned and looked down upon the infant boy, who he would walk with and guide throughout his life. He knew all of the obstacles that would try to keep him from finding his true love. The angel drew in a deep breath, as he knew how difficult the road was going to be for this child. He found peace in knowing the joy that he would feel once he was united with his love. Slowly tears filled the angel's eyes, he also knew the pain and heartache he would feel when the child was taken from his love. The angel smiled as he found the solace in knowing that the love that these two souls felt for each other would bring love to another who was so deserving of it.

Their love is as a circle…it has no beginning and it has no end. Their love is not measured in time, whether it is days, weeks, or months. It does not exist only in living, but also in death.

Michael laughed a loud joyous laughter as he heard the choir of angels in Heaven singing a beautiful song meant for these two gifted souls; for the girl who would grow into a beautiful woman who would pray unto the Heavenly Father for a love that He has already created for her, and for the boy who would grow into a strikingly handsome man and would adore this woman unconditionally. He would become a man— who through an abundance of pain, struggle, and deep sacrifice would understand that love exists in letting go.

Michael's voice sounded across the heavens as he joined in with the hundreds of other angels. Their voices united in splendid harmony as the sun shone brightly on Earth and they all watched as the Circle of Love began to grow.

Chapter 1

Beth quickly wiped the tear from the corner of her eye as she reached down and pulled the covers up around her nude body. Afraid that he would see the sadness on her face, she tried to think of something casual to say to him as he slowly got up from the bed and started getting dressed.

"Your haircut looks real nice, Joe. I thought you were going to let your hair grow a bit", she started.

"Thanks. I was going to grow it out...I am not sure what changed my mind."

Beth knew the next words she said would cause an unwelcome response from the man she had just made love with.

"Why don't you spend the night?" she asked before she lost her nerve. The kids are away for the weekend and I'm here by myself. I'd love the company..."

Joe reached for his jeans that he had laid neatly on floor. He felt his heart beat faster as he listened to her request. He wanted so much to stay in bed with her and for once feel her body next to his as he slept, but he knew he couldn't. Slowly he pulled his pants up and let out a heavy sigh. He did not want to leave her feeling sad and heartbroken as he normally did, but he could not give her the response that he knew she wanted to hear.

"You know I can't stay. We don't have that kind of a relationship. We have an understanding. Please don't start down that road again."

He knew his words would be like a sharp knife cutting deep into her heart. He hated hurting her but he knew that he would hurt her more if he stayed. He quickly picked up his shirt from the floor and pulled it on over his head. Beth jumped up from the bed and grabbed her robe. She tightened the belt around her waist and walked over to where Joe was dressing.

"Joe", she whispered, "Please stay. Can't we be more than sexual partners? I want more than this," she finished then glanced over his shoulder in the direction of the bed.

Joe closed his eyes and drew in a heavy breath. He felt his heart ache as he heard her soft voice pleading for him to stay.

"Beth, why do you always do this? Why? We have talked about this before...this is all we will ever be." He replied in a harsh, angered voice as he spun around and pointed to the bed.

He turned around to see that once again he had caused tears to fill her eyes. In his heart he wanted to take her in his arms and dry her tears, but his intellect wouldn't allow him to. He swiftly moved around her and headed out the bedroom door. Beth followed him down the stairs and painfully watched as Joe quickly slid his feet into his loafers and reached for the front door. For a brief moment he stood frozen holding onto the doorknob before he pulled the door open and stepped outside. The tears quickly ran down her face as she locked the door and watched out the picture window as he jumped into his truck. She wrapped her arms around herself and began to quiver as she watched the man she gave all her passion to back out of her driveway. Finally, when she could no longer

CIRCLE OF LOVE

see the taillights of his truck she turned around and silently walked over to the steps and sat down. She stared aimlessly into space not understanding Joe's actions and words. She had spent many nights experiencing a divine level of intimate pleasure with him. The lovemaking they shared was as breath taking as what could be read in romance novels. She was overwhelmed with sadness realizing she had never spent any other kind of moment with him other than in her bed.

Outside raindrops began to burst from the clouds. "Tap tap tap" they sounded as they hit the glass. Beth raised her head and watched as the droplets steadily flowed down the picture window. She raised her hand and brushed away the tears that had streamed down her face.

"The angels in Heaven are crying with me," she thought, then stood up and headed up to her room.

Behind her in the shadows of the moonlight the guardian angel stood silently, observing all that had happened that evening. He let out a heavy sigh and softly whispered. "Yes, my sweet Beth, the angels are crying. But they are not crying out of sadness, but rather out of joy because they know what is to come.

The angel looked up in the direction to which Beth had gone and smiled. He knew she would be sleeping soon and his presence would not be needed. There was another soul that he needed to attend to. He turned around and stepped into a soft light and vanished.

Chapter 2

It was a beautiful fall day. The trees were all dressed in magnificent colors of rust, red, and yellow. As the gentle wind blew, the branches of the tree swayed back and forth as if doing a slow waltz. Several brightly colored leaves fell from the branches twirling and spinning as they gradually found their way to the ground below. A bright yellow leaf, the color of sunlight, danced with the wind. twirling around and around as if it waited for the perfect moment to come to its resting place. As if being lead by a gentle hand, it floated down from the sky, softly landing on a bronze colored automobile that was moving at a snail's pace down the road.

The dark haired man in the vehicle slowly turned down the side street and headed towards a house he had been to on many occasions. He smiled to himself as he pulled into the driveway. He knew there was a beautiful woman who lived in this house with her two children. He had never had any conversations with her, only delivered his pizza and left. Oddly though, he always had an incredible feeling run through his soul when the two of them were close enough to touch. It only lasted while the two of them were near each other and would fade as the other left. He put his car in park and glanced up to see the young boy looking out the front window as he waited for the pizza to be delivered. The man grinned to himself as he opened his door and quickly got out of the car. He retrieved the red warming bag from his trunk, which held the pizza he knew the boy was waiting for. He put the lid of the trunk down and glanced up at the large picture window to see the boy was no longer standing there. He took a deep breath and headed towards the front porch of the house. He wondered if the feeling would return when she came to the door. He shook his head trying to clear his thoughts and rang the doorbell.

Beth Hanson was a pretty little lady standing five feet two inches. She was of average shape, not skinny, but not fat either. She had nice curves in all the right places. Her hair was shoulder length and the color of golden honey. Often she would wear it in a ponytail high on her head giving her a bouncy young appearance. She had wispy bangs and small strands of hair that had fallen from the ponytail gently framing her face. Her eyes were the color of blue star sapphires and seemed to sparkle just as much. When she smiled it would make them twinkle all the more. She was dressed in gray leggings and an oversized charcoal colored sweater that hung down to the mid-thigh level. On her feet she wore white socks that were pushed down around her ankles. Even though the clothes she was wearing were not something that would make some glamorous fashion statement, anyone who saw her could not deny she was as cute as a button.

Beth was 36 years old and had been divorced for five years. During that time, she had dated a number of men but no one seemed to capture her heart. She would date someone for a while and feel content until the gentlemen would start to get too close to her, expecting her to love them in the same way that they loved her. The moment she felt that they expected her love in return, she would quickly break off the relationship

Dawn Elizabeth

leaving the man completely puzzled as to what he had done to provoke her coldness.

Now standing on their porch stood an extremely handsome, tall, dark haired man. His hair was the color of ebony, his eyes so dark brown that it was hard to tell where the pupils ended and the irises began. The warmth that radiated from his eyes would melt any heart that was guarded by ice. His facial features were soft, having a small thin nose and small lips with the upper lip being covered by a well-groomed moustache. His face was so soft that if the moustache were taken away he would easily be mistaken for a man many years younger than his actual age. He was dressed in a pair of blue jeans and green pullover shirt with the name of Ralph's Pizzeria embroidered with its logo in small white letters on his right chest.

When the doorbell rang, Gregory quickly ran to open the door for the man who was delivering their Friday night dinner. He smiled as he saw the man patiently standing on the front porch holding the warming bag in his hands. The stranger did not flinch when, all of a sudden, a crisp fall breeze blew around him causing his hair to blow back away from his face. For a brief moment, the teenager looked directly into the eyes of the deliveryman and saw the warmth that radiated from the man's soul. He turned his head slightly to the side and wondered if this man would ever be able to touch his mother's heart. Realizing he was staring, the boy quickly asked him the total for the delivery.

"That will be sixteen dollars," he said with a deep voice. He slowly removed the pizza and contents from his warming bag and handed them to the boy.

CIRCLE OF LOVE

Gregory smiled taking the hot box containing the pizza and a small brown bag filled with breadsticks and cheese dip. Politely he asked the man to wait a moment while he went to get the money from his mother. He then turned and stepped back into the house when he heard his mother coming. Beth descended a stairway and moved towards the deliveryman with the money in her hand. She stopped to glance over her shoulder as she noticed her two kids watching her, each waiting to see what her reaction would be to this handsome man on their porch. She gave them both a quick smile, shaking her head, reading both of their thoughts. She turned back to the man and asked, "I'm sorry what did you say the total was?"

"The total is sixteen dollars", he repeated.

As she was giving him the money their eyes made contact for only a second, but in that second a strange feeling rushed through her entire body; a feeling that she had never experienced before. It was an odd sensation that was hard to describe. It was a feeling of warmth and familiarity, a feeling that made her entire body tingle and her heart race, and for that short moment she felt an odd sensation of happiness that she had never known. He took the money and gave her a smile then turned and walked away. She slowly closed the door behind him and the feeling was gone.

"Hey, Mom, what did you think of him? Did you think he was handsome?" Gregory asked.

"Yeah, Mom, did you think he was handsome?" Tiffany also asked.

"Yes, he is very nice looking. But he didn't even notice me," she said as she walked into the kitchen to

Dawn Elizabeth

get dishes for their dinner. She let out a soft sigh as she remembered the strange feeling she had received when their eyes had met. She shook her head trying to block out the thoughts and called to her children. "Come on, guys, let's eat."

Time seemed to pass very quickly and for two years that tall, handsome man would often deliver pizza to her door. Sometimes she would be by herself. She would greet him at the door with towels on her head, or in sweats or sometimes even with her face tear streaked because of the loneliness that sometimes overwhelmed her. He never seemed to notice her, or what she was wearing. It was as if he never really had taken a good look at her. He never said much to her just told her what the total was, handed her order, then took her money and returned to his car.

One evening, when the kids were with their father, she decided that she wasn't going to have her pizza delivered, but rather she would place an order and pick it up herself. The owner of the pizza place was someone whom her family had known for years. He was a kind, caring man who most people found easy to talk to. He was very witty and had a great sense of humor and, on occasion, could be very sarcastic. He had a special way of making a person look to the brighter side of life rather than looking at the negative things. He was a handsome man whose eyes were the color of hazel. He was tall and of a stocky build. As he kneaded his pizza dough the definition of muscles in his arms were very apparent. Any onlooker would know that he was a very strong man both physically and in spirit. During the evenings he could always be seen standing in front of the window of his pizzeria

CIRCLE OF LOVE

tossing the pizza dough high in the air, to the delight of his younger customers, who were amazed that he always caught the dough. Whenever he noticed that he had a captive audience he would show off this old fashioned tradition all the more.

Ralph was the same age as Beth and the kindest man she had ever met. When she was younger he had been someone on whom her younger sister had had a crush. During that time Beth had not really known him because she had been involved with the kids' father and hadn't really paid attention to him. The two of them had kindled a friendship when she became one of his regular customers at his pizzeria.

For some reason, she was feeling down this evening and just needed someone to talk to. She was having a hard time with a man who had been in her life for many years and the relationship was not growing in the way she had hoped. Ralph had known this man too. She thought maybe if she explained to Ralph what was going on he could give her some words of wisdom on what to do. As the two of them were talking, the dark haired man came into the store to pick up his deliveries. She stopped talking to Ralph and looked up at the dark haired man to see he was smiling at her. He had walked in during the middle of the conversation she and Ralph were having and it was obvious he had gotten the gist of what the conversation was about.

"Are you laughing at me?" she asked him feeling embarrassed.

"No, I'm not laughing at you," he responded, looking directly into her eyes for only an instant, then looking down and smiling to himself. He quickly retrieved his order and was out the door.

Dawn Elizabeth

Beth finished her conversation with Ralph and drove home feeling pain and misery. She had been on her own with her two children for seven years now and she had not found that special man. She was beginning to think maybe there wasn't a man out there for her. Maybe God had somehow forgotten her and he hadn't created a man who would love her. By the time she got home, she had lost her appetite. She took her food and put it in the refrigerator with the thought that maybe her appetite would return later and she could then eat. She slowly walked up to her room and closed the door behind her. Even though she tried hard to stop them, tears suddenly swelled in her eyes.

"No, I will not cry. I will not spend another lonely night locked in my room, crying. I just won't do it." She thought. But no matter how hard she tried to suppress the tears the loneliness was too overwhelming and before she knew it the tears were flowing at a steady pace down her face. It was as if someone had opened the gates and let all the tears that she possessed loose. Once that gate was open, no matter how hard she tried to control herself, the tears that she had held in for so many years were determined to be freed and nothing could stop them now. As the tears flowed from her eyes she slowly sank down onto the edge of her bed and reached for her Big Bear. This was a big, stuffed teddy bear that her daughter had given her after her divorce, sweetly telling her that he would be there for her to cuddle when she needed a friend, her precious "Big Bear". He was always there for her when life seemed unbearable. Once his color was as white as snow, but through the years his color had faded to a grayish white, his fur becoming worn due to

CIRCLE OF LOVE

the many times she had held onto him during the sad, lonely times in her life. Her devoted "Big Bear", he was always there on her bed waiting to be picked up and held; as if he were the only thing that could get her through a crisis.

"Oh Big Bear, sometimes it just hurts so much. I pray every night for God to send me someone to love. I wish on every first star that I see, and I toss coins in every fountain I pass. I have so much love to give, yet, after all this time, I am still alone." She wrapped her arms around her bear and buried her face into his worn fur and cried, this time not caring if she controlled the tears or not. The loneliness she felt was overwhelming and it was time to let the hurt that she had held inside her for many years come to the surface. For hours she lay on her bed crying tears that would fill hundreds of buckets. Each tear represented the emptiness and lost love that she had been looking for all her life. It was a love that she was beginning to believe she would never find.

Chapter 3

Beth tossed in her bed reaching for her pillow to cover her head at the sound of the telephone ringing. It was nine o'clock on Saturday morning. Who would be calling her at this time on a Saturday?

"Oh, I am not in the mood to talk to anyone", she thought. Slowly she reached over and turned the ringer off on her phone. "I will just let the answering machine get it. If I am feeling better later I will call whoever it is back." Just as she turned the ringer off, the answering machine clicked on and she heard her own voice saying "Hi there, sorry we can't get to the phone right now, but do us a favor, please don't hang up, leave us a message and we will call you back just as soon as we can. Thanks for calling. Have a great day. Bye." At the end of the message she heard a click indicating that the caller had decided not to leave a message.

"That figures, someone calls me, wakes me up, but doesn't leave a message. Great."

She rolled back to her side and reached for Big Bear. She held him tightly in her arms and remembered how she had cried herself to sleep last night.

Beth had everything anyone could ask for. She had two beautiful children, Gregory, who was going to be fifteen in a couple of weeks; and Tiffany, who was twelve. She had a great job as a legal secretary in a well-known law firm and a brand new house that had been built especially for her and her kids. She had a wonderful family and many friends. The only thing

CIRCLE OF LOVE

that was missing was a special man to share her dreams. She and John had been married a year after they had graduated from high school. For twelve years they had both tried to make their marriage work. They had created two beautiful children and from the outside it seemed they were the "All American Family". Sadly, hidden from the outside they were both miserable, each having different interests, trying to force themselves to be happy when they were not. Rather than growing together as a couple they were both too independent and grew apart. On the day of their divorce Beth had remembered crying, not because she missed John, or thought that the divorce had been a mistake, but because she was afraid that she would never experience a feeling of "true love". As she lay on her bed holding her Big Bear she wondered for a moment whether she had made a mistake seven years ago by agreeing to the divorce. The thought only lasted a second as she shook her head.

"No, John is happy now and I have grown into my own person. It wasn't a mistake. I need to stop feeling sorry for myself. Maybe someday I'll find my knight in shining armor."

She sighed as she thought how hard it had been on Gregory and Tiffany when they were younger prior to the divorce. They had witnessed the constant fighting of their parents and it hadn't been fair to either of them. Fortunately the divorce had been mutual and very civil. John had remained a constant figure in his children's lives and his support had helped the children to adjust. It was obvious as to how supportive their parents were because both Gregory and Tiffany were honor students at their schools and role models for

Dawn Elizabeth

others. Beth smiled to herself thinking how proud she was of her kids. As she started to get up from the bed the answering machine clicked on again. After listening to her message play through she heard a familiar voice.

"Hey, kiddo, it's just me. You seemed so broken hearted last night, I thought I would give you a quick call to see how you were doing this morning."

Beth grinned to herself and rolled her eyes as she reach for the receiver.

"Hi, Ralph. I'm doing okay. I didn't look *that* bad."

"Beth, you know you can't hide things from me. What's really going on with you? Lately you haven't seemed like your old bouncy self. And what's this? You're screening your phone calls now?"

Beth laughed knowing that he was right. She couldn't hide things from him.

"No, I'm not screening my calls. It's Saturday. I was going to sleep in, be kind of lazy today. Someone called at nine o'clock and woke me from an amazing dream. I turned the ringer off hoping I could go back to it."

"Amazing dream, huh? And who was the handsome man in this one? Anyone I know?" Ralph teased.

"Oh yeah, I was just getting ready to seduce Richard Gere. I was so-o-o close, but he was saved by the bell," she quipped.

"Okay, okay, I guess that was a good reason to try to get back into the dream and turn your ringer off. But on a serious note, are you okay? Our talk last night didn't seem to have a good effect on you. I don't know what is going on with Joe. His actions just don't

CIRCLE OF LOVE

make sense to me. It's almost as if he is afraid of something. I hate seeing you so torn apart by it."

"Oh, I'm okay. I don't know why I let it bother me so much. But I am fine now. What are your plans for the day?", she said trying to change the subject.

Ralph could sense what Beth was trying to do and knew he should not push the subject.

"I don't have any big plans. I need to get into the store a little early; I have some paperwork to do. And I have a lunch date."

"Ooh, you do, huh? Anyone I know?"

"Yeah, I think you've heard of her, her name is Cindy Crawford." He laughed.

"Very funny. Seriously, is she anyone I know?

"Ah, she's someone I met through a friend."

"Okay, I get it. You do not want to talk about it. Well, I hope that you and *Cindy Crawford* have a nice time. Thanks for checking up on me. I'm fine … really."

"Well, if you need to talk Beth, you know where to find me. And sweetie, I know you don't want to hear this, but don't try so hard. Love will happen when you least expect it. Really."

"Thanks for the advice, Dr. Ralph. I'll be fine. I just miss the kids when they're not here. Have a good time with Cindy Crawford and I'll talk to you later. Bye."

She hung up the phone feeling very lucky to have a friend like Ralph. During the past couple years their friendship had grown into something quite special. He was her confidant, she could tell him everything and anything without worrying that he was going to judge her or think badly of her. Once or twice she had

Dawn Elizabeth

thought about having a romantic relationship with him and she was very tempted to seduce him, but she knew that if they crossed that line and things didn't work out their friendship would be ruined. It wasn't worth the risk. Real friends are hard to find. Ralph was definitely a true friend and she intended to keep it that way.

She rolled to her back and stared up at the white ceiling. Her thoughts drifted to the night before at Ralph's store. She remembered the dark haired man coming in when she and Ralph were talking. Oddly she had been overwhelmed with the tingling sensation she seemed to feel whenever that man was around. The feeling was actually very wonderful and somewhat magical she thought. As she lay in the middle of the queen size bed, in her mind she could picture his face. Warmth seemed to beam from his dark brown eyes, as their eyes would meet causing her to feel as if she was floating on a cloud. She imagined how soft his thick dark hair would feel to her fingers. She closed her eyes and tried to recapture the magic feeling she had experienced when he interrupted Ralph's and her conversation. She shook her head in disappointment as she desperately tried to conjure up the happy feeling she felt when that man was present. To her dismay, the feeling was lost with the night.

Feeling discouraged, Beth got up and decided she would take a shower and later call a friend to see if she wanted to go shopping. She removed her oversized nightshirt and panties and turned the water on in the shower. As the water was running she turned to glance at her naked reflection in the mirror behind her. Her breasts were round and firm with large nipples. Her stomach was flat from the many hours of dedication to exercising she did each day. She turned to look at her back side and could see that her butt still had a nice roundness to it and on the right side in the panty-line area was a small tattoo of a yellow rose. She closed her eyes, remembering how painful getting that rose had been. Once the water was adjusted to a temperature that was hot enough to steam up the bathroom, she pulled the shower curtain back and stepped in. The water felt wonderful as it hit her back. She stepped to the front of the tub in order to be in a position to tilt her head back directly under the showerhead so the water could massage her scalp. She closed her eyes and stood there enjoying the sensation of the water hitting her head and running down the length of the back of her body. After standing there for several minutes she finally reached for her bath sponge and her vanilla fragrance shower gel. Slowly she started to wash herself, wishing she had someone to wash her back. After she had finished bathing herself, she shampooed her hair. She reached for the conditioner and while she was waiting to rinse out the conditioner she once again allowed her thoughts to drift back to the night before. She remembered the handsome man who worked for Ralph. She smiled as she thought of the feelings she would have whenever he was present. It made her entire body tingle and her heart race. It only lasted while he was in her presence, once he left, oddly, the feeling would leave also. She had meant to ask Ralph what his name was and if he was married, but there never seemed to be an appropriate moment, or she was preoccupied with something else. As she turned to rinse the conditioner from her hair she made a mental note to ask Ralph who he was the next time

Dawn Elizabeth

she spoke to him. She finished her shower, dried herself off and, put on her thick soft robe. She walked over to the round table sitting next to her bed and reached for the telephone. As she dialed her friend's phone number she slowly lowered herself and sat down on the bed. She felt relieved when her friend told her she was free and would love to go shopping. For several moments after she had hung up the phone, she remained sitting on her bed, staring into space. She felt strange as if something was about to happen, but could not begin to guess what it could possibly be. She began to get dressed, the strange feeling lingering for several moments then suddenly vanishing. She was unaware that there was a guardian angel in the room with her, watching her and smiling.

Chapter 4

The young woman paced back and forth in the living room waiting for Beth to find her car keys she had misplaced.

"I had them last night, I normally just set them in the basket on the counter. I can't imagine what I did with them," Beth said, feeling very frustrated.

"Are you sure they aren't in your coat pocket? Why don't you just humor me and look."

Beth walked over to the chair where she had laid her coat when she returned home the night before. She checked her pockets and, sure enough, the keys were there.

"I thought I checked here. Oh well, let's go. Shopping always makes me feel better. What are you looking at?"

The young woman was staring at Beth with a look of concern on her face. She had noticed the dark circles around Beth's eyes that were apparent even with the make-up. Ever since Beth's call earlier that morning she had known Beth had had one of her long, melancholy nights. She knew her friend had been feeling sad due to a relationship that wasn't working out.

Beth had been seeing a man for several years and it was really a no-win situation. Joseph O'Dea was what most women would describe as "tall, dark, and handsome." He stood a little over six feet, and was solid and strong. He had hazel eyes and dark brown, thick, wavy hair. She had met him at one of the firms she had previously worked. He was their process

Dawn Elizabeth

server. The two of them had started talking a short time after she had joined the firm. She had thought of him as only a friend. Due to her being so naïve, it had taken her a long time to realize that he had actually been interested in her as something more. By the time she had realized that he wanted more to their friendship it had been too late; she had bruised his ego. For some odd reason after many years they had remained fixtures in each other's lives. They shared a strange type of bond. Even though they never dated he always was there to help her when she was in some type of jam. Sexually, two people could not have been more compatible. Over the past several years, they had shared many nights of passion. There had been times when he had shown interest in developing the relationship. Unfortunately, whenever he had indicated that he wanted more, it had scared her and she would pull away, throwing the poor fellow into a head spin. He had gotten so used to her being fickle that he eventually had hardened his heart in order to protect himself from being hurt. He would not accept any of her phone calls and would not talk to her for weeks. It was during those times that he pulled away, that Beth had thought that he was the man she really wanted. It would throw her into a state of panic and she would constantly try calling him, leaving him message after message to call. It wasn't until her calls stopped that he would call her unexpectedly, starting the pattern all over again.

The woman knew that it was during these times that Beth would get discouraged the most. She had felt sympathy for her, but at the same time she would get so angry because she knew Beth deserved more than

CIRCLE OF LOVE

the ridiculous emotional roller coaster he had kept her on. It was something that always puzzled her; that Beth would always get back on the ride knowing it was going to take the same course always leading to nowhere. How she wished Beth would meet a man who would treat her with the love and devotion she knew her friend needed. If shopping would get Beth's mind off of the jerk then she would make sure they both had a wonderful time, no matter how many stores they had to go to, or how much walking they had to do to achieve this. She was determined to get Beth back to her bouncy, perky self.

As they pulled into a parking space at the Mall the woman finally spoke and said what had been on her mind during the short drive there.

"Okay something is going on...let me hear about what happened. It is very obvious by looking at your face that you spent the majority of the night crying. What did the jerk face do to you this time?"

Beth knew that if she started talking it would be hard to suppress the tears that were making their way to the surface. She looked at her girlfriend and tried to put on her most convincing smile that she was indeed doing great and her friend should not worry. But for some reason she had lost the strength to do just that and once again the gate opened and the tears flowed down her face.

"Oh, honey, come here. What on earth has you in such a shaken state?" the woman asked moving towards her friend to hug her.

"Honestly, I just don't know. I have felt so lost and empty for the last few weeks. I don't quite understand myself where these feelings are coming from. I think I have even caused Ralph to worry because he called this morning. I had stopped in to talk to him last night but we were interrupted by one of the guys who work for him. I wish I could put my finger on it. But something really strange happened. There is this guy that works for him, he was the same guy who came in when we were talking. Every time he is around I get this weird sensation. All he has to do is look at me, even if it's only for a moment, and I get this strange tingling sensation that flows through my entire body and my heart takes off racing and my knees go weak. It only lasts while he is around, once he leaves the feeling goes with him. And...he has the most magnificent eyes that I have ever seen and his smile is always filled with such warmth. I could have my back to the door and when he walks in somehow I know it's him because that odd feeling begins. I know this must sound crazy but I have never felt like this before...not ever." Beth shook her head and looked out the window of the car as if she were trying to find the answers somewhere beyond the car, the teardrops streaming down her face.

"Okay, I'm a little confused. I don't remember you ever talking about this dark haired man at the pizza place before. You said he has been delivering pizza for two years and the two of you have never talked, yet you get some strange feeling when you see him?" the woman gently asked her friend.

Beth turned back to look directly into her friend's eyes.

"Yes, for two years he has been delivering my pizza. He works for Ralph. When he had delivered pizza a couple of years ago the kids had asked me what

CIRCLE OF LOVE

I thought of him. I had felt the strange feeling then, it was when he looked into my eyes. It was like I had always known him and I had this overwhelming feeling of happiness rush through my body. But once he walked away it was as if he took that feeling with him."

"But if he has been delivering your pizza for all of this time and you get this feeling each time you see him why haven't you said anything to him, or tried to get to know him?"

"Well, the feeling has never been as strong as it was the other night. Usually I just shrugged it off as being attracted to his nice looks. But this last time the feeling was so strong it was like I had been struck by lightening. Am I going crazy? What is happening to me'?" Beth asked as she reached for some Kleenex to dry her face.

"No, sweetheart, you are not going crazy. Unfortunately, I don't have any answers to give you. I don't really know what to say. I can understand why you are feeling the way you are though. If what is happening to you, ever happened to me, I would probably be extremely upset too. Do you still want to go shopping, or would you rather go back home?" she asked.

After Beth had dried the last of her tears she took a deep breath and said, "I want to go shopping. Let me put on a little makeup and try to cover up this red nose."

"Are you sure, we could go rent some movie if that would be better."

"No, I'll be okay."

Dawn Elizabeth

She withdrew her compact from her purse and started fixing her makeup. Once she was satisfied with her appearance she nodded to her friend indicating she was ready to go. As the two women started to walk up to the entrance of the mall, Beth came to an abrupt halt. She stood on the sidewalk and closed her eyes. From out of nowhere she had that strange quivering sensation as she had the night before. This time it was as if numerous lightening bolts had struck her where she stood. The feeling was intensely warm and prickly; giving her a feeling of heavenly calm and peace. As she stood with her eyes closed, the image of the dark haired man appeared in her mind. The vision seemed so real as if he were actually standing directly in front of her. Slowly the vision disappeared and she opened her eyes. The feeling was gradually starting to fade and she turned around. She looked up and was startled to see driving away from her was the dark haired man. She let out a little gasp for air as she noticed he had been looking at her in his rearview mirror as he was driving away. When it had been apparent to him that she had also seen him, he smiled and waved to her. He did not stop, but continued driving away. Beth reached for her friend's arm almost causing her to fall.

"I've changed my mind. I want to go home."

Chapter 5

"Hey Ralph, you will never believe who I saw at the mall today," the dark haired man said with a wide grin.

"I have no clue, who did you see?" Ralph responded with a hint of sarcasm in his voice.

"Beth Hanson. She was with some other woman with long dark hair and glasses. She is so incredibly cute…do you know if she is seeing anyone? I would really like to ask her out and get to know her. Many times when I deliver her pizza there is some guy there in a white van." He silently looked back at Ralph as he patiently waited for his response.

"White van, hmm, I don't know who that could be. There is a guy that she has been interested in for several years…I don't think he drives a van though…and I don't know what the status of their relationship is. You can try asking her out, but I can't say whether or not she will accept the invitation. She is kind of having a hard time right now…and I am not so sure she is interested in dating someone new."

As Ralph spoke the words, in the back of his mind, he hoped silently to himself that Beth would reject this man if he did ask her out. He wasn't sure that he was someone he wanted his friend to be involved with. He liked Alex, but knew him to be quite a lady's man. He had seen Alex get close to someone then suddenly lose interest for no reason. He didn't want Beth to be another woman added to his list of broken hearts. Yet, he knew Alex was a good man and, maybe he and Beth would be good for each other.

Dawn Elizabeth

"Would you mind if the next time she places an order I talk to her for a little while when I deliver her pizza?"

"As long as we're not busy I don't see where I would have a problem with that." Ralph replied.

The dark haired man smiled to himself and hoped that Beth would place an order this evening. He only worked a couple days a week and would not be working again until the following week. For some reason he had strong longing to see her; he could feel that she was suffering a strong pain and heartache. There was a strange feeling deep in his soul telling him that it was important to see her. His smile broadened as a peculiar feeling also told him he would get his chance to talk to the pretty, blue-eyed woman very soon.

Beth was doing her normal workout, which began with a thirty-minute walk on her treadmill, when her son approached her.

"Mom, can we order pizza tonight?"

As Beth reached to take a sip of her ice water sitting close by, she thought of how she had felt earlier that day when she and her friend were at the mall and how she had seen that dark haired man. She wasn't quite sure she wanted to deal with those overwhelming emotional feelings tonight.

"I guess", she said not really being overly enthusiastic with the idea. "But tell Ralph we'll pick it up. I want to talk to him."

Gregory gave his Mom a smile and spun around heading for the phone to order their pizza. Beth shook her head as she continued doing her walk. She was

CIRCLE OF LOVE

going to take this opportunity to ask Ralph questions about this handsome stranger. Maybe, if she found some information out about him, it would help to her understand why she got these strange feelings when he was around.

The young boy returned to the family room and plopped down on the couch as he reached for one of his many magazines.

"Okay, Mom, the pizza will be here in about twenty minutes."

For a moment the words that Gregory had said did not sink in. When she finally realized what it was that her son was actually saying and that the dark haired man would be coming to her home, an electricity of panic overpowered her and she nearly tripped when her steps faltered on the treadmill.

"What did you just say, Gregory?" she blurted, practically pouncing on her son who was deeply engrossed in one of his magazines.

"I said the pizza would be here in twenty minutes. Ralph is so funny mom…"

"No! No! *I* said I would pick the pizza up. You march right upstairs and call Ralph and tell him I will pick it up. I don't want it delivered," Beth said interrupting her son in mid sentence.

Not understanding why his mother had suddenly became so angry, he did as he was told and went back upstairs to call Ralph to tell him that his mother would be picking up the pizza. She did not want it delivered. He hung up the phone and looked over at his sister who had witnessed the whole event that had just taken place. She put her hands up in question, wondering what had come over their mother. Greg shrugged his

Dawn Elizabeth

shoulders and shook his head silently indicating to his sister that he was just as puzzled as she was.

"What was that all about?" Tiffany whispered to her brother as he brushed passed her to go inform their mother that they would now be picking the pizza up. He once again only shrugged his shoulders.

"All right Mom, I told Ralph we would be picking up the pizza. He made some comment about Alex being disappointed and that the pizza would be ready in twenty minutes."

Gregory looked at his mom to see if she was going to display any of the behavior she had previously. Beth was continuing her workout and was walking at a steady pace once again. She hesitated only for an instant when her son advised her of what Ralph had said. It took a long moment for it to register to her that he had mentioned something about "Alex being disappointed." She glanced down at the odometer to see how far she had walked. Her goal was to walk three miles this evening and according to the odometer she had only walked half the distance. She knew she would not be able to reach the three miles in the time remaining before she had to go pick up the pizza. Suddenly, as if someone had just turned a light on, or slapped her in the face, she recalled what her son had said about "Alex". She stopped walking and quickly asked her son,

"Who's Alex? What do you mean he's going to be disappointed?"

Tiffany entered the room also wondering what some Alex guy being disappointed meant. She was not about to miss how her brother was going to respond to their mother's questions.

"I have no idea, Mom. That's just what Ralph said. I told him that you were going to pick it up and he asked me "Why?" Then he commented about some guy named Alex being disappointed."

By this time Beth was extremely curious and decided not to wait, but, go now and talk with Ralph. She went upstairs and let her hair fall gently down around her face freeing it from the ponytail it had been in while she worked out. She ran a brush through her shoulder length hair quickly and changed out of her workout clothes into a pair of jeans and sweater. She refreshed her face and applied a small amount of makeup. She stood back and looked at her reflection feeling confidant with her appearance. She wasn't sure if she would run into the dark haired man, but in case it happened, she wanted to at least look her best. As she came down the stairs the kids were standing by the front door waiting for her. Both of them were somewhat nervous about the strange manner, which their mother was exhibiting. Gregory was the first to open the door and Tiffany followed. Neither of them were making any comments whatsoever. They both got into the car swiftly and waited patiently for their mother to get in and back out of the driveway. Tiffany was sitting in the front passenger seat and she turned herself in order to be able to see her brother who was situated in the seat directly behind their mother. Trying to catch his attention, she coughed. Gregory looked at her with a look of question in his eyes. As Beth turned her head in the opposite direction to look and see if it was clear for her to back out, Tiffany quickly mouthed the words "What's going on with Mom?" to her

Dawn Elizabeth

brother. Gregory shook his head to her indicting that he had no idea.

During the car ride to the pizzeria, Beth had strange feelings going through her mind. Hopefully, the dark haired man would be out on one of his runs and she would be free to talk to Ralph. But as she pulled into the parking lot she saw the dark haired man exiting the pizzeria with his arms full with the red warming bags they used for the pizzas. She took a deep breath and started to get out of her car. As she was closing the door she could feel herself being drawn to the man. She turned around to see him smiling at her, and then much to her surprise he motioned for her to come over to his car. She felt her knees go weak and turned back to see both of her children watching the events that were taking place. It seemed to take all the energy she had to say, "You guys, he wants me to go over to his car. What do I do?"

Tiffany was the first to speak up, "Duh, you go over to his car, Mom, that isn't hard to figure out," then the young teenager crossed her arms over her chest and smiled mischievously.

Beth took a deep breath and slowly started walking over to the dark haired man's car. As she came close enough to touch him those same wonderful feelings overwhelmed her body once again. She felt her cheeks turn hot as she blushed at the wonderful warmth that constantly radiated from his eyes when they made contact. She came to a stop standing directly in front of him.

"Hi, Beth. You and I have never been formally introduced. My name is Alexander Fuentas. My friends call me Alex. I hope that you don't mind, but I left one

CIRCLE OF LOVE

of my business cards on your order. I have to admit I was a little bit disappointed when you called back and said you were going to pick your order up rather than have me deliver it. I was looking forward to seeing you," Alex said in a deep husky voice.

Beth felt as if she had been in some beautiful dream and at any moment she was going to be awakened by the alarm clock. The sound of Alex's deep voice pulled her back into reality.

"Beth, did you hear me?" he asked letting his eyes slowly go up and down her body stopping to look directly into her beautiful blue eyes. As he stood there taking her beauty in, he experienced the same feelings that Beth had felt. For some reason, he too always knew when she was present. Without even seeing her, he always knew she was there. His heart raced at such a speed that it felt at any moment it was going to come pounding right out of his chest. There had been so many times during the past two years when he had delivered pizza to her door that it had taken every bit of energy that he possessed not to take her in his arms and kiss her. There were times when she had met him at the door wearing a towel on her head and he thought she had looked so adorable, and then there were the times when he had noticed the puffiness of her eyes due to something that had made her cry. It was during those times that he wanted to wrap his arms around her and let her cry on his broad shoulders. He remembered driving away wondering what had caused her so much pain? Often he wanted to turn around and go back to demand her to tell him the reason for her sadness. But no matter what the circumstance was, there was always that feeling that overwhelmed him. It was a feeling as

Dawn Elizabeth

if he had known her always, that he could look into her very soul. When she was in his presence he felt so complete. The wonderful feelings always seemed to vanish the instant they were apart. Now those feelings were so strong they were almost intoxicating. He had never mentioned the way he felt to a single soul for fear someone would think he was insane. But for some odd reason the feelings had become more intense and there was no denying that they did exist.

Afraid that she would be able to read his thoughts he turned around and opened his car door and sat down putting the key in the ignition. He looked back at her and smiled.

"Would you do me a favor and page me later tonight? I would love to have a real conversation with you. My number is on the business card."

Beth was caught off guard by his request and only smiled and nodded. She moved away from his car giving him the opportunity to safety back out of his parking space. She looked up and saw Ralph observing the whole scene from his window as he was preparing his pizzas. The two kids had already gotten out of the car and were waiting inside of the pizzeria letting their mother have some privacy as she and Alex spoke with each other.

As Beth entered the pizzeria, her complete attention was directed to Ralph.

"All right, Ralph, tell me about Alexander, or Alex whatever his name is. Is he married? Does he have a girlfriend? What kind of person is he?" Beth was asking one question after another not pausing long enough to get an answer.

CIRCLE OF LOVE

Ralph took a deep breath and wondered to himself how he should answer Beth's numerous questions. He had come to truly care about her and was uncertain as to whether Alex was the type of person he wanted to see his dear friend involved with. He knew the last thing that she needed was someone tearing her heart to pieces and he knew Alexander Fuentas was known for breaking many women's hearts. He did not want to see her name added to this long list.

"Well no, he's not married. He is divorced. And no, as far as I know he doesn't have a girlfriend." So far everything Ralph had said was all true. To his knowledge at the present time Alex did not have a girlfriend. "He has worked for me for about two years, and he's a nice guy."

"Ralph, he said he left his business card on my order. He wants me to page him later. Do you think I should?" Beth asked with a hint of skepticism in her voice.

"Sweetie, you have to do what you are comfortable in doing. If you want to page him, then do it. If you are uneasy calling him, then maybe you shouldn't. I hate to say it, but it's your call."

Ralph was hoping that somehow Beth would hear the concern in his voice and decide against calling him. But unconsciously he knew she would.

Beth hated to ask the next question. She was uncertain how to ask it so as not to offend Ralph. With a hint of hesitation she proceeded.

"Does he have another job? I mean does he do anything else besides deliver pizza?"

Ralph looked at Beth and chuckled. "Yes, Beth, he does have a full-time job. It is on his business card. He

Dawn Elizabeth

only delivers pizzas on a part-time basis to help me out."

As Ralph finished making his pizza, he put it into the huge oven and reached overhead to retrieve the order Gregory had placed. He walked over to the cash register and began ringing up the order. He always charged Beth only half-price for her orders. She was a valued friend, as well as customer, and he never felt comfortable charging her full price.

When Ralph told Beth what the total was she quickly flashed him a look of question. She had thought the total would be much more than what he had given her.

"Ralph, are you sure? Check the slip I think you may have forgotten something. That just doesn't seem right," she said.

"Beth, I know my own prices. The total is eight dollars," he replied.

Shaking her head in disbelief, but knowing full well that her friend was indeed giving her a large discount, she reach into her purse and pulled out a ten-dollar bill. As she handed the money to Ralph she nodded towards Gregory to pick up their order. Ralph started to hand Beth a dollar back but after seeing the look in her eyes he decided against it. He put the money in the cash drawer and closed it.

"So do you think you'll call him?"

Beth looked down to the floor then back at her friend.

"I'm not sure, Ralph. Maybe. He is handsome, so incredibly handsome. I guess I will have to wait and see what happens."

CIRCLE OF LOVE

She turned to give her friend a hug and reached up to give him a peck on his cheek. She then turned and headed to the door, but before she pushed it opened she turned back to him and smiled.

"Hey, you never told me about your lunch date. How was it?"

"It was fine. I'll you tell you about it some other time. You need to get your kids home, your pizza is getting cold."

Beth shook her head, knowing this was Ralph's polite way of saying he didn't want to talk about it. So, rather then pushing him into talking, she let it go. She turned back to the door and she and her kids headed for the car.

As she drove home, her mind was filled with thoughts about the brief conversation she and Alex had. She was tempted to say something to Ralph about the feelings she felt whenever Alex was around, but decided against telling him. She remembered how her heart had raced when she was actually close enough to reach out and touch him. It was strange, but somehow she had felt like the two of them were connected when their bodies were so close to one another. She could feel each and every emotion he was feeling. She knew that he had gotten into his car quickly because he had been experiencing the same odd sensation as she had at that moment and was terrified that Beth somehow could read his thoughts. The feelings were not frightening, but rather completely amazing and calm. As the two of them stood together they were two puzzle pieces that fit perfectly together.

The three of them ate their dinner in silence but all of them were thinking the same thing. Would she call

Dawn Elizabeth

him, or not? When they finished their dinner they each cleaned up their plates and went to do whatever they had to do to prepare themselves for the next day. She ironed the clothes she needed for work then headed to the bathroom to take a quick shower.

For several moments she silently stood under the showerhead and let the water beat down on her body. It felt so wonderful as its warmth relaxed her tired muscles. She had felt so tense since her trip to Ralph's. She couldn't erase the image of Alex's face from her mind. The feelings that appeared whenever he was present seemed to be lingering with her. She sighed as she felt the water beating down on her back. It felt like tiny little fingers massaging her tight skin. The water felt splendid as she regrettably reached for the faucet and turned the shower off. She knew it had to be fairly close to ten o'clock and it was time for her to get ready for bed.

As she was stepping out of the tub there was a knock on the bathroom door. Suddenly, a prickly awareness ran through body when she heard the soft sound of her daughter's voice.

"Mom," Tiffany said, "You have a phone call. I think it may be Alex. Do you want him to call back?"

Beth's heart began to pound at the thought of talking to Alex.

"No, that's okay. Tell him I will be right there."

She wrapped a towel around her and stepped out of the tub. She reached for a second towel and wrapped it around her soaked hair. Once both towels were securely draped around her body and head she opened the door to her bedroom. She walked over to the side of her bed where the phone was sitting on the round

CIRCLE OF LOVE

table. She slowly sat down on her bed, took a deep breath and reached for the receiver. She had no idea that in the corner of her bedroom an angel stood watching her in the dim light. A smile slowly formed on his face as he watched her raise the receiver to her ear. He looked up towards the Heavens and nodded as he heard the thousands of angels singing joyously as they all watched as the two special souls were finally becoming united.

Chapter 6

"Hello," Beth said as she closed her eyes and waited to hear the voice of the caller.

"Hi, Beth." Alex replied in his deep husky voice. "I hope it isn't too late for me to call. I wasn't sure what time you went to bed."

"Oh, no it's not too late. Actually I was just getting out of the shower." Beth said feeling slightly awkward.

"I wrote your number down from the order you placed today. I hope you don't mind. I didn't know if you were going to call me or not, so I thought I would take a chance." He too, felt a little uncomfortable and strange.

"Oh it's fine. I don't mind at all. Actually it is nice to finally have an opportunity to talk to you. I always wanted to hear you say something other than what my total was." Beth blushed.

Alex grinned to himself thinking if she only knew how many times he had wanted to say more to her. How he had wanted to take her in his arms and kiss her inviting lips. There had been so many times that he had been totally drained after he walked away, due to the fact that he had used every ounce of his energy to fight the temptation.

"So, how are you going to feel on Friday night when I show up at your house to take you out rather than deliver you pizza?" he asked her.

"You are planning to take me out, huh? Tell me, sir, do I have a say in this matter? Or do I behave like a good little girl and be here ready and waiting?" And willing, she also thought.

Alex laughed at her teasing and then responded, "Oh but of course you have a say in the matter. You can tell me "no" you do not want to go out with me. But then you would have to deal with the idea of breaking my heart. And how could those beautiful eyes of yours ever look into mine knowing I was feeling so rejected and crushed?" He teased back.

"I don't think I could ever look into your eyes, knowing that something I had done could make you feel crushed," she tried to say kiddingly back to him. But for some odd reason she felt deep inside that she could not ever do anything to intentionally hurt this man.

The two of them laughed and joked with each other for hours on the phone. They talked about everything from each others' jobs, to kids and their families, to their likes and dislikes. In the middle of the conversation it had been agreed that they would go out on a date on Friday of that week; but that day seemed like an eternity away. Quickly, Beth had made the suggestion that he stop by the house on the following day for a short visit. It would give them both a chance to relax and get to know each other without the awkwardness of being surrounded by many people in a public place. It wasn't as if they were total strangers and needed the security of others around. In fact, in some ways, they already knew each other. All the while as they talked Beth felt the most wonderful feeling of happiness. It was as if every word he spoke was a gentle caress to her ear and on her face. There was something in the tone of his voice that calmed ever part of her being, erasing away every sad moment that had clung to her.

Dawn Elizabeth

Neither of them had wanted to end their conversation, but each had to get their rest for work for the following day. It was already extremely late and it was only hours before Alex would have to get himself up and ready for work. They both said "Goodnight" and looked forward to tomorrow evening when they would be able to spend a short time together.

As Alex hung up the phone he lay on his bed staring up at the ceiling. If he closed his eyes he could picture her face and her expressions when he spoke to her in front of Ralph's. He had noticed how initially she had blushed when he had first called her over to his car. When she moved closer to him he could see the smile in her eyes and he knew that he hadn't made a mistake by calling to her. He remembered the way her hair looked as it gently blew in the breeze. He had taken in every curve of her body with a quick glance and had thought that the clothes she had been wearing had flattered her sensuous figure.

As he turned over and shut off the light, he reached for a pillow to put under his head. He pulled the covers up over his naked, strong body. He had never been able to sleep wearing any type of nightclothes, even if they were only briefs. But he did like to have the secure feeling of the covers. He tossed from one side to the other trying desperately to get comfortable. It was no use. His mind was filled with thoughts of Beth and how badly he wanted her. He could not understand why she caused him such desire. He had been with many other women, yet none could cause his body to be aroused at the mere thought of them. He sighed heavily and shook his head; he looked down and saw that it was obvious, due to the rise in the covers, that it was going to be a long night.

Chapter 7

As Beth's alarm clock sounded at 6:00 a.m. she slowly reached over and pushed down the snooze button. She had not slept very well and she could use the extra nine minutes the snooze would give her. She reached for Big Bear underneath the warm covers. After she found where the cherished teddy bear was, she wrapped her arms tightly around him and turned to lie on her left side in order to have a clear view of her alarm clock. As she quietly lay there she remembered the wonderful conversation she and Alex had the night before. During the whole time they spoke she felt the tingly warm sensation. It was like she had known him her whole life and was not afraid or embarrassed to say anything to him. His voice was so deep, yet so soothing. The thought of having him over to her house was extremely thrilling to her. It would seem strange to have him enter the house rather than just waiting on the porch, but he would be welcome to come in and see the interior of her home. He would be able to look around the house and go from room to room seeing how Beth's personality had been expressed in her decorating. He would see all of her many photographs of her friends and family that were displayed throughout the house. By allowing him to pass through the doorway, she would be opening herself to him. Somehow she would have to keep her guard up because she would be allowing this handsome man into her life, into her private world. No longer would he be delivering pizza and leaving, he would now be entering into her world. It was a world that was very special to her. Not very many men had been allowed to enter that world; her world that was safe and secure. Oddly, for some reason she knew things would be fine. She also had a strange feeling that Alex Fuentas belonged in her world.

The alarm clock sounded again, it's loud continuous tone disturbing her wonderful thoughts. With her right hand she reached over and turned the noisy alarm off. She then unwrapped her arms from Big Bear and gently laid him beside her on the bed. She then quickly got up and rushed to the bathroom to take her morning shower. She and her kids had a set schedule and if she took any extra minutes it would throw them all off. She grabbed a towel and turned on the water so that it could start warming up. She slid the straps of the red nightgown off her shoulders and allowed the garment to fall down to the floor. Usually she slept in an oversized nightshirt and boxer shorts, but Alex had made her feel sexy and she decided to wear the pretty red nightgown made of satin. It was a beautiful nightgown; it hung down to her ankles with slits that rose on either side to expose her hips. The bodice was plain but swooped down exposing the top roundness of her breasts. There were spaghetti straps, which connected with other straps forming a web pattern on her back, the back of the gown dipping slightly above her buttocks. It was a beautiful gown that she only wore for special occasions. As the water was running she stood in front of the mirror wondering what had made her wear that gown rather than her nightshirt? Why did Alex have such a strong impact on her? She tilted her head back and closed her eyes. As she stood in the cold bathroom nude, her mind was

Dawn Elizabeth

filled with a vision of Alex and her standing in front of each other. He slowly lowered his head down to her and gently kissed her waiting lips. His hands reached for her waist and gently pulled her to his body. His kisses, which had started off slow and gentle, suddenly turned passionate as his tongue encouraged her lips to allow its entry. As the vision became more and more intense Beth felt as if she was losing all of her control, but somewhere deep inside of her mind she knew she had to pull away. Suddenly she opened her eyes and looked at her reflection in the mirror of the vanity.

"What is happening to me?" she wondered. I can't be fantasizing about such things, I don't even know this man."

She tested the temperature of the water and after feeling that it was how she liked it, quickly jumped in. It took all of the control she had to focus on taking her shower and then getting her children up. Somehow she would have to block Alex Fuentas out of her mind, otherwise, she would be totally unproductive at work today. She knew that she had an appeal brief due that afternoon and it would take all of her complete concentration. She briskly dried herself off and went to get Tiffany and Gregory up.

"You will never believe what has happened. I talked to *him* last night and he is coming over this evening for a visit. His name is Alexander Fuentas." Beth rapidly began as soon as her friend walked into the office.

"What did you say?" the young woman asked, as she turned to open the closet door located in the suite's lobby.

CIRCLE OF LOVE

"I said I talked to "him" last night. You know the handsome, dark haired man. His name is Alex. He is coming over tonight! Can you believe it?"

"Slow down, Beth, let me get my coat off. What are you talking about? Who is Alex?"

"Remember the man I told you about? Remember the mall yesterday? Well, the kids wanted to order pizza, so I did. I decided to go in and pick it up rather than have it delivered. I wanted to talk to Ralph. When I pulled in, he was coming out of the store. He motioned me over to his car! I was so nervous, I really thought I was going to faint! But the kids encouraged me to go see what he wanted. He told me he left his business card on my order and he wanted me to page him later. Anyway, I didn't call him, but as I was getting out of the shower Tiffany said he was on the phone. He had written my number down from my order. We talked for hours and hours he is going to take me out on Friday, but he is stopping by for a visit tonight. Can you believe it?"

By this time Beth was so wound up it felt good to be able to let some of the excitement out and share it with her friend who stood there silently amazed by everything she had heard.

"Beth, I think it is great. Are you nervous? What about those feelings you said you get whenever he is around? What was it like when you were actually talking to him? Were the feelings there then?", the friend asked, amazed at all the events that had taken place the night before.

"Yes, the feelings were there when we talked. It felt like I have always known him. His laugh is so wonderful, and his voice is so-o-o, so soothing. I felt

Dawn Elizabeth

that I was in some magnificent dream during the whole time we spoke. We talked about everything. I have to admit that I didn't sleep very well. After we hung up I lay on my bed and tried to remember every word he said. It's funny, because somehow, I know he didn't sleep very well either. We both kept each other awake. I have heard that if you find yourself constantly thinking about someone it means that they are thinking about you too. If that is true, he must have been up all night because I could not get him out of my thoughts. It was strange, but yet it was wonderful at the same time." Beth reached up and put a strand of hair behind her ear. "What do you think?", she finally exclaimed.

The young woman stood silently, bewildered by what she heard her friend saying. The events that had taken place during the past few days had sounded like something out of a romance novel. There was no way this could actually be happening. It was fascinating, yet hard to believe. She didn't want to offend her friend so instead of conveying her true feelings of doubt, she reached out and patted her friend's shoulder and unconsciously began to pace back and forth, swinging her arms as she walked.

"Beth, this is really exciting. What time will he be over?"

"Oh gosh, in all the excitement I don't think we even talked about a time! I suppose he will call first and it will be some time this evening. I am so nervous. How am I going to be able to work?"

She had a voluminous brief to type. Once the typing was completed, she would have several exhibits to copy.

CIRCLE OF LOVE

"I wouldn't want to be in your shoes. You have to pull yourself together though. You have that appeal brief to get out, so somehow block him out. I'll keep my eyes open and see how you're doing. This is going to be a long day for you. The anticipation alone is a killer. Don't worry, I'll help you get through it.", she said in an attempt to distract her friend.

The day was indeed a long one for Beth. She was extremely excited, but somehow her professional side stepped in and took over. In no time at all she had the brief typed, exhibits copied and ready to be filed with the court. Somehow she was able to block out her anticipation of the evening that was to come. Little did she know that the night would lead to the answering of all of her wishes, dreams, and prayers. God himself was smiling down on her. The long awaited day had finally come when His special souls would finally be united.

The angels in Heaven began to sing a beautiful melody as they too beamed with joy at the event that was about to take place. They merrily watched as the man and woman began to get ready for a meeting that had been ordained prior to their births. Neither person knew this was not their first meeting, but rather the reuniting of their souls. A precious, beautiful love that had patiently waited for the time when it was allowed to be expressed, would soon be freed...a love that would last throughout all of time.

Chapter 8

Alex pulled off the flannel shirt that he had tried on. "No, this isn't good," he thought. He wanted to wear something that made him look handsome, yet classy, not rugged. He pulled a multicolored crew neck sweater from his drawer. He eased it over his head then stood back looking at his reflection in the mirror. The soft colors of the sweater accented his dark skin and hair. "Yes, he thought, this is good." He wanted to look his best. He reached for his cologne and splashed it on his face. For some reason he was extremely nervous. Normally it wasn't a major task to go visit a beautiful woman. He had had many women. He had lost count of the numerous women that he had used. Beth Hanson was different. He didn't want to use her and toss her aside as he did the others. There was something about her that pulled at his heartstrings deep down to his very soul. He wanted to hold her and shower her with love and affection. Strangely, he knew that if he ever had to, she was someone he would walk through fire to rescue, without even hesitating for a brief second. She was someone he would gladly sacrifice his life for. This was a new feeling for Alex. Beth wasn't a conquest to him. He had felt some strange type of connection to her. He didn't want to seduce her, but rather he wanted to impress her, earn her respect, and if possible, earn her love. He wanted her to love him in the way he had always loved her.

He went to the closet and pulled out his black long leather coat. He grabbed his car keys and turned on the living room light. He didn't know how long he would

CIRCLE OF LOVE

be out and didn't want to return to a dark house. He walked out the front door turning back to make sure he had locked the door.

It was a cold, crisp night and it seemed like it took forever for his car to warm up. He anxiously waited for the warm air to flow from the vents. He leaned back in his seat and began to listen to the song that was playing on the radio. He smiled to himself as he heard the artist's lyrics: "A new beginning, a reason for living, a deeper meaning...yeah." Could this be a new beginning for him? He had never felt so nervous and extremely excited when he went to a woman's house. He grinned broadly as he thought, "This was no ordinary woman. This *is* Beth Hanson." She was the most beautiful woman he had ever laid his eyes on. There was something about her that was extraordinary.

He put his car in reverse and backed out of his parking space; soon he would be knocking on her door and entering her home rather than just waiting on the porch. He would soon become part of *her* world. It was a world he had often wondered about whenever he would walk back to his car after making his delivery. His heart told him that beyond those doors was the key to what was missing in his life. It was a place where he belonged. He felt tiny goose bumps rise on his arms as he tried to envision what it would be like to cross the threshold and enter the world that belonged to her. He knew that Beth Hanson was the one woman who could make him feel complete.

As he drove out of his complex he thought of the extreme loneliness he had felt all his life. It was true; he had been involved with too many women to mention. There were times that he had felt close to falling in love with someone, but then suddenly without any specific reason, the feeling would be gone. He knew that he had broken many hearts and felt horrible for doing so. He could never justify his actions for ending a relationship. It was almost as if some higher power was leading him to someone specific. He shook his head as he tried to block those thoughts from his mind. There were too many strange things happening already, he did not want to add anymore to his list.

As he turned down her street, a route he had taken on many occasions, he could feel the anticipation rising in his stomach. His heart was racing at a speed that was so rapid he expected his heart to rip out of his chest at any moment. He knew he had to calm himself down, otherwise he would scare her. He took a deep breath and pulled into her driveway. He took this time to look at himself in his rearview mirror. After he was satisfied with his appearance he turned the engine off and reached for the handle to open the car door. He slowly began to walk up to her front door, a walk he had done on numerous occasions, yet this time it was different. His heart began to beat faster and faster as he walked up the steps leading to the door. A quiet voice in his mind told him that the answers to his questions would be found once he crossed through the doorway, the answers to why he felt completely connected to her. He paused for a brief moment and then rang the doorbell. He stepped back, crossed his hands down in front of him, and waited for the door to be opened. The door would not only be the entrance to her home, but most importantly was the key to opening his heart.

CIRCLE OF LOVE

Beth was upstairs in her room when the doorbell rang. She finished brushing her hair and looked up to see Tiffany standing in the doorway.

"Mom, Alex is here. Are you ready?" Tiffany asked, knowing that at that moment her mother must be fighting the numerous butterflies in her stomach. She walked over to her mom and gave her a quick kiss on her cheek.

"Mom, you are absolutely glowing! You are so beautiful. Take my word for it, one look at you and it's going to take his breath away."

"You think so T? I am so nervous. I feel like a schoolgirl."

Beth looked at her daughter, thinking that soon Tiffany would be going through the dating stage. Hopefully, her daughter would be able to handle it better than she had. For a moment Beth just stood there staring into space, until the voice of her daughter snapped her out of it.

"Mom, he's waiting. Gregory is down there talking to him. If you don't get down there soon it will be hard to pull him away from whatever it is guys talk about."

Tiffany gently grabbed her mother's arm and led her to the door. Beth took a deep breath and walked down the steps. She could hear the voices of Gregory and Alex. The two of them were laughing about something. As she descended the stairs leading into her family room, she realized that the voices had suddenly become silent. She turned her head to see Alex stand up and walk in her direction. As she watched him approach her, her knees became weak. Somehow he

Dawn Elizabeth

must have sensed that she was losing her balance because he was at her side in one quick movement with his hand around her waist, catching her before she fell. She turned towards him and grabbed onto his arms for support.

"Beth, are you okay?" Alex asked with concern in his voice.

"Yes, I'm okay. I don't know what came over me. I guess I just wasn't paying attention to what I was doing."

Beth's heart was beating rapidly as she looked directly into Alex's eyes. His hands remained around her waist until he was sure that she had regained her balance. He let them linger there for many moments until he finally released her and slowly stepped back. As he stood there looking down into her blue eyes, he felt the warm sensation run through his body. It was a combination of excitement, anticipation, desire, happiness, and serenity all rolled into one emotion. He had never experienced this feeling with anyone else in his entire life.

"Mom and Alex, why don't the two of you come over here and sit down. You both look like you are in some strange kind of trance."

Beth was the first one to move towards the chairs. Alex followed her and the two sat down on the couch. Tiffany descended the stairs and looked at the scene of her mother and this handsome man together. She had seen men that her mother had dated since her divorce, but she never noticed her mother to radiate such a glow as she had now. She had heard adults mention of love at first sight. She had never understood what that meant, but she was beginning to believe that she was

CIRCLE OF LOVE

observing it now. As she looked at the two adults before her she couldn't help but begin to giggle. They looked as if they were lost in each other, oblivious to anyone or anything around them. An earthquake wouldn't be able to distract them. Tiffany felt as if she was an intruder to a magical moment that her mother experiencing. She wished that she could capture the magic in a picture to hold onto forever. She started to go over and sit next to her mother but decided against it and sat down in a chair closer to the television instead. Alex leaned back and looked at Beth. Without even realizing what he was doing, he slowly moved his hand over and took Beth's tiny hand into his. His fingers parted, opening spaces for hers to entwine with his. Once their fingers were together he slowly closed his hands locking her fingers with his. Beth looked at Alex and smiled, feeling that his gesture was the most natural thing to do.

"I must say it is nice to finally be inside of your house. In some ways it feels weird because I thought I would never pass through that doorway." Alex said, and then glanced up towards the front door where he had stood on the outside for many years.

"You shouldn't feel weird. But I guess it does seem a little strange for me too. But it is strange in a good kind of way. In some ways I feel as if I am dreaming."

Alex gently squeezed Beth's hand.

"No, I assure you we are both wide awake, this is most definitely not a dream. And if it is…I don't want to wake up."

Tiffany turned her head back to look at the two adults. She let out a little giggle, thinking the whole scene was too unbelievable. She had never seen her

Dawn Elizabeth

mother behave like such a schoolgirl and found it sweet and romantic.

"Mom, would you or Alex like something to drink?" Tiffany asked.

"Oh my goodness, where are my manners? I should have asked, Alex would you like something to drink?" Beth replied.

"No thanks. I'm fine. And thank you, Tiffany, too. How was your day at school today? Gregory was telling me about signing up for driver's training. Before we know it you'll be doing that too," Alex laughed.

"No it will be a long time before I will be doing that. Gregory gets to do all of the fun stuff. I just go to boring school. I do have cheerleading practice though. Speaking of which, Mom we have a game tomorrow, you are coming…right?"

"Of course I will be there. But I might be a little late. Traffic is always so bad coming home at the time of the day."

Alex turned towards Tiffany and asked, "What time is the basketball game tomorrow, Tiffany? If you wouldn't mind, I would like to come."

"Really? Well the first game starts at four o'clock. We normally have two games…that would be nice of you to come…maybe you and Mom can come together," Tiffany said excitedly.

"Hey, what about me? I would like to go to the games too!" Gregory interjected.

Alex turned to Gregory. "What time do you get home from school? I could stop by and pick you up and then we could meet your mom there… that is if it's

CIRCLE OF LOVE

okay with her." He turned back and looked directly into Beth's eyes.

Beth was a little surprised that Alex would want to come to her daughter's games so soon. This was really the first time that the whole group had actually been together talking. But her heart felt a warm, calmness that told her that everything was okay. She felt Alex's hand gently squeezing hers, she looked up into his beautiful warm brown eyes and somehow she felt his anxiety as he was waiting for her response.

"I think that it would be great to have you at the game, Alex. The traffic is usually heavy when I'm on my way home, so I can meet you and Gregory at the school."

"Really, mom? Alex, it will be so cool to have you there. Don't laugh at me though, because I cheer really loud," Tiffany said.

"Why would I laugh? Cheerleaders are supposed to be loud." He turned to Gregory, never letting go of Beth's hand. "Gregory, what time should I pick you up?"

"Well, I usually get home at 2:30. If the games start at 4 o'clock you can pick me up whenever you can," Gregory answered.

"Let's see, I don't get out of work myself until four, so, how about I pick you up as soon after that as I can? We will miss the first game, but we can make the second."

"Sounds good to me," Gregory said. He got up and headed for the stairs. "I'm going to get myself a Coke, anyone want one?" Once he saw that no one in the group wanted one he headed up the stairs leaving Tiffany alone with their mother and Alex.

Dawn Elizabeth

Tiffany looked at the two adults sitting on the couch together. She once again felt as if she was intruding on something that was extremely magical. These two adults radiated such a glow. They made a perfect picture sitting next to one another on the couch holding on to each other's hand. Tiffany had never seen her mother behave this way. Her cheeks were slightly pink with a natural blush and her blue eyes seemed to sparkle. Alex's appearance was just as magical. His brown eyes were beaming, as he would ever so slightly steal glances at Beth. His cheeks too, were slightly colored pink. Tiffany felt that her mother deserved to be happy and for some odd reason she had the feeling that this was the beginning of happiness for her. Suddenly the young girl had a wonderful thought. She remembered her camera had a few pictures remaining on it. She would take a picture of them so they too would be able to see how perfect they looked sitting together. Who knows, they may even end up becoming a "couple" and this picture would be a beautiful remembrance of their first day together.

Excited with her idea she quickly jumped up from her chair. Her impulsive move startled Beth and Alex and they both jumped. Once again, Tiffany started to giggle.

"I am sorry. I just had a really neat idea. Excuse me for a moment. I will be right back."

In an instant the young girl was running down the stairs with a small black camera in her hands. The adults both laughed when they realized what she was going to do. In unison they both turned to pose for a picture.

CIRCLE OF LOVE

"No! Don't pose. Be natural. Alex just look at mom the way you were. Talk to each other…"

Alex quickly relaxed and turned back to face Beth. He gave her a wink, which caused her to smile. There was the sound of a soft "click", then a bright white flash. For a moment Beth and Alex remained looking into each other's eyes.

Deciding she should give the two adults some time alone, the young girl stood up and walked towards the stairs. Not knowing if the adults would even hear her she said, "I have some things I need to do to get ready for school tomorrow so I'm going to go upstairs. It was nice seeing you, Alex, and I'll look for you at the games tomorrow."

Alex pulled away from looking into Beth's eyes and responded to the young girl, "I'll look forward to hearing your loud cheers, Tiffany. I'll see you tomorrow." He then gave her a broad, warm smile and nodded his head and winked. Tiffany smiled and gave them a quick wave and bounced up the stairs with the camera. She smiled to herself knowing she carried a touch of magic inside that box. She knew it would be a picture he mother would always cherish.

Beth's heart began to race as she realized that she and Alex were finally alone. Sitting next to her holding on to her hand was this wonderful man. This was a man who gave her the most wonderful feelings that she had ever experienced. Having her hand in his she felt as if they were two puzzle pieces that fit perfectly together.

"Beth, you look so beautiful," Alex said as he reached up to remove a piece of hair that had fallen down around her face. "You have such a lovely home.

Dawn Elizabeth

It beams with the same warmth as you do. It is a wonderful reflection of you. Thank you for inviting tonight, and I hope you don't mind my inviting myself to the games tomorrow."

"I'm glad that you're coming tomorrow, and I'm glad you're here now."

Alex reached down and took both of Beth's hands into his and raised them to his lips and gently kissed each one. His heart was racing at a speed so fast that he was certain that at any moment it was going to burst out of his chest. This woman sitting next to him made him feel emotions that he had never experienced before. He wanted somehow to hold on to them and never let them end.

"So...tell me about yourself. Even though we did talk a little bit last night, I want to hear more. Tell me more about your other job that doesn't deal with delivering Ralph's delicious pizzas to women."

You want to hear about my real job, huh? Well, I work with computers and lasers. Our company engraves machine parts and tools. We do engraving on medical instruments too. It is an interesting job. As for delivering pizzas, I do that as a part-time job. I enjoy working for Ralph. He is a good man. I understand you have known him for a long time."

"Well, actually I have known of him for many years, ever since I was a young girl. My sister had a crush on him when she was younger, but I was involved with Gregory and Tiffany's father and wasn't really around much. I didn't really get to know him until the kids and I moved here and I started ordering his pizza. He and I have become very close friends. Enough about work...tell me more about *you*. Why

CIRCLE OF LOVE

does such a handsome man as yourself not have a girlfriend?"

Alex laughed and looked at Beth. He wasn't quite sure how to answer her question without sounding like Don Juan. He had been with many women. He wanted to give her an honest answer without scaring her away.

"No, Beth, I don't have a girlfriend and I'm not seeing anymore. I was married once. But that was a long long time ago."

Beth felt a small tug on her heart. Even though Ralph had told her that Alex was divorced, for some reason she couldn't imagine him "playing house" with any one. After a long silence she continued with her questions.

"So how long were you married?"

"I was married when I was very young. We were both just kids and the marriage was annulled after several months. I haven't seen or heard from her since. Does that bother you?"

"Of course not. What about a girlfriend? Why don't you have a girlfriend now?"

Alex took both of Beth's hands in his and raised them to his lips. He kissed them both tenderly then looked into her eyes and smiled.

"Princess, until now I didn't think I would ever meet someone who could capture my heart. No other woman has ever intrigued me in the way that you do. I have dated quite a few women, I won't deny it. But there was always something missing, a feeling of warmth."

He slowly released her hands and glanced around the room. He had wanted to reach out and take her in his arms and tell her exactly how she made him feel.

Dawn Elizabeth

He wanted to release the heat of desire that burned inside of him whenever she was present. But he didn't want to scare her away.

Beth could sense his anxiety and reached up and caressed his cheek with her small hand.

"I don't care how many women you have been with. It doesn't matter. All that matters is at this moment in time, right now, you are sitting here with me."

Without hesitating for a second, she leaned forward and gently kissed his lips. She did not feel embarrassed or awkward but rather as if it was something she was meant to do. A feeling deep in her soul was telling her do kiss him. Alex smiled at her and once again took her hands in his.

"Now, it's your turn to answer *my* questions. Are you ready, Princess?"

Beth let out a little giggle knowing she was about to be given the twenty questions routine.

"I'm ready. Shoot."

"Why does such a beautiful lady live here with her two children without a man taking care of them? How is it that some man has not caught you? Or do you have a boyfriend and he's hiding here somewhere?"

Alex turned and stretched his head up to looked behind the furniture as if he were looking for someone who might be hiding. Beth started laughing as Alex got up and started walking around the room, searching for some helpless man that was hiding from them, waiting to jump out from his hiding place at any moment. Alex made one trip around the room whistling and then suddenly stopping to look behind the furniture and opening the closet doors. Any person entering the room would die of laughter at the silly scene of Alex trying so hard to act like the jealous man looking for his fictitious opponent. Finally, the performance was more than Beth could take. She had been laughing so hard at his dramatic over-acting that her stomach felt as it was going to split open. Her eyes began to water uncontrollably and it made it difficult to see.

"Stop! No more. There is no man hiding. We're alone. I p-p-promise."

Alex turned around and headed for the couch. He looked at Beth and grinned as he watched her wiping the tears of laughter from her face. He sat down beside her and helped her wipe the tears.

"So seriously, Beth, are you involved with someone? What has made you cry so many times? I've noticed your sad, tear-streaked face many times when I delivered your pizza. What is causing you so much pain?"

Beth looked at the handsome man sitting beside her and could read the sincere concern in his eyes. She was overwhelmed with joy at the comprehension that he had noticed her sadness, and he had remembered it.

"Oh, I don't know. I guess at times I just feel so lost and incomplete. It is as if something or someone was missing from my life. There are times, when the kids are with their father, that I am very lonely. I never thought my crying had been that noticeable. And you were only here long enough to drop off the pizza. I never imagined that you had actually noticed me."

"A blind man would be able to see how deeply you were hurting. There were times that you seemed overwhelmed with so much pain. It took all the energy I had to resist taking you in my arms and holding you.

Dawn Elizabeth

I couldn't bear to see you hurting so badly. Was it loneliness or did someone break your heart?" the dark haired man said as he reached up and tenderly caressed her cheek.

"Maybe a little bit of both. Alex, do we have to talk about this? Right now, all I want is for us to get to know each other. I don't want to think about things that happened in my past, or in yours. Those things don't really matter. What matters is you and I are sitting here now. And I am the happiest that I have been in a long time." She softly smiled.

As if a magnet were pulling the two of them together, the two went into each other's arms. Beth wrapped both of her arms around Alex's neck as his arms slid around her, pulling her body to his. He released his hold gently and with one hand reached up to touch her cheek. He slowly moved his face down to hers and tilted his head slightly to the side. His lips parted as they tenderly touched hers. As their lips met, Alex's arms tightened around Beth drawing her as close as was possible to his body. His tongue gently parted her thin lips allowing its entry. At first, their kiss began slow and tender causing Beth's body to quiver. She opened her lips allowing his tongue to enter, touching and caressing hers. Alex's hand began to move slowly up and down her back until it stopped at the bottom of her sweater. He moved his hand to the front of the sweater and as his kisses became filled with heated desire, he reached up under the soft garment and began caressing the soft skin on her stomach. With ease and control his hand moved upward until it found her full, firm breasts. He reached for the bra fastener holding the bra closed and with a

CIRCLE OF LOVE

quick movement of his fingers unfastened it. Her breasts were now exposed to his wandering hand. He slowly began to caress her breast feeling its fullness. His fingers grasped it and cupped it. With his forefinger he searched for its nipple and found it standing hard and erect waiting for his touch. He pulled away from Beth's lips and slowly moved his head down to her beautiful breast. At first his tongue played with her hard nipple making small circles around it. His lips parted as he took it into his mouth, allowing his hand to remain cupped around the firmness. Beth tilted her head back and let out a little moan at the warmth of his mouth around her breast. She felt as if she was melting as the heat of desire burned in her body. Never had she wanted to give herself so completely to any man before.

Chapter 9

Joseph O'Dea leaned back in his chair and laid the pen down on his desk. He glanced at the clock sitting on the shelf. It was ten-thirty. He was busy doing paperwork getting ready for the next day. His briefcase was open on the floor with several documents hanging from its sides. On his desk lay several forms and papers scattered in an unorganized fashion. No matter now hard he tried to concentrate, his mind was constantly filled with thoughts of Beth.

He had met Beth almost eight years ago. He could remember vividly the first day he noticed her. He had walked into the office and saw her sitting busily working at her desk. Because her desk was facing the doorway, he had a perfect view of her. For a moment he remained standing at the entrance and tried to discretely look at her. As she quietly stared at her computer monitor he could easily see her beautiful blue eyes. He studied the way her long golden hair lay on her shoulders with pieces tucked behind her ears and the headphones. He watched as she stopped typing and removed the headphones from her ears placing them down on her desk. She pushed herself away from the desk and quickly got up to retrieve a file from the filing cabinet. He continued to watch as she walked to the back of the office, stopping for a moment to pick up a book lying on a nearby desk. She was wearing a navy blue suit with matching pumps. The skirt was short in style and showed off her shapely legs. He sighed as he continued to watch her, but quickly turned his head when he saw she was retuning to her desk. He

CIRCLE OF LOVE

did not want her to notice that he had been watching her. His heart pounded wildly.

He knew the firm was hiring a new secretary but was unsure when she was to begin her position. No one had told him her name or any information about her. He took in a deep breath as he realized he would have to walk past her desk to deliver his papers. As he began to walk past her desk to drop off the papers for another secretary, she glanced up at him and their eyes met for a second. Her eyes were as blue as sapphires and seemed to twinkle. She gave him a quick smile, but did not say a word. He quickly glanced at her fingers that were rapidly typing on her keyboard to look for any rings that she might be wearing, specifically a wedding band. To his dismay, there was a diamond ring and gold band on her left ring finger. He felt his heart drop as he felt the disappointment of the ring confirming that she was married. No woman had ever captured his attention like she had.

He had been twenty-eight then and never been married. He had never found the woman of his dreams, someone who he could give his love to. But as he walked past Beth, something in his heart had told him that the woman he had always dreamed of was sitting right there, only a few feet away from him. Sadly, some other lucky man had found her first and had stolen his chance to be with her.

As the memories started to flood his thoughts, he leaned back in his chair and reached up and ran his fingers threw his thick, dark, wavy hair. Even though it had been eight years, he could still feel the excitement, then disappointment he had felt on that day when he had first seen her. He shook his head recalling

Dawn Elizabeth

how he had envied the man who had put those rings on her finger. He would never have an opportunity to get to know her, nor would he ever be able to open his heart to her, the woman of his dreams.

For seven months following that day he made trips to that office dropping off the documents that he had filed with the courts for the various secretaries. Once in a while he would drop off papers for Beth. But she never showed the slightest interest in him. She would only take the papers and thank him. She never would start any conversation or small talk. This was unusual for him because most secretaries in this office and other offices that he did filings for had always flirted and thrown themselves at him.

Joseph O'Dea was extremely handsome. He had thick, wavy, dark brown hair and warm, hazel eyes. A well-groomed moustache covered his thin upper lip, lips that surrounded perfectly straight, white teeth. On the right side of his face, about half an inch from the bottom of his nose was a mole, which gave his face character. He stood slightly over six feet tall and was of a strong, solid, muscular build. He was most definitely a man who caught most women's eyes. He was able to dress casually and the women seemed to love the way he filled out his jeans. In the warm months he would wear shorts into the offices to retrieve the papers that needed to be served. He would always laugh to himself as he felt the many eyes surveying his strong, muscular legs. He most definitely fit the description of "tall, dark, and handsome". He was used to getting the attention of many women, but for some reason she never paid him any mind.

CIRCLE OF LOVE

On the days he had documents to return to her office, he would purposely find some reason to pass the area where she sat. Even though she never noticed him, he always enjoyed stealing glimpses of her. On some days he would notice that she would be wearing her wedding rings, and on other days her finger would be bare. He was not sure as to whether she had forgotten to put them on that morning, or if she was having marital problems. Finally, one day he got up the courage to ask one of the secretaries in her office whether or not she was married. He was told that she had been married, but was going through a divorce. Even though he knew that it was wrong to be happy that someone's marriage had failed, he was ecstatic because it meant she would soon be free, and it would give him a chance to possibly be with her.

It was a sunny spring day when his prayers had been answered. He walked into her office expecting it to be the same as any other day when he dropped papers off for the secretaries. He would do his usual walk past her desk and deliver the documents he had filed that morning. He would try to steal glimpses of her as he usually did. Sadly, he had gotten used to the fact that she didn't seem interested in him. But on this particular day something had happened. As he walked past her desk he could feel her eyes on him for longer than just a moment. He felt her eyes survey his behind just as the others had done. As he stopped, he turned to look at her and actually caught her looking at his backside.

"Beth, what are you looking at?" He asked.

Beth's face turned as red as the slacks she was wearing.

Dawn Elizabeth

"Ah, nothing. I wasn't looking at anything."

He walked over and sat on the corner of her desk.

"Yes you *were*. What were you looking at?" he whispered.

He looked at her and could see the redness in her cheeks as she became more and more embarrassed after being caught "checking him out." Joseph felt that this was the moment he had always hoped for. Beth Hanson had actually noticed him. He was not going to walk away from this opportunity, especially since he knew she was a free woman. Beth turned back to her computer, hoping he would leave. She was extremely embarrassed being caught doing what every other woman in the office had been doing for months. She picked up one of the files sitting on her desk and began to open it. She thought that if she pretended to be busy he would forget about it and leave. Joe realized what Beth was trying to do but did not want to forget about what he had seen. This was the opening that he had been praying for. Now that the door was open, he was determined to go in.

"C'mon, Beth, tell me ... what were you looking at?" He bent down close to her face and whispered in her ear.

Beth looked at him and smiled. She took a moment to really look at him. He was truly handsome and had a beautiful smile, especially when he was flirting.

"Okay, if you must know. I was looking at your nice jeans. I was trying to see what brand they were. Now could you please get off of my desk and go. I have work to do."

Joe felt like he had just won the lottery. Beth Hanson had just admitted that she indeed was looking

CIRCLE OF LOVE

at him. She did know that he existed! As he stood up, he looked directly into her beautiful blue eyes. They were so full of light. He felt a small tinge of happiness as he realized that he could be credited with, at that particular moment in time, putting that light in them.

"Okay, I will leave." He started to walk away, but stopped and turned back to once again look at her. "But I am going to find out exactly what it was that you were looking at." He gave her a broad grin, turned and walked away.

Joe had driven only a few miles from her office when he impulsively pulled over to a phone booth. He wanted to talk with her more, and maybe even ask her out. When the receptionist answered the phone she didn't even sound suspicious as to why he was calling Beth. He often called the secretaries when he had questions about the pleadings he was filing with the courts. To the receptionist he was only calling with some questions about some paper Beth had given him. He couldn't hold the smile back when he heard her voice on the other end of the receiver.

"Hello, this is Beth. May I help you?" she asked.

"Yes, you can help me. You can tell me what exactly it was that you were looking at."

"Ah...I wasn't looking at anything. I promise." She replied in a whisper. She looked around the office to make sure no one was nearby listening to her.

"Yes, you were, I saw you. Tell me."

"Okay." she laughed, "I was looking at your butt. There are you happy? I admitted it." She spoke in a low tone so the other secretaries wouldn't hear what she was saying.

Dawn Elizabeth

"I thought so. And why were you looking at my butt?" he kidded.

By this time, Beth had become so embarrassed and was concerned that one of the other secretaries would notice and wonder why her face was beet-red when she was talking on the phone.

"Can you hold on for a moment. I am going to go to another phone. Hold on a sec." She put him on hold and went into one of the vacant offices and closed the door. She went over to the desk and picked up the receiver.

"Are you still there?"

"Yes, I am here. Can I say something? Joe asked, his tone softly changing to serious.

"Sure, what do you want to say?"

"Do you realize that ever since you started working with Jones and Jones I have had a crush on you?"

Beth rolled her eyes, not believing what this handsome man was saying to her. She closed her eyes and remembered how handsome he had looked when he was flirting with her just moments earlier. This was probably the line he used with many women. Maybe it had worked with them, put it wasn't going to work with her.

"Do you tell all of the secretaries that?" she laughed.

Joe suddenly felt crushed. He had been very honest and very serious. He could tell by the tone of her voice that she thought it was only some kind of line.

"I'm serious. Ever since you started working at that firm, I have been mesmerized with you. I looked at your hand when you first started working there and

CIRCLE OF LOVE

noticed that you had on wedding rings. But I would come in the office and one day you would have them on, the next day you wouldn't. I had no idea what was going on. Finally, I asked one of the girls and she told me that you were going through a divorce. Is that truer? Are you going through a divorce, or are you already divorced?"

Beth was completely surprised with what she had just heard. First, this man had said that he had a crush on her, then he had taken the time to notice whether or not she was wearing a wedding ring. She was extremely amazed, yet at the same time she was tickled and flattered. She had overheard the secretaries commenting on his good looks on numerous occasions and knew that there were many women who worked at the courthouse that were interested in getting to know Joseph O'Dea, and perhaps dating him. Now this man was telling her that he had been mesmerized with her so much so that he made a point to notice whether or not she wore any wedding rings.

"Hey, are you still there, or did I lose you?" Joe asked.

"I'm still here. A little in shock, but still here."

"I hope I didn't offend you by asking about the divorce."

"Oh no, it's okay. In answer to your question, yes, I am divorced. My divorce was final a month ago. But he and I had been separated for quite a long time before that. The divorce just made it final, and legal."

"Well, I hope you don't think I am being too forward. But, I was wondering if I could give you a call later tonight?"

Dawn Elizabeth

"You want to call me tonight?" Beth asked, still amazed with the idea that Joseph O'Dea was interested in her.

Joe laughed at the sound of astonishment in her voice. "Yes, I would like to call you tonight. But in order to do that I need one thing."

Beth took a deep breath before asking her next question. She wasn't sure whether or not she was ready for his answer. "And what might that be?"

"Your phone number," he laughed. I guess I could look it up, but I would rather that you gave it to me.

Beth giggled and started to recite her number to him.

"Uh oh," he teased. "You live right around the corner from me. The two of us are going to really get into trouble."

What do you mean you live right around the corner?" she quietly asked.

Joe grinned to himself because after hearing Beth's phone number he knew she lived in the same area as he did and it would be easy for them to run into each other. Actually, their town was small, so it surprised him that they hadn't run into one another at one of the shopping centers or even passed on the street. Of course, he had never thought that she lived in his town. He had always thought she lived in the town in which the firm was located.

"I live in the Heather Lake Apartments. I believe they are close to where you live. Do you know where they are?"

Beth put her head down and reached for pen that was lying next to phone. She started to doodle on a piece of scratch paper that was sitting to the side of the

CIRCLE OF LOVE

phone. She knew exactly where the apartments were that he had mentioned. Not only did she know them but, her house was right around the corner from them, just as he had said.

"Yes, I know where those apartments are. I drive by them on my way home everyday. I didn't realized that we lived so close to each other."

"Well, it looks like we do...so, would it be okay if I called you tonight? Maybe I could even drop by for a visit if you wouldn't mind. Then you could tell me why my jeans seemed to interest you so much," he teased.

Beth laid the pen down next to the phone and smiled, "It's okay for you to call me tonight, that would be nice. And I would love it if you stopped by...but...don't expect me to tell you what I found so interesting about your jeans...because that is my little secret."

Joe got up from his desk and walked into the kitchen. He knew that he had a lot of work to do for the next day. Unfortunately, he couldn't concentrate because his mind kept drifting back to that night, the night that had been their beginning. He reached for a glass in the overhead cupboard to the left of the kitchen sink. He withdrew a tall, blue tumbler and placed it down on the counter. He turned and walked over to the refrigerator and opened the door looking for something that contained caffeine in order to keep him awake. He did not drink coffee; otherwise, he would be making a pot. He moved a few of the items around the shelf and noticed a liter bottle of Coke behind a jug of milk. "This would do it", he thought as he poured the soda-pop into his glass. As he drew the glass to his

Dawn Elizabeth

lips to take a sip, memories of that night came flashing through his mind like a scene on some television show that he was observing.

The telephone was on the third ring when Beth reached for the receiver hanging on her kitchen wall. It was eight-thirty and she had just finished tucking her children in their beds and kissing them goodnight.

"Hello," she said cheerfully into the mouthpiece.

"Hi there, this is Joe. Is it too late for me to be calling?" he asked.

Beth was extremely surprised that he had kept his word and was calling. She actually had given up on him calling an hour earlier. The sound of his voice made her shiver for some odd reason. She turned and leaned against the kitchen wall and started to twirl the phone cord around her finger.

"Hi! No, it's not too late for you to call. Actually I had just finished tucking the kids in bed…"

"You have kids?" he quickly interrupted.

Beth felt her heart sink when she heard his question. She hadn't thought to tell him earlier that she had two kids. She had thought it was common knowledge. Her son and daughter were her world. She thought everyone knew that.

"Yes, I have a little boy and little girl. Does that bother you?" she asked.

"Not at all, I love kids. Do I need to let you go so you can take care of them?" he responded.

"No, they are both tucked in for the night. They are usually in bed by eight-thirty."

"Well then, would you like some company? As we discovered earlier I am just around the corner. I could stop by for a little while."

CIRCLE OF LOVE

Beth's heart began to pound. It had been so long since she had dated and she wasn't really sure how to play the game. She wanted him to come over but she didn't want to appear too eager. She gently bit her lower lip and looked down. She took a deep breath before responding to his question.

"I would love some company. Are you sure you want to come over tonight?"

"I have never been more sure. How about you give me directions and I'll drop by in an hour or so? I have some things I need to do to get myself ready for work tomorrow. If I get everything organized now, I won't have to rush to leave when I get there. That way we can both relax and get to know one another."

Beth quickly gave Joe the directions to her house then hung up the receiver. She smiled to herself in disbelief as she stood in her kitchen letting the idea that Joseph O'Dea was actually coming over to her house sink in. She was so nervous that she decided she would have a glass of wine to calm herself down a little so it wouldn't be obvious to him. After pouring herself a glass of wine she went to her room to change into something that would flatter her figure. She took a pair of jeans and a pale blue, short sleeve sweater from her closet. She held the sweater up in front of herself and looked at her reflection in the mirror. She had been given many compliments when she wore this sweater. It had a scooped neck that emphasized the roundness of her breasts without appearing sleazy or distasteful. The soft color brought out the bright blue color of her eyes. She removed the clothes that she was wearing and went to the bathroom to freshen up. She really didn't have time to take a full shower but

Dawn Elizabeth

decided to have a quick sponge bath. She washed her face and removed the makeup that had faded. She carefully reapplied a touch of makeup and tied her hair up in a bouncy ponytail. She pulled a few strains of hair from the ponytail and let the soft hair frame her face. She reached for her glass of wine as she stood back and glanced at her reflection in the mirror. The sweetness of the wine lingered on her lips and made them tingle. As she took another sip she thought to herself, "I am so nervous. I think I should pour myself more of this." She quickly finished the remaining wine and headed for the kitchen to pour her another glass. She didn't realize that the wine was slowly starting to have an effect on her. A waive of happiness traveled through her body and she began to giggle.

"I cannot believe Joseph O'Dea is coming over to my house...my house!" She giggled. She picked the glass of wine up and without realizing what she was doing drank the whole glass without stopping. As she sat the glass down on the counter she heard the doorbell ring. She walked to the front door stopping briefly to glance at her reflection in the mirror to make sure she looked nice.

Joseph rang the doorbell then stood on the long front porch and waited for Beth to come to the door. He was fighting the butterflies in his stomach as he glanced around the beautifully landscaped yard. It was obvious that someone had taken special care in keeping the bushes and trees trimmed. The hedges that encircled the large yard were all neatly and evenly cut. The lawn was also freshly cut and the smell of fresh grass filled the air. To the right of the door was a long park bench with black cast iron sides. On the left side

CIRCLE OF LOVE

of the door was an antique metal milk jug that had been painted dark black. The house itself was a large two-story colonial. The upper section of the house was painted a pale yellow, the lower section was dark brick.

The butterflies in his stomach seemed to be at war with each other as he patiently waited for her to answer the door. He wished that he would have had a beer before he left to relax him a bit, but had decided against it. He didn't want to make a bad first impression. He hadn't smoked a cigarette because he was afraid that he would smell like smoke and that would turn her off, or offend her. He didn't know if she smoked or not, and didn't want to take a chance in spoiling things.

As Beth opened the door, Joseph's heart started to beat so fast that he felt she would notice it beating and pounding against his chest. He took in a deep breath as he looked at the woman of his dreams that was standing only arm lengths away. He smiled to himself thinking she looked like an angel in her pale blue sweater. He glanced at her and noticed that she had pulled her hair up and allowed a few strands to fall loose in order to frame her face. With her hair up it exposed her beautiful neck. Seeing this evoked in him an incredibly strong urge to kiss it. It took all of his energy to refrain himself from doing just that.

She smiled at him and opened the door, welcoming him into her home. As he stepped inside he came close enough to smell the faint scent of alcohol on her breath. He recalled how he had been so nervous and had wanted to have a beer to relax him before being alone with her. He wondered if she had drunk the

Dawn Elizabeth

wine for the same reason. He stepped inside and slowly looked around her home. It was decorated with various country crafts that gave it a warm, cozy atmosphere.

"You have a beautiful home. It suits you. It is warm and cozy," he began as he continued to glance around the room.

"Thanks. Come into the family room and make yourself comfortable. Would you like something to drink? You'll have to excuse me, but I have had a little bit of wine. I needed something to relax me a little bit."

The handsome man looked over at Beth and noticed the slight flush in her cheeks and wondered exactly how much wine she had had. He didn't think it would be a good idea for him to have anything to drink.

"Oh, no thanks. I am fine."

He walked into the family room and sat down on a big puffy beige recliner. He quickly glanced around and noticed there was a matching chair on the other side of the room. As he continued to look around he saw a television sitting in the corner. The family room and kitchen were adjoined. There were two bar stools pushed up under the counter that extended from the kitchen into the family room. On the far end was beautiful fireplace with a mantel that extended the full width of the wall. Decorating the mantel were various pictures of all shapes and sizes. The people in the pictures were small children and other people who Joe decided must be her kids and family members. On the right was a large door-wall. The blinds hanging on the window were partly opened and it appeared that the

CIRCLE OF LOVE

doorway lead to a huge deck overlooking her backyard. As he continued to survey the room he noticed an adorable large sized Raggedy Ann and Andy sitting on a beautiful rocking chair that appeared to be hand painted. The room was definitely enchanting and somehow put him at ease.

Beth followed him into the room and sat down in the matching recliner opposite Joe. The effects of the alcohol were starting to hit her and she felt as if she were in some strange type of daze, not really in total control of her actions.

The two both feeling a little awkward, began talking about small things. They talked about what she thought about the firm and the people she worked with. He asked her about her children and she proudly began to describe her son and daughter to him. As she spoke about each child her eyes filled up with a beautiful light. It was very obvious to Joe that these two children were her world. After talking for a while, Joe decided he wanted to share with her the way he had felt.

"Beth, I meant what I said today about having a crush on you. I am not very good with words, so I really don't know how to say this…but in my eyes you are the most beautiful woman that I have ever seen. I have been dreaming about you all my life."

The wine had finally hit her hard and she was now feeling slightly intoxicated. She listened as best she could to the words that he had said and when he had finished she began to laugh.

"My gosh, do you tell all of the women you see that?"

Dawn Elizabeth

The blood rushed to his face, as he felt somewhat humiliated. He had been honest and was speaking from his heart. He had poured his heart out to her and she was actually laughing at him. He took a deep breath and looked down at his hands. Slowly he looked up and took another breath before he began to speak to her again.

"I'm serious...it isn't some line."

As he began to say something else the phone began to ring and interrupted him. Beth stared at him for a moment, caught off guard by what he had just told her. She gave him a tender smile and then got up to answer the phone.

Joe felt crushed. He silently wished that somehow he could retract the words that he had spoken. He was foolish to believe that someone like him could ever capture the heart of a woman like her. He had never acted in such a foolish way before, telling a woman how he felt. In the past he had always tried to keep his feelings buried deep inside of his soul, never allowing them a chance to be shown. As he waited for her to return from her phone call, he spotted a remote control sitting on the floor next to the chair she had been sitting in. He got up and walked over to retrieve it. He turned back to the T.V. and turned it on. He lowered himself down on the floor in front of the chair and stretched his long muscular legs out in front of him. Quickly, he started to switch the channels searching for something to get his mind off what he had just done.

As Beth walked back into the room she saw Joe sitting on the floor with his legs outstretched in front of him, leaning against one of the chairs. He held the T.V. remote in front of him and was rapidly changing

CIRCLE OF LOVE

the channels. She noticed the sadness on his face as he stared at the screen of the television. Suddenly, she realized what she had done. Twice today he had tried to tell her his true feelings of interest in her and she had laughed at him. She felt horrible for bruising this man's ego. She deeply regretted drinking so much wine, it always made her say and do stupid things. Unfortunately, it also took away her inhibitions and gave her courage to do things she normally wouldn't. Slowly, she entered the room and, without hesitating, walked over to where Joe was sitting and sat down on his lap. Joe grinned and laid the remote down on the floor next to him.

Beth drew her lips in a childlike pout and asked the man she was now comfortably sitting on. "Joe, I am sorry, do you hate me?"

Joe was extremely surprised at her actions but could not stop himself from taking advantage of the wonderful situation. He pulled her to him and began to slowly kiss her beautiful wine sweetened lips. His kisses began slow and tender. He felt Beth hold back at first, but suddenly as if someone had unlocked the door to her control, she began to return the kisses with fire and passion. She briefly pulled away from his lips and began to kiss his neck. She moved up to his ear and started nibbling the lobe. She began to breathe heavily into it allowing her tongue to move into his ear as she softly moaned. He felt the walls surrounding his heart grumble as he pulled her back to him and once again began to kiss her passionately. His tongue parted her lips and searched for hers. Her arms went around his neck and she pushed her body as close as she could to his. He wanted her so badly and was

Dawn Elizabeth

afraid that he was going to burst from his desire. Slowly, he pulled himself from her in order to look directly into her magnificent blue eyes.

"I want to ask you something, and it is going to be hard for me to do…but I am going to ask anyway," he asked, his eyes never leaving hers.

Beth was puzzled as to why he had stopped. "What, Joe?"

"Beth, you are so incredibly beautiful…I was wondering if you would put a teddy or nightgown on for me."

Through the effects of the alcohol she listened to the words the man had spoken. She felt as if someone had abruptly slapped her across her face. She was deeply shocked as to what he had asked her to do. In her mind she could hear herself saying, "No, Beth, don't do it." But the alcohol was overpowering and she slowly lifted herself up off his lap. She looked down at Joe, knowing he was anxiously waiting to hear her response.

"Yes, I will…I will be right back."

As she walked into her bedroom her mind was telling her that she shouldn't be doing this. She didn't even know this man. It was wrong for her to put on a "teddy" or, nightgown like he asked. But it had been so long since she had been with a man. She wanted to be touched. She wanted to be made love to. She walked over to her dresser and withdrew a beautiful peach nightgown with matching panties. The gown had spaghetti straps and a plunging neckline that would barely cover her firm, full breasts. The material was silk and clingy which would emphasize her curves. As she held the garments in her hands she felt

CIRCLE OF LOVE

the anticipation as to what kind of response wearing the negligee would provoke. It was extremely sexy and there was no doubt as to what reaction it would cause. She lowered herself down on her bed and shook her head trying to focus, unfortunately, the alcohol was too strong, and she felt as if she had no control. She quickly changed into the negligee, grabbed a robe, and returned downstairs to seduce Joe.

As she walked into the room, Joe looked up and smiled. He had gotten up off the floor and was sitting comfortably in one of the recliners. She walked over to him and knelt down in front of him. She rested her hands on his knees and looked up into his eyes. She felt the loneliness in her heart battling its walls to get out. She wanted to be held and touched, even though her mind was telling her this was the wrong way to pursue it.

In a soft whisper she said, "Now it is my turn. I have a question to ask…"

Joe could see that something was bothering her and he did not want to do anything to scare her or make her feel uncomfortable. No matter how badly he wanted her, he did not want to push her into something she was not ready for. He reached down and began to caress her cheek in an attempt to put her at ease.

"What is it, Beth? What do you want to ask?"

For a moment she pulled her eyes away from his and looked down at the floor. She took a breath and raised her head so that she could again gaze directly into his eyes.

"Is this going to be a one night stand, Joe?"

Joe felt his heart drop; he was ashamed of himself for causing her to feel this way. He bent down and

Dawn Elizabeth

scooped her up into his arms, gently sitting her on his lap.

"Oh, Beth… no… no, this definitely is not going to be a one night stand," he moaned.

He drew her body to his and slowly started kissing every part that was exposed to him. It took all of the control that he possessed not to take her right then and there when he heard her moans of pleasure. He eased her down onto the floor and removed his shirt. Her hands quickly reached up and started caressing his back, exploring each and every muscle on his arm as they made their way around to his chest. She started kissing his neck and moved her way down to his chest, always exploring. He closed his eyes and silently said a prayer of thanks for having his prayer answered. He opened his eyes and saw the woman who was now surrendering herself to him.

Joe returned to his desk and looked down at his paperwork. He knew that he should sit down and finish it, but he had no motivation. In his mind he could still see the way she had looked at him that night many years ago. He remembered the way her eyes had looked into his, pleading with him not to hurt her. All she wanted was to be loved. She deserved to be loved. He loved her more than she could ever imagine, but it was the love that he felt for her that had kept him at a distance. He would never be able to give her the love she had wanted and also deserved, but he could not allow himself to stop seeing her either. So he continued to see her, using her, even though he knew it tore her heart apart each time.

Chapter 10

Beth shook her head and let out a heavy sigh as she picked up the file and tape sitting on her desk. There was a note on the tape indicating that it was a full two-sided tape. It was bad enough that the tape was so long but the thing that made it even more burdensome was the file the tape belonged to. It was a file that Beth hated to work on. Her stomach turned each time this particular file crossed her desk. Any work done on it was always time consuming because there were so many defendants involved. Numerous defendants meant numerous attorneys that would have to be copied on every document that was prepared. She bit down on her lower lip and placed the tape into the transcriber and quickly pressed the rewind button. She turned to her computer and located the area where the documents relating to this filed had been saved. Once she heard the high-pitched tone on the transcriber indicating the tape had been rewound she picked up her headphones and began listening to the instructions her boss was giving her. She closed her eyes as she listened to the deep voice of her boss advising her that they would be preparing yet another motion on this case. After his instructions he began with his dictation and she began to type rapidly word for word.

Just as she had finished typing the first page, her senses were filled with the wonderful tingling sensations she always felt whenever Alex was near. She tilted her head to the side and closed her eyes. In her mind she could vividly see his face, his warm brown eyes and the smile he had whenever he was

Dawn Elizabeth

comforting her. Pulling her from her thoughts, she heard her friend's voice on her intercom.

"Beth, you have a call, on line one. It's…"

Beth shook her head and grinned to herself. "It's Alex, isn't it?"

"Yes, it is. How did you know? Did you just page him?"

"Nope, but I got that feeling again. Somehow I always know when Alex is around, or thinking of me. Thanks." She quickly reached for the receiver. "Hello, this is Beth."

"Hello, Princess. We're not busy at the moment so I thought I would give you a quick call. How is your day going?"

"Oh, it's going okay," she said with a sigh.

"That didn't sound very convincing. What's up? Are you having a bad day?" Alex said with concern in his voice.

"No, not really. I just hate working on this file. It is always so time consuming. It wouldn't be bad if it was an interesting case. But, unfortunately, it's a boring one. How is your day going? Do you miss me?"

"You know the answer to that. Just like I knew you were dreading working on that file. I felt it. That's why I called. I was working and I felt you give out a heavy sigh. It hit me like a ton of bricks. Are you sure you're okay?"

"Yes, I'm sure." Beth lowered her voice to a whisper so someone wouldn't overhear what she was going to say next. "Close your eyes Alex. Feel it? I'm okay now. Isn't it amazing how we both get these feelings and we seem to know what the other person is feeling?"

CIRCLE OF LOVE

"Yes, it is extremely amazing. The love we feel for each other must be true. I hope we always can feel what the other is feeling. Well, honey, I need to get back to work. If you need me, page me. Otherwise, I'll see you tonight."

"Okay. See you tonight." Beth picked up her headphones and started working on the tape. She didn't dread doing it so badly now. She knew that by the time she finished it, it would only be a short while before she would be with Alex.

It had been a month since they had started seeing each other and for some reason they were both able to feel each other's feelings. At first it had scared both of them, but after having it happen a few times they had both gotten used to it. Even though neither had actually said the words, "I love you" they both felt a strong love for the other. Beth smiled to herself knowing that tonight was going to be a special night. This was the kids' weekend to be with their father and she and Alex had a wonderful evening planned. Beth had an amazing dinner planned and had bought a couple dozen candles to scatter throughout her home. They would have a romantic candlelight dinner, which she would prepare, then they would dance to beautiful love songs, with only the glow from the flames of the candles giving them light. Swaying back and forth in perfect harmony in each other's arms, she wanted the night to be as perfect as possible. In her heart she was hoping that this would be the night that they would become one.

As her fingers started to fly across the keyboard she was interrupted by the intercom again.

Dawn Elizabeth

"Beth, you have another call. Pick up the phone for a second."

Beth took the headphones off and laid them on the desk and reached for the receiver.

"It's Joe. Do you want me to tell him you are away from your desk?" her friend suggested. She did not want this man to wiggle his way back into her friend's life. The last thing Beth needed was to have this jerk screw up her relationship with Alex.

Beth was a little surprised by the call. She had not spoken to Joseph O'Dea in almost two months. She really didn't want to take the call but she knew that if he thought she was away from her desk he would be persistent in continuing to call back until he finally spoke with her directly. Rather than delaying the confrontation she decide to take the call.

"It's okay. I'll talk to him."

"Are you sure? I can tell him you're in an all day meeting or something."

"No, I'll talk to him. What line did you say he was on'?"

"He's on line three ... I hope you know what you're doing. Remember that handsome man named Alex? That man who is so good to you?"

"I'm not going to see him. If I don't take the call he will keep calling back. I will just talk to him now rather than delaying the inevitable. Have a little faith in me. I know what I'm doing. I promise."

The young woman shook her head. She knew the kind of control this man had had on her friend for many years. He would tell her to jump and she would say "how high" without thinking twice. Beth was actually happy now. It made her cringe to think that he

CIRCLE OF LOVE

would do something to spoil her friend's happiness. Beth had asked her to have some faith in her so without any unwanted comments she hung up her phone to let her friend handle the caller on her own.

"Hello, this is Beth."

"Hey, lady, I haven't heard from you in awhile. I thought I would give you a call and see if you would like some company tonight." Joe said confident that she would be eager to see him. He knew that in the past that Beth had never said "no" to him. It had been two months since she had called and, truthfully, he had missed her.

"No, Joe, I don't. I don't know how to say this except to say it straight out. I am seeing someone. I have been for the past month. It's an exclusive relationship. I have no desire to see you or anyone else besides him."

Joe felt his stomach twisting in knots. He and Beth had had a physical relationship for eight years. She had dated other men in the past but she always made time for him.

"Hey, you can give me twenty minutes of your time. I know I haven't called in awhile, but I have been really busy. I miss you, Beth. C'mon, I know you miss me too. Why don't you stop by my apartment on your way home...we can get re-acquainted with each other's bodies."

Beth, beginning to feel frustrated by his persistence, lowered her voice so someone wouldn't hear her. "Didn't you just hear what I said? I said no! I am seeing someone who I care for very much. I don't need, nor do I want, a quick roll in the hay. Don't call me anymore. Go find someone else to use.

Dawn Elizabeth

Okay? Bye." Infuriated with his attitude she quickly slammed the receiver down on its base.

Joe's eyes widened as he heard the phone being slammed in his ear. He sat in his chair for what seemed like an eternity to him. He could not comprehend, nor did he accept, what Beth had just said. He slowly put the receiver back onto the base of the phone and reached up to rubbed his forehead. He had always known in his heart that sooner or later Beth would give up on the idea of the two of them ever having a relationship other than physical. Their physical relationship had lasted for almost eight years and he had used every ounce of constraint that he possessed to not let her see his true feelings for her. He loved her and always had. But in his soul he felt that she deserved more than what he had to offer. In her presence he had always acted as if the sex were the only thing he was interested in. What she didn't know was, that in all the years that he had known her, he had never touched another woman. No woman would ever be able to touch his heart in the way she had. She was the most perfect woman there was. She had always tried so hard to win him over, when all along she had held his heart in the palms of her little hands.

He reached for the nearest object next to him and picked it up and threw it across the room. The glass hit the wall and shattered into tiny pieces, then scattered all over the floor. The liquid in the glass streamed in various directions down the wall leaving a brown stain on its path to the floor. "Damn it", he yelled. He looked at the pieces of glass that were scattered all over the floor and the streams of coke finding their way to join the shattered remains of glass on the floor.

CIRCLE OF LOVE

He stood up and went to the kitchen to retrieve the broom and dustpan. He also grabbed a dishrag and ran it under the water getting it wet to wash off the stained wall. As he reached the space on the floor where the broken glass laid he couldn't help but feel that it was his heart that had been broken and was lying on the floor in a million pieces and it would take more than a broom, dustpan, and sponge to clean it up. He knew that someday he would lose Beth. He just didn't think it would be this painful when it finally happened. He took a deep breath and bent down and started sweeping. She deserved to be happy, he thought as he swept. In his mind he heard someone say, "If you love her, set her free. She'll come back if it's meant to be." As he turned to wipe the stain off the wall he felt the warmth of tears fill his eyes. The tears were a symbol of his acceptance that she wasn't going to come back to him. All those years he had loved her enough to keep their relationship at a distance, purely physical and unemotional. He never let her see the love that he held hidden in his heart. He had always been afraid that he could never live up to her expectations of the man she thought he was. So he had pretended that he wasn't interested in her in any way other than in the bed. With the back of his hand he quickly wiped the tears that had escaped from his eyes. Now he would have to pretend that he was glad she was gone. He would be the only one who would know the pain he felt caused by her absence. No one would ever know how deeply he loved her, no one except him.

Chapter 11

Beth drew the shower curtain back and reached for a thick, navy blue bath towel lying on floor next to the bathtub. She first patted the water from her face and then slowly started to dry herself off. She wrapped the towel around her shoulders and slid the towel from side to side drying off her back, then moved the towel to the front of her body drying it. She wrapped the towel around her body and tucked the end into her cleavage keeping the towel securely closed. She bent down and picked up a second towel. She lowered her head letting her long wet hair hang in front of her body. The water quickly found its way to the ends of the strands and dropped to the floor leaving several tiny drops giving the effects of a little cloudburst in the bathroom. With her head lowered, she skillfully wrapped the towel around her head, then twisted, it drawing the end up over and to the back tucking the twisted end under the back part of the towel. After making sure the turban was securely attached, she walked over to the vanity and looked at the mirror, which was covered with the steam from the hot shower she had just taken. She reached for a dry wash cloth to wipe the fogged up mirror. In a circular motion she started to wipe the moisture from the mirror. It seemed an endless battle though because shortly after she wiped the mirror the fog would again appear.

"This is useless," she thought. "This bathroom resembles a sauna."

She walked to the bathroom door that adjoined her bedroom and opened the door allowing the steam to

CIRCLE OF LOVE

escape into that room. She turned and walked to the bathroom door that lead to the hallway and opened that door also. She wasn't worried having the doors opened because she knew that she was alone in the house and it didn't matter if she was naked. No one would see her.

She walked to the vanity once more and looked at the fogged up mirror. She smiled to herself than leaned and reached over the sink. In large letters she wrote, "I love you Alex." She enclosed the words in a large heart then stood back to look at what she had written. As she stood looking at the words on the mirror the fog slowly disappeared and the mirror dried. As if someone had taken a rag and wiped the mirror the words vanished. Now, with the mirror clean and dry she could see her reflection. For several minutes she stood there gazing at the woman in the mirror with the towels wrapped around her body and head. She looked at the blue eyes that sparkled brighter than stars, the eyes that belonged to her. No longer were they filled with sadness or a feeling of emptiness. Those eyes sparkled due to the love that she felt for her handsome Alex. Her heart was no longer empty and lost. It was overflowing with a love and joy that was evident in the twinkling of her eyes.

Tonight was the night that she and Alex would have completely to themselves. They had debated on what they had wanted to do with their time alone and had decided that, rather than going out on the town, they would have a romantic evening at Beth's. She had prepared a wonderful dinner for the two and had shopped not only for the perfect dress for her, but also had picked up a new beautiful elegant tablecloth made

Dawn Elizabeth

of lace with a matching solid piece that lay beneath it. She had chosen new, matching linen napkins which she had folded and fanned, placing them next to the table settings. The table was elegant and romantic. Any onlooker could not mistake that it was a table set for two lovers. With the leaf removed the table formed a small circle. Its lace tablecloth hung down forming perfect points at all four corners. Sitting directly in the middle of the table was a vase filled with beautiful flowers. There were roses and carnations with baby's breath and greens interspersed. To each side of the flower arrangement were brass candlesticks, which held long pale blue taper candles. There were two table settings sitting on either side of the flowers and candles. The settings were of beautiful china that Beth only used for special occasions. The plates were white with tiny, pale blue flowers in the center. The ends of the flowers were tipped with white while the center of the flowers had a hint of a darker shade of blue. Circling the flowers was a band of white gold. The dishes' edges were also surrounded by white gold. There were exquisite crystal water and wine goblets to the right of the plates. The glasses stood on beautiful crystal stems with diamond designs engraved into the top half of the crystal. Scattered around the place settings were red rose petals. It was a table designed out of love and romance, a table such as this could not be found in the most exquisite of restaurants.

Alex and Beth had decided that, even though they were not going out, they wanted this evening to be perfect. They both decided that they would dress for the evening. Beth had bought a dazzling black dress. It was plain, yet extremely elegant. It had spaghetti straps

CIRCLE OF LOVE

that attached to a form-fitting bodice that dipped slightly at her cleavage exposing the roundness of her breasts. The skirt of the dress was full and flowing and fell two inches above her knees. Beth had first noticed the dress hanging on display in the store. She had thought it was rather plain but had decided to try it on. She had been pleasantly surprised at how beautiful the dress was. It was as if the dress were designed specifically to fit her body. She has chosen sheer back hose and black Patent-leather pumps. The shoes were of a medium heel so that they would be elegant, yet comfortable.

As she stood in front of the mirror she closed her eyes and could see Alex smiling at her. Her heart started to beat rapidly as she felt that he too was anxious and excited thinking of this night that they had planned. Somehow, she knew that he was a little nervous, but that his heart was overwhelming with love for her. She knew that he had been with many women, but that for some reason she was different to him. She smiled to herself knowing that she had been the woman who had captured Alexander Fuentas' heart. Tonight was the night that their love would be expressed in the most intimate, magical way. Instead of being two hearts beating separately, they would become two hearts intertwining until each beat was in unison with the other becoming one connected soul.

"Thank you, Father", she whispered. She turned around and walked into her bedroom. Alex would be there in less than two hours; she had a lot to do to get ready.

Dawn Elizabeth

Alex opened his closet door and moved to stand in front of the clothes hanging on the hangers. He was looking for the new black dress slacks that he had just purchased. He had shopped for hours looking for the perfect outfit to wear on this special night. He had had his slacks tailored so that they fit him perfectly. They had several pleats at the waist and cuffs at the bottoms. He had decided on wearing an ivory turtleneck sweater rather than a dress shirt and tie. His ebony hair hung down just above the top of the neck of the sweater. The young woman who had helped him pick it out had told him that the white sweater accentuated his coloring and gave him an appearance of a movie star. He smiled to himself, remembering the way she had blushed when he came from the fitting room to get her impression. He was hoping that Beth would have the same reaction. He wanted to please her in every possible way. As he removed the slacks from the hanger he laid them at the foot of his bed. For a moment he gazed at his bed and imagined what Beth would look like lying there. She would be so beautiful, like an angel, with her hair fanned out on the pillows, those wonderful eyes smiling at him. He felt his heart starting to race with the anticipation of the memories that they would create this evening. It would be a night that neither of them would ever forget. It would be the beginning of the rest of their lives.

He looked up trying to somehow see Heaven. "Father, I know that in the past I haven't been such a nice guy and I may have hurt many woman. I am sorry, Father. For some reason you have brought Beth and me together. And, Lord, these feelings that I get with her ... It's as if the two of us are connected.

Sometimes, I can I can actually feel what she is feeling. I know her fears and her joys. I know when she's worried, even when we're miles from one another. I feel her. Maybe there is such a thing as "soul-mates". I don't really know about all of that, but I do know that I love her. And I know that I have always loved her. I promise you, Father...I will never hurt her. I will always protect her and give her all the love that she deserves. I don't know how to say this, but I just wanted to thank you, Father, for bringing us together." Alex turned and walked to his dresser. He felt a peace in his soul knowing that his prayer had been heard, just as he knew that all the angels in Heaven were smiling down on him. This was a night that was created in Heaven, a night that was pure destiny.

Chapter 12

Beth looked up to see Alex smiling at her from across the table. She couldn't help but smile back at him. She could feel her heart flutter as their eyes looked into each other's. Her heart started to beat faster as his hand reached to caress hers. "Beth, dance with me." he softly said, then slowly stood up and walked to her side.

"Dance with me. I want to hold you in my arms," he said, as he looked down at her and gently eased her to her feet.

A beautiful soft love song was playing softly on the stereo as they walked to the center of the room. Slowly, Beth turned to stand directly in front of Alex. He smiled down at her and took one of her hands in his as their fingers intertwined. She rested her other hand on his shoulder as he pulled her close to him. His hand slid around her waist. Their bodies slowly started swaying in perfect motion to the music. Their eyes never strayed away from each other's gaze. As the song played, they moved with each other like they had been dancing forever, both turning and swaying with the other. They each felt the love that was radiating from their partner's heart, the emotion deep and intensely strong.

As they danced, Beth felt that there was no place that she would rather be than in Alex's arms, dancing as they were now. She felt Alex gently pull her closer to him as if he could feel what she was feeling. He leaned down and whispered into her ear, "No, Beth, there is another place that is just as beautiful, where we

CIRCLE OF LOVE

will still move in perfect rhythm. Let me show you." Pulling away from her he looked down into her eyes waiting for her response.

"Show me," she softy whispered.

Alex felt his heart pounding in his chest as he saw the want and desire in her eyes. He bent down and picked her up carrying her in his arms, he turned and headed for the stairs leading to her room. He was going to show his beautiful Beth the true meaning of making love. It was time for them to move in perfect rhythm.

Beth's heart beat rapidly as Alex carried her up the stairs to her bedroom. As he stepped up each stair, she could feel his warm breath on her face as he exhaled. No words were spoken, or needed, as he reached the top of the staircase and entered her bedroom. He walked over to the side of her bed and gently released her so that she was in a sitting position on the edge of the bed. He bent down in front of her, never breaking their eye contact, or ending the silence, and carefully removed her shoes. He slowly sat down next to her and reached down to tilt her chin up. He bent down and tenderly kissed her lips. As their lips met he felt her let out a soft moan, as he tasted the wine that sweetened her lips. All of his senses seemed to be intensified, as he could smell the fragrance of her perfume and his ears echoed with the rhythm of her breathing. He felt that at any moment his heart was going to rip apart the walls of his chest as it pounded wildly, pleading with him to be released and allowed to be out of control. Beth's arms reached up and circled around his neck. Slowly, she lowered herself, leaning back on the pillows drawing him close to her. As Alex followed her their lips never parted. Gently, his tongue motioned

Dawn Elizabeth

her lips to open allowing it to enter. As it explored her welcoming mouth, he could feel her fingers running through his hair moving with the same motion as his tongue, both moving to a magical beat that only they heard. For a month he had held back and denied himself the pleasure of her body. In his heart he had wanted this to be something that would be magical and beautiful, not hurried or rushed. He wanted this moment to be something that the two of them would always remember and cherish. As their kisses became more passionate his hand moved to her shoulder and slowly removed the strap to her dress. He slowly pulled Beth up towards him as he turned her slightly to her side, never breaking their kiss. His hand moved up to the zipper and quickly moved it down releasing her full breasts from its secure hold. In a quick motion he pulled the dress down and removed it, exposing Beth's beautiful, wanting breasts. For a moment, he broke the kiss and gazed down into Beth's beautiful eyes.

"Show me. Show me the rhythm," she looked up at him and whispered.

Alex let out a moan as he quickly removed her remaining garments. He stood up and rapidly removed his own clothing. For a brief moment he stood next to the bed and let his eyes gazed at Beth's nude body. Never before had he wanted a woman as much as he ached for her. She looked like a goddess with her hair fanned out across the pillow. It was just as he had imagined earlier. Her breasts were round and full with nipples that were light colored and standing hard in anticipation of his touch. His eyes moved down to her small stomach, stopping for only a moment, then continued down to looked at her beautiful, shapely

CIRCLE OF LOVE

legs. When he thought that he couldn't bear holding back any longer, he eased himself on top of her. Her arms went around his back and she slowly started caressing his back. She too was holding onto desire that was close to tearing her apart from restraining its passion. She moved her lips to his ear and once again whispered. "Show me. Show me the rhythm, Alex."

Upon hearing her soft whispers he could not hold back any longer and gently parted her legs to allow his hardness to enter her warmness. As his maleness entered her, he heard her let out a whispered, "Yes", as her fingers gripped his back and opened her legs wider welcoming him to her. Slowly their bodies started moving together in perfect rhythm as he pushed farther and deeper into her. He felt her raise and lower her hips following the movement of each of his thrusts. He lowered his chest down to her, slowing the motion and reached for each of her hands. One by one he took her small hands into his and intertwined his long strong figures into her tiny ones. He leaned down to her and tenderly started kissing her lips. As he tenderly kissed her and held her hands in his, he once again started the rhythmic motion, starting slowly then moving faster and faster, with each movement going deeper and deeper. He felt her hands grip his tighter. He could feel her heart pounding against his chest. He felt the warmness of her contract around his hardness and he was thrown over the edge of ecstasy, he could hold back no longer. With one final thrust he exploded into her as she raised her hips in anticipation of his final thrust.

Alex slowly broke their kiss and raised himself above her. He gazed down into her beautiful face.

Dawn Elizabeth

Beads of perspiration ran down his face. The room was dimly lit by the moonlight. A beam of its light shone through the window and gave Beth's face a magical glow.

"Do you know how beautiful you are? You look like an angel," Alex said with emotion that came from deep in his soul. As he looked down on her face he felt as if this woman had opened an emotion in him that he had never known or experienced. Her beauty was something he had never seen before and there were no words that had been written that would do it justice. Their lovemaking had been the joining of their souls.

Neither knew that a magnificent angel had been with them the whole time. He stood in the shadows in the end of the room as he watched over the two sleeping lovers. He stood silently and smiled as he watched the souls that he had been guiding throughout all of their lives, leading them to this specific moment in time. The angel quietly walked to stand at the side of the bed and looked down at the couple that now slept intertwined in each other's arms. As he gazed down on them a beautiful spectrum of light encircled him. In his heart he could feel the warmth of the love that they felt for each other. He smiled and then looked up towards the heavens. He heard the magnificent sound of the angels in Heaven singing as they too had watched the reuniting of the couple's souls. He closed his eyes and bowed his head as he listened to words that God was whispering to him. He felt a deep emotion in his heart, as he understood that it was now time for them to experience the feeling of true undying love. He opened his eyes and turned to walk back into the shadows. He remained in the room, kindheartedly watching over the two souls as they slept peacefully.

Chapter 13

Beth slowly turned over and reached her arm out searching for Alex; to her alarm, he was not there. Startled at the emptiness of the bed, she bolted upright. She grabbed the sheet and wrapped it around her nude body. Last night she and Alex had spent an entire evening of passion, each of them intimately getting to know the other. She was looking forward to waking up and seeing him and feeling him next to her, but to her dismay he was not in the bed, nor was he anywhere in the room. With the sheet wrapped around her she headed for the bedroom door stopping abruptly as it opened before she reached it. With a tray full of a variety of different breakfast foods ranging from pancakes, eggs, fruit, wheat toast and Cheerios, Alex entered the bedroom beaming. He stopped and slowly gazed at Beth standing before him with a sheet knotted around her naked body. He grinned as he watched her quickly and nonchalantly attempt to move her mussed up hair out of her face, while trying to look cute at the same time.

"Going somewhere?" he chuckled.

"Ah, no. I was... Oh, Alex, I woke up and reached for you and it scared me because you weren't there. I guess I was going looking for you."

Alex looked down in Beth's face and saw the fear and loneliness that someone in the past had caused her. He walked over to the dresser and placed the tray of food on it. In a swift motion he swooped her in his arms, carrying her back to the bed. Careful not to pull

CIRCLE OF LOVE

the sheet from her, he gently sat down lowering her to his lap.

"I'm sorry I wasn't there when you woke up. I wanted to surprise you with breakfast in bed. You were sleeping so peacefully, I didn't want to disturb you." He wrapped his arms around her and pulled her to his chest. "Beth, I'm not going anywhere. I know that someone has hurt you deeply in the past. I can feel your pain. I know that someone has used you and now you doubt that someone, me, will remain with you after the passion. I can feel your emotions, your thoughts, close your eyes and feel mine."

Beth looked into Alex's eyes and saw the sincerity in them. Without hesitation or question, she closed her eyes. Her heart was suddenly filled with overwhelming warmth, which brought her an unspeakable joy. As if she had somehow been drawn into Alex's very soul, she could feel his deep, pure love for her. In her mind she could see him standing before her smiling. Her body was filled with an incredible peacefulness that assured her that he did indeed love her. She opened her eyes to see him looking down at her smiling in the exact same way as she had seen him in her mind.

"I saw you. The vision was real. I could feel you as if I was part of you, part of your soul. What is happening to us? How is this possible?"

Alex's arm gently encircled Beth pulling her closer to him. As she nestled up against his chest, he gently brushed a strand of her hair from his face.

"I'm not sure what's happening to us. I can feel you as if we are connected, as if our souls are one. When we are together as we are now, I feel complete, whole. It's as if all my life I was missing half of me.

Dawn Elizabeth

The emptiness that I use to feel has disappeared. Beth, I love you. I love your smile, the way your eyes sparkle with this radiant light. I love the sound of your voice… the way that you smell. But all of these things are familiar to me, as if I've always known them. At first I was afraid. I would be alone watching T.V. or perhaps driving in my car and I would have these intense emotions, your emotions, hit me with such an impact that it would almost knock me out. It would happen mostly when you were afraid of something or maybe overwhelmed. A few times I tried to block them out, thinking it was all my imagination. But something told me that it wasn't something that I was imagining, it was real. So I began to talk to you in my mind, assuring you that you were going to be okay and gradually your fear would subside and I would know you were okay."

Alex tenderly pulled away in order to allow Beth the freedom to turn her face up towards his. Her beautiful blue eyes were now beaming with an incredible radiance of light. Her cheeks glittered with a joyous glow. A mischievous grin suddenly appeared on Beth's face as she looked up at Alex.

"If what you say is true, and you do in fact know me so well. You can feel my emotions then what is that tray of food for? Did you think or feel that I was so famished that I would eat all that." She giggled as she pointed to the array of food, which he had placed on her dresser. Alex laughed as he too looked at the amount of food he had prepared. It indeed could feed an army.

"Well, that is something that is hard to explain…" he began. "Somehow I know that you do like each of

CIRCLE OF LOVE

those things on the tray. The question I had was which one would you be in the mood for when you awoke? Rather than just deciding on one, I made or prepared them all. Look at that tray of food Beth, is there a single item on there that you do not love?"

Beth got up and walked over to the dresser where the variety of food was sitting. She looked down at the pancakes with the butter and syrup on them in just the exact same way that she herself would have prepared them. Her eyes widened as she saw the delicious bowl of fresh honeydew cut up in different sizes of cubes. Sitting next to the bowl of fruit was another plate with two eggs prepared over medium. As she continued to view the tray she smiled at the four slices of wheat toast, which had been spread with butter and grape jam, and cut into diagonal halves. She let out a laugh as she looked at the bowl of Cheerios, which had been poured into her favorite country heart bowl. The final item on the tray caused her heart to beat rapidly. There, in her special, secret mug, which she only used on weekends without her kids because it displayed a cartoon picture of a damsel in distress asking the question "Where is my knight in shining armor?" was her yummy French vanilla hot chocolate. Beth spun around to see Alex grinning from ear to ear, knowing that his morning preparation was indeed appreciated. Without warning, Beth leaped on top of Alex covering his face with tender little kisses stopping between each kiss to say the words, "Thank you". As Beth was about to plant another kiss, this time on Alex's neck, he pulled himself out of her reach.

"Now now, if you start to kiss me like that, that food that I worked so hard to prepare is going to be

Dawn Elizabeth

cold and you probably won't have the chance of eating it because we will be busy… ah, finding the rhythm…"

Beth lifted herself off Alex and lay next to him resting her head on her elbow. She slowly bit her lower lip, trying to hide a seductive grin while raising her eyebrows twice.

"Oh, but Alex, we can do both. I know how we can have our breakfast and each other too."

Alex let out a deep knowing laugh. He knew that when the two were finished with their breakfast they would both be in desperate need of a shower.

Chapter 14

Although Joseph knew it was wrong, he slowly turned into the subdivision where Beth and her two children resided. He had been up all night thinking about the past several years and how he had felt about himself since Beth had come into his life. He had felt so ashamed of himself as he remembered all of the horrible, unkind words he had used to discourage her from pursuing him. There were numerous occasions that he had left her crying due to his harsh cruel actions. Those words had been his defense, his only means of protecting himself from losing his heart to her. He had tried to tell himself throughout the years that their relationship could only be physical. Somehow he had convinced himself that he was not wrong because he had told her he was not interested in anything other than sex. It wouldn't affect his conscience if she cried or hurt because of his words, he was only being honest. Last night he had realized that he had never been honest with her and what he had done to her all of these years was unforgivable. It had been months since they had been together and he missed her. When she had told him she was involved with someone else it had torn his heart to pieces. He desperately tried to convince himself that she deserved to be happy. It was true. He did want her to be happy. But he wanted to share the happiness with her. He had decided that he would go to her and tell her the truth about his feelings for her. He would never lie to her again, nor would he ever say anything to intentionally

Dawn Elizabeth

break her heart. Rather than pushing her from him, he would do whatever he could to bring her closer to him.

As he turned the corner heading down her street he noticed a car in her driveway. One he had seen on numerous occasions, not knowing to whom it belonged. He passed her house and reached for his cell phone. Quickly, he dialed her number and waited for her to answer her phone. To his disappointment the phone rang repeatedly without being answered. He slowly flipped the phone shut and placed it on its cradle.

Somehow, he knew that he would never get his chance to tell her his true feelings. She had spent several years trying to prove to him how much she loved him. He shook his head, remembering the many times he had seen the tears stream down her face when he told her that she was not the kind of woman he could ever love. As he sat at the stop sign waiting for it to be clear for him to proceed, he thought of a way that he could prove to her that he did indeed love her.

In his heart he knew, the only true way to prove his love was to let her go. If she did, in fact, have a new man in her life, the last thing that she needed was to have him step in and try to complicate it, or destroy it. He would wish only good things for her and pray that this man was worthy of her love and treated her as a princess. Joseph knew that the best thing would be to let go of her. If for some reason, or by some miracle he were given the chance to see her again, he would tell her of his true feelings and not have doubt in himself. All he could do now was to go on with his life and let her have hers.

CIRCLE OF LOVE

As a car passed his, he proceeded down the street. As he exited her subdivision he quietly whispered, "I love you, Beth. If you ever need me, I will be there for you."

He pulled out onto the main road and did not look back.

Dawn Elizabeth

Chapter 15

Beth slowly pushed the grocery cart up the aisle, her eyes surveying the shelves searching for egg noodles. She was not familiar with this supermarket so she was uncertain as to which aisle they might be in. She had tried to read the sign that hung directly above the center of each aisle listing the contents of that aisle, but no matter how hard she squinted her eyes she could not bring the words into focus. She had taken her glasses off before she exited her car out of vanity. Now she wished that she hadn't been so vain. She realized that leaving her glasses in the car had been stupid and immature. A shopping trip that was supposed to take only a few minutes had turned into a half hour due to her blindness. As she finally spotted the section of egg noodles, she was stopped by the sound of a familiar deep voice.

"I wondered what it was that you were desperately searching for. It was starting to become apparent that you were frustrated because you couldn't seem to locate something."

Beth turned around to see the warm smile of Joseph O'Dea. It had been months since the two had seen each other, since her involvement with Alex. Something about his appearance was different and for a moment she was unsure as to what it was.

"Hi there," she said cheerfully, "How are you doing?"

"Hello, I'm fine. I have heard through the grapevine that you are floating on cloud nine due to some fellow. What is his name ... Alex?"

CIRCLE OF LOVE

Beth pulled her cart to the side to allow another shopper room to pass.

"I guess you could say that I am happy, very happy in fact. And yes, there is a very special man in my life whose name is Alex."

The grin on Joe's face slowly vanished. In order to hide the hurt that suffocated his heart and overwhelmed his emotions, he turned his head to the side pretending to be searching for an item on the shelf opposite from Beth. He was desperately trying to hide his heartache at her confirming the rumors; that she was indeed involved with another man. He placed two cans of tomato paste in his cart.

"I know what it is that's different!" Beth exclaimed. "You shaved off your moustache."

Joe turned his face towards Beth's and saw the excitement that filled her eyes was brought about because of her discovery of his now clean-shaven face. Through his eyes he saw the beautiful glow of her face, a radiance of light that beamed from her eyes. Without realizing he was doing so he let out a chuckle. His hand reached up to touch his now exposed upper lip.

"I haven't had my moustache for several months now. I shaved it off one day impulsively. What do you think?"

Beth turned her face from side to side and bit her lower lip. She wasn't quite sure what her opinion was. He didn't look like the Joe she had known for so many years. In some ways that moustache was his character, his trademark.

"Well, I think it makes you look younger. But to be honest, I liked your moustache. It gave you character."

Dawn Elizabeth

"Character, huh? I guess I like not having character. I appreciate your comments and opinions though. I haven't really gotten any reaction from anyone since I shaved it. I guess people are afraid to be honest."

"I didn't say it looked bad. I was just used to the old Joe. He had a moustache. It doesn't matter if you have a moustache or not, you are a very handsome man."

Trying to change the subject Joseph quickly asked, "How are the kids doing?"

"Oh, the kids are doing great. Both of them do exceptionally well at school." Beth moved her cart down a little searching the shelves for her favorite spaghetti sauce. "How about you, are you seeing anyone?"

Joe took in a deep breath, unsure as to how he should respond to her question. She was the only woman he wanted, even now after all this time. There was never any interest to pursue another woman.

"Actually no. I have been pretty busy. I can't seem to fit a relationship into my hectic schedule." Afraid that she would question what he had been doing to keep him busy, he quickly continued. "Hey, it was really nice seeing you. I am glad that you are happy and that you have found a special man. I better get going, I have a few more items that I need to pick up and I have an appointment I don't want to be late. Take care of yourself."

He put both hands on the handle of the buggy and pushed it forward. Beth nodded as he walked away from her. She watched as he walked up the aisle and noticed him quickly turn back to look at her as he

CIRCLE OF LOVE

reached its end. Realizing that she was watching him, he lifted up his left hand and waved. Swiftly, he turned the corner and headed towards a check out line. Although there were other items that he did need to purchase the thought of being in the same store as she was tugged at his heart. The best thing for him to do was to pay for his groceries and go home. He could always stop at another store or pick up the items he still needed later.

After he paid for his few groceries he walked out to his truck carrying his groceries in the plastic bag. As he put the key into the keyhole of the car door he glanced around the parking lot to see if he could spot where she had parked. To his surprise, he had parked two vehicles away from her. He smiled as he saw the sporty, little, red Sunbird Convertible that she drove. That car suited her he thought. He couldn't imagine her driving some huge four-door car. It wouldn't fit her bouncy personality.

As he pulled out of the parking lot and headed towards his home he thought back to their conversation. In his mind, as if he had recorded it, he played back the whole event. He remembered every detail ranging from the clothes she was wearing, the style of her hair, the fragrance of her perfume, and the color of her lipstick to the expressions on her face and sound of her voice. Every detail was etched into his memory to be kept forever. He had noticed the way her face glowed at the mention of Alex's name. It was very evident that she did have very strong feelings for this man and, in a loving way Joseph was happy for her. Oddly, he did not have any hatred or contempt for this man who now possessed Beth's heart. He did,

Dawn Elizabeth

however, feel empty and lost knowing that he would never be able to express the love he felt for her. His love would always remain buried deep in his soul, with no one but he and God knowing how deep it was.

As he continued to drive down the highway thoughts of their years together raced through his mind. He had never seen the light in her eyes as he had today. His memories were full of the sadness he saw in her eyes caused from his cruel words or actions. He knew the tears that he had caused her to cry could fill up several buckets, tears that she was never meant to cry. He could hear the sound of her voice pleading him to give them a chance. He hated himself for the pain that he had caused her during all of those years. He was grateful that God had brought a man into her life that treated her with the love and respect that she deserved. Somehow knowing that gave him a quite peaceful feeling. Perhaps in his cruel, but caring way, he had accomplished what he had meant to do. He had pushed her away and opened her eyes. He had given her the chance to experience love in the way it was supposed to be felt. She had met a man who loved and cherished her. From what he had heard from their mutual friends, she had never been so happy and this Alex loved her as much as he himself loved her. To some degree, Joseph was overwhelmed with emotion. Even though men aren't supposed to cry, tears swelled up in his eyes. With the back of his hand he quickly brushed them from his face before they flowed down his cheeks. In his sacrifice he had been able to prove his love and it had worked out. The woman, whom he loved with all his heart and not felt worthy of, was happy and content. He knew that he had proven his

CIRCLE OF LOVE

love by walking away. She would never know the amount of pain and restraint it took for him to not pick up the phone and call her. Nor would she know the way his heart pounded when he saw her in the store today. She would never know of the many nights he lay in his bed staring up at the ceiling just remembering her smile or voice, or the way his arms ached to hold her. She would not know the long duration of time it took for him to let go of the hope that she would be on the other end of the line each time his phone rang. No, all that she would know, all she needed to know, was the happiness that Alex brought her. Joseph reached for the button to turn on the radio. Tears swelled up in his eyes once again as he heard Brian Adams sing, "Everything I do, I do for you." No song could ever convey his love any better.

Dawn Elizabeth

Chapter 16

Beth slowly reached up and removed the hair that the gentle breeze had blown in her face. It was a beautiful spring day as she sat out on her deck. The chaise lounge that she sat in was covered with puffy, beautiful cushions with large yellow and white daisies, the reverse side of the cushion being solid bright green. Next to the chaise was a matching chair with a similar cushion. A beautiful oval patio table with an umbrella, which coordinated with the chaise and chair cushions, sat in the center of the deck. Around the table sat six smaller swivel chairs, each having the same cushions. A variety of flowerpots containing geraniums and impatients in dark shades of red and pink in all shapes and sizes decorated the deck.

The deck itself was stained in a natural oak color and was octagon in shape. A railing protected all the sides; it was several feet off the ground with two sides of the deck having built-in benches. To the far left hand side of the deck there were five steps that led to a smaller deck, which also held chairs and several flowerpots. At the lower deck's center were three more steps that lead to the yard.

To the left of the deck was a natural pond, which was home to a family of ducks and a Blue Heron. The mother duck swam from side to side as five ducklings followed in a line directly behind her. The father duck kept close by guarding his family, uncertain as to what prey inhabited the area surrounding the pond. It was his duty to keep his family safe as his mate taught their ducklings how to fish. The Blue Heron, being

CIRCLE OF LOVE

oblivious to the duck family, walked around the pond searching the water for the small goldfish that swam in the pond's shallow water.

As Beth watched the birds swim back and forth in the pond her thoughts were of Alex. She knew that he had an important meeting that morning and through their special bond she was trying to determine how the meeting was going. She closed her eyes and cleared her mind of any thoughts that would distract her concentration. Slowly, as if they had become connected into one spirit, she could feel Alex's thoughts. She smiled to herself as she heard Alex assure her that the meeting was indeed going well. She also giggled when she felt him warn her not to stay in the sun for too long. In her mind she told him that she loved him and would see him when he was finished. He sent the same thoughts to her and she then opened her eyes allowing him to continue his meeting.

Gregory and Tiffany were at their friends and she was home by herself. The four of them planned an evening at the movies and it was her job to get the movie schedule.

The kids loved Alex and he had developed a fatherly love for them also. He never missed one of their school events and helped each of them with homework assignments should it appear that they were having a problem. He never tried to take the place of their natural father and respected and encouraged their relationship with him. He and Greg laughed and joked about the awkwardness of dating and how disappointing and trying it could get at times. He tried to be supportive and let him know that if a certain young lady didn't return his interest there were "other

Dawn Elizabeth

fish in the sea". As for Tiffany, he was very protective. He knew that she would be approaching the dating age soon and he was not looking forward to that time. Tiffany was a beautiful, sensitive, young lady and he knew her heart was going to be broken many times by insensitive teenage boys.

Alex and Beth had decided to keep their special bond for one another to themselves. As they did not understand it, there was no way that it could be explained without sounding as if they were both insane. On a few occasions Tiffany had noticed that something very special was shared between these two adults but she wrote it off as being an aspect of being in love and never gave it another thought.

Beth got up and walked over to the table and picked up her glass of ice water. After taking a small sip of the cold water, she replaced the glass and returned to the chaise. She knew that she had some time before the kids and Alex would be home and she enjoyed leaning back and relaxing. She repositioned the chair so that it was in a reclined fashion and she then sat down. She placed her arms on her lower stomach and closed her eyes. As she lay in the chaise, she listened to the sound of the ducks splashing around in the water. It was a soothing sound that if listened to for any long period of time was sure to hypnotize. The day was especially warm and the sun brightly shined on her entire body. She felt a great deal of the warmth radiating from her own body in harmony with the rays of sunlight. She felt her spirit dancing high above the sky as though she was floating with the billowy, white clouds. Each breath she exhaled commanded the Earth's gentle breeze.

CIRCLE OF LOVE

As she gradually fell into a dazed state she recalled how lonely she had felt a year before and how her life had taken an almost magical turn. All her life she had wished and prayed for a man to come into her life and love her. She never imagined it would be someone as wonderful as Alex. In the nine months that they had known each other, they had become inseparable. Unless they were working or attending meetings, they were always together. They always maintained a physical contact whether it was by holding hands or embracing one another; one arm around the other. Even when she was preparing dinner he was right by her side washing vegetables or peeling potatoes. He helped in setting the table, as well as clearing it, and loading the dishwasher when the dinner was done. The two moved together in harmony as if they were one person occupying two bodies.

For some unexplained reason they were able to feel each other's emotion and communicate through thoughts even if they were miles apart. At first this had frightened them both but they had gradually lost their fears and were able to use this power to their benefit. In the nine months that that had been together they had never once fought. Their love was enchanted. It was as if God had smiled down on them both and blessed them with happiness. The hurt that Beth had felt after her divorce was a vague memory. The nights she had spent holding on to Big Bear and crying, overwhelmed with loneliness were forever lost in the past. Her nights were now spent holding onto Alex, the two of them tenderly kissing one another throughout the hours of the night.

Dawn Elizabeth

Strangely, the past several nights she had dreamed of Joe. Although she could never make out what the dreams were about, she was sure he was a participant in them. Her thoughts and feelings of him were one emotion Alex never felt. She had been honest with Alex at the beginning of their relationship and had confided the details of her relationship with Joe. She had explained that there had been a time that she truly believed she loved him, even though at times he was extremely almost over-exaggerated in being cruel to her. For some reason she always looked past his cruelness and saw a gentle man hidden behind a cold cruel façade. Perhaps he was a man who was frightened with love. She described him to Alex as a magnificent puzzle that had its borders but was missing the centerpieces where the true picture lies. Alex listened intently to every word she had spoken about him and, unlike most men, he never was jealous or put out. Rather, he was sympathetic towards him and felt that he never really meant to hurt Beth, but, that there was some reason that made him push her away. Somehow he had felt that he had made some sort of sacrifice when Alex and Beth started dating, almost as if he thought she would be better off with someone other than himself.

Alex never questioned Beth about Joe's appearance. He was never concerned with his physical being and had never seen pictures, nor asked what he looked like. This was not something he thought had any significant value or meaning. To him, what was important was this man's spiritual being. This was an emotion that Alex had never experienced before. In his past relationships he never wanted to hear about another man with whom the woman had been involved. He had been arrogant and possessive at times and the mention of another man's name would overwhelm him with anger. Many times the past relationships would end due to his jealous nature. Something had changed him when he met Beth. Those former feelings were lost in his past. As much as he loved Beth, he never felt threatened of the love she had felt for another man. The emotion of jealously or envy was not one that he could comprehend. He knew that another person could not take the love he and Beth shared away whether it was a man or woman. The bond the two of them shared was sacred and could not be duplicated.

Chapter 17

Alex glanced at his gas gauge. His car was low on fuel. He thought this was strange and was sure that he had noticed almost half a tank when he left home that morning. He had not driven a great distance that day and surely could not have used such a significant amount of fuel. He had just purchased his car a month ago and had not had any problems with the vehicle. To the contrary, he had been quite satisfied with the purchase. He had kept a regular report of its gas mileage and was pleased at the miles per gallon it was getting. As he looked at the gauge he was confused as to why it indicated the fuel was near to being empty. He slowed his speed as he recalled a gas station being a few miles down the road. Turning on his right turn signal, he watched for traffic to clear and then merged into the right lane.

It was a beautiful spring day with temperatures being at a record high for that time of year. He preferred driving with his window down and feeling the fresh air to the manufactured cool air of the air conditioner. As he surveyed the area looking for the approaching gas station, he rested his arm on the door's open window and hummed along to the song that was playing on the radio. As the car's tires hit a small bump on the road's surface he felt a small tap against his chest. He smiled to himself, knowing that the tap was from the tiny, black, velvet box, which was safely hidden in his inside jacket pocket.

Beth had thought the important meeting he was attending was regarding work. This had been a ploy to

CIRCLE OF LOVE

cover what he actually had been doing. He had been with a friend of his who was a jeweler and whom he had commissioned to create a spectacular engagement ring. The two of them had met on several occasions, working together to design the perfect ring. His friend had called him last week to notify him that the ring was now finished. It was quite a task keeping his excitement from Beth. Normally, the bond that they shared wouldn't allow them to keep secrets from each other, but when there was a special occasion approaching, the bond permitted the secret to be kept. This was indeed a special event and Beth was unaware of what Alex was planning.

Alex felt proud of himself as he thought about the romantic and lovely evening he had planned. He had told Beth that he wanted the four of them to go out to dinner and to a movie. Little did she know that the four of them were involved in an evening straight from a fairytale.

Beth was always mesmerized by the era of knights in shining armor and damsels in distress. She had referred to Alex as her Sir Lancelot on many occasions and commented that when he had entered her life he had been a knight rescuing her from a dredge of emptiness and loneliness. It seemed only fitting to him that on the day that he ask for her hand in marriage they should be clothed in garments befitting a knight and his beautiful damsel. He had researched many of the costume stores in the area until he found the perfect costumes. The kids were also a part of this joyous event and they too would be dressed in costume, Gregory, as a squire: and Tiffany, as Beth's young lady-in-waiting. He had picked them up from school

Dawn Elizabeth

one day early in the week and the three of them had gone to the costume store and chosen their apparel. There was no need for the kids to choose their mother's gown as Alex had spotted the perfect dress as he entered the store. On his way to his meeting that morning he had told Beth that he would drop the kids off at their friends. He had actually taken them to the store to retrieve their costumes and they were now waiting for him at a neighbor's house down the street. This particular neighbor was also involved in the event. They owned the most magnificent white stallion, which they were honored to let Alex ride. He had also set the anticipation and atmosphere by having a dozen long stem yellow roses delivered to Beth. The roses were to be delivered in sets of three each arriving on the hour beginning at two o'clock. Enclosed with the first box of flowers would be an unsigned card which read, *"If ever asked, Have I known love? My answer would be honest and true. I would answer that I fell in love ... on the day that I met you."*

The next box of flowers was to be delivered at three o'clock. It also would contain an unsigned card with it reading, *"I would tell them how right it feels, when your arms are holding me. And how if I had my choice... there is no other place I would wish to be."*

The gown chosen for Beth would accompany the third box of flowers. The delivery person was an older lady from the costume store. She had been working the night that Alex and the kids had come into the shop looking for costumes. He had told her about the fairytale type proposal he had planned. She thought it was such a beautiful and sweet idea and asked if she could participate in the surprise. She explained that

CIRCLE OF LOVE

she could assist Beth into the beautiful gown, almost as if she was her fairy godmother. She would advise Beth to please put on the gown she had brought for her because on this night her dream and wish would come true. The older woman would advise Beth it was her job to make sure that she was into her dress by five o'clock because she then would be presented with another package. Once this woman was convinced that Beth was getting into her costume, she would then arrange the first nine roses in a beautiful crystal vase. After seeing that Beth was in the dress she would present her with the vase of flowers and another unsigned card. This card would read, *"I would tell them how complete I felt each time you stood by my side, And how my heart was filled with joy on the day I asked you to be my bride"*. It would then be up to Alex to get to the neighbor's home where the kids were now dressed and waiting, get himself into costume and on the horse. The kids would walk a few paces ahead of him carrying the remaining three roses. This time the roses would be wrapped in pale pink tissue paper with a white satin ribbon tied in a beautiful bow around the bottom of the triangle. As the trio approached their yard, it would be Tiffany's responsibility to get her mother's attention and lead her out to the yard. Gregory would remain at Alex's side and take the horses reins remaining with the white horse once Alex dismounted. Tiffany would guide her mother to stand before Alex and she would then take her place with Greg by the horse. Alex knew that when it reached this point he would then be flooded with deep emotion. He would lower himself down on one

Dawn Elizabeth

knee and recite the poem he had composed for Beth in its entirety, this time including the final verse.

> *If ever asked have I known love?*
> *My answer would be honest and true.*
> *I would answer that I fell in love,*
> *on the day that I met you.*
>
> *I would tell them how right it felt,*
> *When your arms were holding me,*
> *And how if I had my choice,*
> *There would be no other place,*
> *I would rather be.*
>
> *I would tell them how complete I felt,*
> *Each time you stood by my side.*
> *And how my heart was filled with joy...*
> *On the day I asked you to be my bride.*
>
> *The question I ask today comes from my heart,*
> *Knowing our love was meant to be.*
> *Will you answer the question "Yes?"*
> *And say you'll marry me?*

As Alex hummed along to the song on the radio he felt an overwhelming energy of happiness. He could feel Beth's rising excitement and knew that she had just been presented with the beautiful gown. As if she were sitting by his side in the vehicle he could hear her shrieks of utter delight as she first gazed upon the gown chosen for her. In his mind he heard her voice saying, "I love you, Alex, I love you, Alex." In his

CIRCLE OF LOVE

mind he responded, "I love you too, Princess. I love you too."

He had known at the very beginning that she was the woman he wanted to make a life long commitment to. He could not, or would not, comprehend his life without her in it. She was his soul mate. In their hearts and souls they had already made a pledge to each other. It was time that they stood before their family and friends and exchanged their vows in front of God and witnesses. More importantly Gregory and Tiffany were at very impressionable ages and the adults wanted to instill the sacredness of matrimony in them.

Everyone who knew the couple was aware of the special love the two shared. It was said by many that their love was a special blessing from God Himself, and many wished that they had a love that was close in comparison. Viewers and passer-bys would often stop and stare in amazement and awe as the couple passed by on one of their evening walks. Their paces were always in unison, never becoming out of step with the other. Their hands were always held tightly with their fingers entwined as they swung back and forth. The sound of their laughter would echo down the block and bring smiles to any that heard it.

Pulled abruptly from his thoughts, Alex spotted the service station and turned into its driveway. As he pulled up to the pump his senses were overwhelmed with an almost knowing feeling, the effect causing him to feel dizzy and shaken. He sat in his vehicle and tried to focus on Beth, wondering if this strange feeling was brought on by something she was experiencing. As if there was an unknown presence with him he was assured that Beth was fine. He glanced around the inside of the vehicle searching to make sure that he was alone. The only thing in the vehicle besides him was his knight's costume. He shook his head and tried to regain his balance. "What's happening here?" He questioned himself. He glanced at the digital clock and saw that he had better hurry and get his gas, otherwise the night that he had so carefully orchestrated would be delayed. As he reached for the door's handle, he was once again thrown into a state of bewilderment. He was sure that he could feel the presence of someone else inside the car with him. Again he looked around the car. There was nothing there. He reached up and rubbed his head trying to pull things into focus, confused as to what was happening to him. For some reason he sensed that there was something he needed to know. What was it? Slowly he made an attempt to reach for the door handle, afraid that he would be stricken with the dizziness again. This time there was a peaceful calm surrounding him and he was able to open the door. Confused as to what had taken place in the car, he walked around the vehicle and removed the gas cap. He then retrieved the pump's nozzle and began inserting fuel. He was astonished when the pump came to a sudden stop. He looked up and noticed that the pump had stopped after he had only pumped a few dollars into the car's tank. Completely confused, he shook his head and replaced both the nozzle and gas cap. He was sure that he needed gas, so why had the pump stopped after only a few dollars? Convinced that his gas gauge was not working properly he proceeded into the station to pay. As he passed one of the other gas islands he spotted a small, teal colored truck. The

CIRCLE OF LOVE

truck was empty, which meant its driver must be in the station as well.

As Alex came a few steps within reach of the door, it opened. Exiting the store was a tall man with dark hair. Just as Alex, this man had a groomed moustache. On his cheek directly out from his moustache was a large mole. The stranger noticed that Alex was staring at him and said, "Hello". At the sound of the man's voice, Alex was once again overwhelmed with a knowing sensation. He felt as though someone had spun him around in circles several times like a top and he lost his balance. The stranger quickly reached for Alex and caught him before he hit the pavement. As the man helped him stand he heard a soft voice whispering in his head, "Remember him, Alex, he is the one."

"Hey...are you okay?" the stranger asked.

Alex felt extremely dizzy and confused but allowed the stranger to help him regain his balance. For a moment he stood and stared at the dark haired man who had come to his aid. Deep in his soul, he felt that he somehow knew this stranger but he could not recall from where. He shook his head trying to clear his thoughts and looked directly into the man's eyes.

"Yeah... I'm fine. I don't know what came over me. Actually today is a very special day for me. I am proposing to a very special lady. I didn't think that I was nervous...but I guess I am. Hey, thanks for your help. I feel better now."

The stranger looked at Alex with concern in his eyes.

Dawn Elizabeth

"Hey, no problem. Don't be so nervous. I am sure whoever the lucky lady is...she is going to say yes. I wish you the best."

The man patted Alex on his back and turned and headed toward his vehicle. He opened the truck door and started to climb up in but paused momentarily and turned back to wave to Alex. Alex smiled and waved back at the stranger who had been so kind to him. He then proceeded to enter the gas station. As he approached the register he once again turned to glance out the window, watching the stranger pull out onto the road. He felt as if someone was standing directly at his side then he heard a faint voice whisper. "Remember him, Alex...he is the one." Alex frightened by the voice quickly turned around to see if someone was standing behind him. No one was there. The sales clerk gave him an expression indicating that his actions were odd.

Feeling uncomfortable, he quickly paid for his gas and exited the store. As he opened the door of his vehicle he glanced at the knight's costume that had been put neatly into a garment bag. Inside the bag he could see the blade of the sword sparkle as the sunlight hit through the thick transparent plastic. He knew that Beth was now in her beautiful gown and her emotions were extremely high. He, too, was starting to feel overwhelmed with emotions as he realized that this was going to be one of the happiest days of his life. This would be the day that the two of them would cherish and remember always.

As he pulled out into the traffic, he reached to turn on the radio hoping to hear a beautiful love ballad. He turned the small black round knob clockwise until he

CIRCLE OF LOVE

heard the sound of music blare from the speaker. He jumped a little in his seat as the hard rock music blasted from his radio. Shaking his head, slightly he allowed the fingers on his right hand to randomly search for an easy listening station. Once he was pleased with his selection, he leaned back in his seat and continued to drive home.

Beth's heart was pounding wildly as she held the vase of nine roses in her tiny hands. She had been delivered nine, beautiful, long stemmed yellow roses and presented with a beautiful costume from the Renaissance period. The beautiful clothing that the ladies-in-waiting wore in that period had always fascinated her. In her heart she knew that Alex had been her "knight in shining armor" rescuing her from the sea of loneliness.

At the beginning of their relationship, she had been frightened at the bond that they somehow shared, always knowing how the other felt. In some ways she felt as if their souls were joined, connected. She knew that all of the wishing and praying that she had been doing throughout her life had not been in vain. She sincerely felt that God Himself was smiling on her, blessing her with Alex. He had added to his blessing by giving them their gifted connection.

Oddly, she could not use her insight to see what Alex had in store for her for that evening. She had reached the conclusion that it must be extremely special, otherwise she would know. She placed the vase with the beautiful flowers on the counter and stepped back and gazed at them. Their color was a magnificent shade of bright yellow. She had always loved yellow roses. The flowers had always been her

Dawn Elizabeth

favorite because she felt that a rose radiates beauty in a variety of different ways. As a rose bud, the flower is holding itself tightly as if fingers entwined holding the petals closed. As the flower gradually opens, it is as if the flower is shyly asking the world to enjoy its beauty. The fragrance it omits is sweet. The most commonly loved color of a rose is red, but Beth loved the yellow rose more. To her it was one of God's beautiful creations. He had taken the beautiful, sculptured flower and added the bright color of sunshine. Now, before her in a crystal vase there stood nine long stemmed yellow roses surrounded by greenery and delicate white Baby's Breath.

She tilted her head back and concentrated on Alex. She forced all thoughts and surroundings to fade from her mind, allowing Alex's soul and her soul to join. As if she were watching a movie which Alex was playing the leading role, her thoughts took on the effect of a cinema screen in which she was observing. At first she was a little frightened as to the ability she was experiencing in seeing Alex so clearly. As if someone was standing at her side, she felt a presence with her telling her she must continue to watch. As if in slow motion, she watched as Alex pulled out onto the road from a service station. She watched as he leaned forward to turn on the radio, and smiled to herself when he jumped when he was startled as the rock music blasted from the speakers. She recognized the area in which he was driving and knew he was right around the block. Oddly her thoughts were turned to the road ahead of Alex. A black pickup truck was speeding towards Alex, weaving back and forth in its

CIRCLE OF LOVE

lanes. She watched as it headed faster and faster towards Alex.

Beth shook her head, trying to clear the thoughts. "No, God... please no," she whispered then quickly searched the counter for her car keys. Uncontrolled by herself, her mind was once again filled with the vision of the black truck racing down the road. The vision was directed back to Alex driving along the road. Clearly she heard him sing the words... "A reason for living, a new beginning, a deeper meaning..." Quickly the vision once again changed to the black truck darting back and forth from left to right lanes.

"Oh my God, something is trying to tell me something... God, please...not Alex!" She pleaded.

With her heart pounding wildly, she watched the events that were taking place in her mind. Trying to shake them from her thoughts, she threw her head back and forth and from side to side. Suddenly she felt the coldness of the metal keys on her fingers and quickly picked them up. She took the floor length gown she was wearing and lifted it up to her knees allowing her the freedom to run. For some reason her legs didn't want to cooperate with her as they weakened beneath her and she fell to the floor. The gown that she had once thought was so beautiful had now become an obstacle, hindering her from running to Alex. It took several minutes to unknot the dress, which was now tangled around her. Tears were streaming from her eyes as she unwrapped the gown from her legs. In her mind she tried to communicate with Alex.

"The truck, Alex...there is a truck...look, Alex...there is a truck."

Dawn Elizabeth

Once again her mind was filled with the vision of Alex in his vehicle. For some reason he could not hear her warning him. The vision moved to the seat directly behind him. There on the seat in a transparent garment bag lay a knight's costume complete with sword. The vision moved to the front seat where Alex was sitting. Beth watched as Alex's hand reached inside of his interior coat pocket and retrieved a small black velvet box. He held the black velvet box tightly in the palm of his hand. She heard him say, "I love you, Beth. I hope you say yes."

She watched as his vehicle hit a bump and he accidentally dropped the little box. Frustrated, he tried to lean to the right searching for the little case. His hands searched the vehicle's floor as he tried to locate where the box had fallen. He reached up and unsnapped his seatbelt, allowing him freedom to move. After several attempts, he finally felt the softness of the velvet and grasped his fingers around it. As he lifted back upright in his seat, he observed a black pickup truck speeding uncontrollably in his direction. He tried to swerve out of its reach, but it was too late. Time seemed to distort as his surroundings changed to slow motion. There was the sound of tires squealing as their rubber burned on the pavement when they were forced to halt, the explosive sound of the metals colliding, and the high pitched sound of the glass shattering into millions of tiny jagged pieces. He felt the incredible pain as his body was thrown through the windshield, the jagged pieces of glass ripping and tearing his flesh. He heard the violent sound of bones breaking as his body bounced on the hard pavement of the road. Then, in a flash, Alex's world turned black.

Chapter 18

Beth's hands trembled as she forced the key into the ignition. She did not bother to fasten her seat belt as she shifted her car into reverse. She turned her head and looked over her right shoulder. She slammed her foot on the accelerator and rapidly backed out of her driveway. Dirt and pebbles scattered and a cloud of dust flew as the wheels shoved them out of its path. She swiftly moved the car's gears into drive and sped down the street once clearing the driveway. Ignoring the stop signs, she flew through the intersection.

Her body had started to shake convulsively as she tried to control her sobs. Tears flowed from her eyes at a rapid pace as she reached up and wiped them from her face with the back of her hand.

"Please, God", she pleaded, "Please let the vision be wrong, please let it be wrong. Don't take my Alex."

Various neighbors ran out to their front yards as they heard Beth's car racing down the street. Gregory and Tiffany raced to the sidewalk to see the commotion their mother was causing. Standing at the street's curb, the two teenagers stood bewildered in their Renaissance costumes. Realizing that something was seriously wrong, Gregory grabbed his sister by the sleeve and hurriedly pulled her down the street in the direction their mother was headed. Tears began to swell in Tiffany's eyes as she heard the sound of emergency sirens. Picking up the end of her gown, she quickly moved her legs down the sidewalk keeping next to her brother's side. As the two reached the end of the street, the young boy let out a painful yell as he

Dawn Elizabeth

realized what his mother was racing to reach. The young girl stopped momentarily and then darted across the street to where groups of people were gathering. Greg joined his sister as the two began to push their way through the crowd.

"Let us through, damn it! Let us through!" Tiffany screamed as she pushed the gawkers out of her path. "I said let us through…" she continued to scream. The group of people parted, allowing both teenagers to pass. Men and women stood silently watching the heart-wrenching event, which was taking place before them. Tears were shed from the eyes of many onlookers as they recognized the people who were involved. As the teenagers reached the end of the crowd, they instantly halted as they, too, watched in horror the scene that was now before them.

Two vehicles had collided in a head-on collision. Lying on the ground to the left of the road was an elderly man with two paramedics speeding to attend to his mangled body. On the right side of road was what had been a white Jimmy, its front-end pushed in and mangled almost beyond recognition. A few feet from the vehicle laid the body of another man with several paramedics working on him as well. A woman dressed similarly to the kids in a Renaissance costume was running towards the injured man, screaming.

As Beth reached Alex, she quickly pushed one of the paramedics to the side and knelt down next to his crushed and bloody body. Taking the end of her gown she quickly wiped the blood that was pouring from the gashes in his face. Against the instructions of the medical technicians, she leaned down over him and

CIRCLE OF LOVE

turn her ear almost touching his lips in order to hear what he was desperately trying to say.

"I am here, sweetheart. I am here," she cried, as the teardrops quickly escaped her eyes and ran down her cheeks.

Slowly Alex's eyes opened, flickering, as he tried to bring her face into focus. Observing that the energy was fading from him, she pulled inches away from his face in order to look directly into his eyes. Her heart was torn and ripped apart as she felt the intense pain of utter sorrow he was feeling as he looked into her blue eyes.

"Baby, it's okay…save your strength. I won't leave you. I'm…I'm right here. You're going to be okay. Just try to be still…I won't leave you Alex, I'm right here with you."

Something inside of her knew that he wanted very much for her to hear what he was trying to say, so once again she leaned her ear down next to his lips.

"What is it, Alex? What do you need to say?" she whispered, tears steadily streaming down her soft cheeks. Her body started to tremble as she became overwhelmed with emotion.

For a moment he lay on the hard ground and looked into the eyes of woman he would love forever. He felt the pain she was experiencing as she held his battered body in her arms. He felt his own heart breaking, as he knew he would be leaving her alone.

In a weak whisper he said, "I will always love you, Princess…". Slowly his eyes closed and his last breath left his body.

Trembling, she cradled his head in her lap. Caressing his blood stained cheeks she cried, "No,

Dawn Elizabeth

Alex...don't leave me...Alex...no, don't you leave me. Come back...come back. I got the flowers, the poem...the gown...look, sweetheart, I am wearing the gown...it's beautiful...honey, open your eyes...please Alex, don't leave me...I need you...I love you, Alexander...open your eyes, Alex, open your eyes..." Slowly she started to rock back and forth while continuing to stroke his face.

One of the paramedics knelt down beside Beth and put his arm around her. "I am sorry, ma'am, he's gone. Let us take care of him now." Beth pushed the man's hand from around her.

"No! You're wrong! He is just weak. I have to hold him. He needs me to stay with him. He needs me to hold him and keep him warm. Isn't that right, Alex?" Unconsciously, she began to run her fingers through his dark hair as if she was trying to sooth him and comfort him. She continued to rock back and forth and with pleading eyes she looked at the stranger kneeling next to her. She tenderly looked down at Alex's motionless body and then back at the man. Gradually, she started to carefully wipe the blood that had oozed from the numerous cuts on his face. Gently, she picked the fragments of glass that were scattered throughout his dark, thick hair, careful not to allow any to fall on him. Several of her teardrops began to fall down on his battered silent face as she leaned down over him.

"Isn't he the most handsome man you've ever seen?" she stuttered. "He is going to ask me to marry him today. He knows I'll say yes. I love him so-o-o-o much. He is so sweet and romantic...he sent me roses...and a poem...isn't he wonderful? I need to wash his face...he has a beautiful face and beautiful eyes...don't you, Alex..."

"Yes, ma'am, he is very handsome...but we need to take care of him now. Will you let us take care of him?"

Beth looked into the man's sympathetic eyes and knew that she had to release Alex to his care. Slowly she nodded her head, allowing the man to get near Alex. Another medical technician was standing directly behind Beth, as she allowed one technician to attend Alex, the man behind her quickly reached for her knowing she was in shock. Beth slowly stood up, allowing the paramedics to support her as she silently watched two other men carry a stretcher over to where Alex's body was lying. The two men slowly lifted his motionless body and placed it on the stretcher, pulling a white sheet up across him. As the man covered Alex's face with the white material Beth began to force herself loose of the man's hold, then began to scream.

"No! Alex...my Alexander...God, no...he is mine...No.!"

Chapter 19

Alex felt as if he was traveling, almost being pulled, by a magnetic force towards a light filled with a spectrum of colors with a magnitude that radiated warmth. He felt no fear or pain, as his soul became a part of the colors, each as if gentle arms were embracing him. He then felt his spirit being tenderly lowered to stand on a ray of light.

His surroundings were illuminated with the brightest brilliance of colored light that no human could behold. He did not blink or try to shield himself from the intensity of its glow, but rather allowed the light to encompass his soul, becoming a part of it. He knew that he was not alone and that someone was with him. Little by little a figure started to take form to his side. He waited patiently as the form slowly took on the appearance of a man. The man was dressed in a flowing white gown that extended down covering his feet. The sleeves of his gown were full and hung loosely around his arms. The man was slightly taller than Alex. His hair was the warm color of wheat and flowed down to his broad shoulders. The stranger's eyes were the color of sky blue and from them beamed great warmth and kindness. His facial features were soft, his nose very small, with its tip slightly rounded and smooth. His mouth consisted of soft, thin lips. His face was gentle and did not have a single glimpse of hair on it. As he approached Alex a soft breeze blew his long hair lightly back and forth away from his kind face.

CIRCLE OF LOVE

The stranger offered his hand to Alex and softy began to speak.

"Hello, Alexander. My name is Michael. I am your guardian angel. I have been with you since the day you were born. I have been with you, watching over you…guiding you to this day…the day that leads to you fulfilling your destiny."

As Alex extended his hand, it too started to take upon his human form. He looked down to see that he also was dressed in white, although his garment was not that of a gown but rather a suit. Even the shoes that were on his feet were white.

"My guardian angel? I don't understand," he responded.

"It is too soon for you to fully understand. You have just reached us. But your soul is strong, it feels no fear."

Strangely, what the stranger was saying was correct because Alex was not at all afraid. He listened intently to each word the angel spoke.

"You are one of His most precious souls and are very special in His eyes. When you were created you were not created alone. He enjoined you with another. He allowed you to love in the way love was created. You were in unison in thought and in spirit. From the day you were born the two of you were connected. He watched over you both as he watches over all. Yet, he kept his distance allowing time to reunite you. There are many who may get a small glimpse of what humans call "true love", but there are few who actually experience it. You and she have the gift of true love. Love is a circle, there is no beginning and there is no end. She will love you throughout all of eternity. Her

Dawn Elizabeth

love will never end. Just as your love for her will be without end."

"What do you mean my soul was connected with another? Beth...my soul is connected with hers...isn't it?"

As Alex spoke he felt the heaviness in his heart. He felt the pain that Beth was feeling at his loss. He looked into Michael's warm eyes.

"Michael, I don't understand. If this is Heaven why do I feel her sorrow, her grief? Her heart is bleeding and I cannot ease her pain. What kind of love would allow two souls to be torn apart?"

Michael looked into Alex's eyes and saw the pain that he felt. He rested one hand on Alex's shoulder and again began softly speaking.

"Alex, you have not fulfilled your destiny yet. That is why I am here to guide you. You are at Heaven's gates; once you have fulfilled your destiny I will be there to witness you walk through them. It is not time yet. The love that she feels for you keeps you from passing through the gates. She holds onto you and does not allow her soul to live. It is not her time to leave that place that you know as Earth. She has many things yet to do. There is another soul that desperately needs her love. Someone who has been spent too much time alone and deserves to be loved. In some ways, He created the two of you to bring love to this other soul."

"Is it one of the children?" Alex questioned.

"No, Alex, not the children. There is another soul, another man who loves her with such deep conviction, yet he denies his love. It is his love that will release you."

CIRCLE OF LOVE

"Another man loves Beth?" Alex whispered.

"Yes, another man who also loves Beth. His soul is good and kind, just like yours. He has suffered greatly and does not believe in himself. He has built a wall up around his heart to protect it, yet the heart is strong and it cannot be denied. He is deserving of her love Alex, and it is you who will bring them together."

"But if Beth and I have this love that is never-ending, how can she love another man?"

Michael reached up and rested both hands on Alex's shoulders and peered down directly into his eyes as he continued to speak.

"The love that you and Beth have is never-ending, Alex. It will always exist no matter where your souls reside. But she must be allowed to live, and she cannot as long as she holds onto you. Love exists in letting go. The other soul needs her love and it is his time to be loved. I was with you in that car. You felt me there, though you did not understand. I whispered something to you. Do you remember?" Michael questioned.

Alex turned his head to the side and tightly closed his eyes. The moments prior to his death were repeated through his mind. He recalled a voice saying, "Remember him...He is the one." Slowly, Alex looked back at Michael.

"Yes, I remember hearing a voice at the service station. I remember the odd sensation that surrounded me while I was in my car. I felt so dizzy when I pulled into the station. I looked around the inside of my car because I felt like I wasn't alone." Alex reached up and rubbed his chin as he recalled those last moments prior to his death.

Dawn Elizabeth

Michael walked a few paces around the area that they were standing then turned back to Alex. He knew the man was trying to remember the events that had taken place.

"Do you remember the man, Alex? There was a gentleman that crossed paths with you on that day. The man that was very kind to you."

Once again Alex closed his eyes tightening them as he tried to focus on a memory. His thoughts were filled with an image of a tall dark haired man exiting the service station. He remembered the strong feelings of loneliness that he felt flood his soul when the stranger had looked into his eyes. Somehow, he had known that the lonely emotion he felt at that moment was what the stranger carried deep in his heart. He recalled the way the man had not hesitated, but had helped him when he had stumbled. The vision was incredibly clear, as he remained standing with his eyes closed, remembering. Alex slowly opened his eyes and turn to look back at the angel.

"Yes, he helped me. I was about to fall and he caught me... He is the one who loves Beth?" opening his eyes wider he looked to Michael for the answer.

Michael slowly nodded.

"Yes, he is the one. You knew of him before that day at the gas station. She spoke of him, yet you never saw his face, until that day."

Puzzled, Alex shook his head from side to side as he tried to recall if Beth had ever spoke of another man who had been in her life. Then as if the area of which they stood had become brighter he remembered.

"She spoke of one man. It could not possibly be *him*. He treated her badly. There is some kind of

CIRCLE OF LOVE

mistake here, Michael. He is not deserving of *my* Beth's love." He yelled as he shook his head from side to side rapidly.

"Alex, remember what I said. You were listening, but yet, you did not hear. I shall repeat it. His soul is good and kind, just like yours. He has suffered greatly and does not believe in himself. He does not believe he is worthy of *anyone's* love. So, he has built a wall up around his heart to protect it, yet the heart is strong and it cannot be denied. He is deserving of her love. The reason for his cruelty, although it may be hard for you to understand, was a means of protecting her from being hurt. It was not done out of malice or hatred. It was done out of an unselfish love for her. He has pushed her away because he does not feel worthy of her. He did not feel he could give to her all that she needed. He was afraid that he would not live up to her expectations. He felt that she deserved someone like you Alex. He knew that she had found you and, even though it tore at his own heart to realize that he had lost her, he never hated nor felt any jealousy or contempt toward you. He is a good soul, Alex. He *is* deserving of her love, you will come to see that for yourself."

Although he heard every word the angel spoke, Alex could not comprehend how a man who had been utterly cruel to Beth could possibly be deserving of her. He did not feel that he would ever be able to walk through the Gates of Heaven because, in order to do so, he would have to allow her to love another. He did not feel his soul was strong enough.

Michael could read Alex's every thought and slowly he approached Alex and stood by his side.

Dawn Elizabeth

"Your soul is strong, as is your love. You are relying on past memories and that is why you will go back and discover the circle of love that exists."

"Go back...what do you mean? I have died. Surely you know that I am not alive anymore. I cannot go back," Alex quickly stated sarcastically, thinking the angel hadn't realized that he was only a spirit.

The angel's face sparkled as he began to smile, he softly laughed knowing the thoughts that were going through Alex's mind.

"Alex, I am an angel. I know your thoughts. I have been at your side always. I have been *your* guardian angel. I was with you in birth and I was there when you died. I am aware that you are a spirit now. You will go back and I will go with you. You will not go back as a man, but rather you will return as a spirit." Alex turned his head as he started to speak but paused as he saw Michael's hand come up to stop him.

"You will still feel the love for her when you see her. And she will feel your spirit there with her, yet she will not understand."

"Will she see me?" he interrupted.

Michael closed his eyes and slowly nodded. "There will come a time that she will be able to see you and touch you. And when this day comes, you will know that your destiny has been fulfilled."

Alex recognized the mixed emotions that appeared on the angel's face. It was clear that on the day that Beth would look into his eyes would be a day filled with joy and happiness, yet, it would also be a day filled with some sort of sadness as well. As he remained standing on the beautiful ray of light with the angel, he felt his heart being ripped and torn by the

CIRCLE OF LOVE

overwhelming grief Beth was experiencing. He felt the pain in her tired eyes from the many tears she had shed as she tried to face his absence. He felt her body ache as she longed to feel safe and secure in his arms. He knew that she had withdrawn into a silent world of emptiness when he had been taken from her. This was not what he wanted her to feel. He did not want their love to be a constant torture for her. He wanted her to live again, even if it meant living without him. He knew what he had to do and he would do whatever it would take to give her life. Tears slowly filled his eyes as he realized how difficult going back would be for him. She would be so close, and yet so completely far away. His feelings for her had remained with him and he also felt ripped and torn apart from her absence. He wanted to do whatever he could to ease her pain, even if it meant bearing it all himself and allowing her to love another. He slowly let out a soft sigh and glanced over to the angel who now stood directly to his side.

"I am ready. When do we go?" Alex asked.

The angel looked sympathetically back at the man at his side. He too knew how painful and difficult the journey back would be for Alex. As the light around them became brighter and glorious, he searched his own soul to find the words he could use to give Alex comfort.

"Alex, remember and never forget, the love you and she share will remain throughout all of eternity. The angels in Heaven have all smiled at the gift of love that He blessed to you and Beth. But keep close in your mind that *love exists in letting go.*"

Dawn Elizabeth

"I will keep that in mind," Alex said, his heart aching at the thought of letting go of his love for Beth.

Michael slowly nodded towards a ray of light that's beam was dimmer than the others. His beautiful hair was lifting off his shoulders as a gentle breeze blew it back. Alex looked over at the angel and the two slowly started walking towards the dim light, leaving behind them the radiant colors and beauty that showered the gates of Heaven.

Chapter 20

The day was gloomy and gray as the raindrops trickled down the windows next to where Beth was sitting. She silently hugged her knees and rested her chin on them as she blankly stared out the glass. Her hair was knotted up and clipped to the back of her head with several strands fallen from the clip. Her face was pale without the slightest makeup. Her eyes that once had sparkled were now puffy and bloodshot due to hours of crying. As if in a daze, she just stared out the window, numb to anything around her.

It had been a month since Alex had died and with him a part of her had died as well. She had collapsed after they had taken his body away and she had fallen into a world of silence. Her firm had granted her family's request for her leave of absence as they all desperately tried to bring the light back into her eyes.

The nine roses that he had had delivered to her on that day still remain in the crystal vase. The flowers had wilted and turned brown but she would not allow anyone to touch or remove them. For her to remove those flowers would mean letting go and she was not ready to do that. As she sat by the window she glanced over at the wilted flowers that sat on the counter. Again tears filled her eyes and slowly started down her cheeks.

Tiffany, heartbroken at the sight of her grieving mother, walked over and knelt beside her. As she watched the many tears flow from her mother's eyes she stood up and walked to the counter and retrieved several tissues. Gently, she wiped the tears from her

Dawn Elizabeth

mother's eyes. She then reached down and tenderly hugged her.

"I love you, Mom. You still have Greg and me. We need you too."

Beth's hands slowly reached up to caress her daughter's hair. She knew what her daughter was saying was true as the tears poured from her eyes and she started to sob.

"I am sorry, Tiffany. I just miss him so much. It is so unfair." She cried.

Tiffany tightened her hug as the tears started to swell up in her own eyes. "I know, Mom. I know. But, Mom, he wouldn't want you to be so unhappy." She released the hold and knelt directly in front of her mother.

"Mom, Alex loved you so much. His love radiated the rooms of this house. I remember the first night he came over for a visit. I recall thinking that there was something so magical about the two of you being together. I know that your time together was short, but, Mom, most people never share the bond that you two did… that beautiful love. You hold on to that, those memories, and he will always be there."

Beth slowly nodded as she looked into the precious face of her teenager daughter. She was so young, yet so grown up. Instead of she taking care of her daughter it was her daughter who was now taking care of her.

"Oh, honey, I am sorry. I love you and your brother so much. I need to snap out of this and start being your mom again."

As she leaned forward to hug her daughter, the telephone rang. She quickly looked at Tiffany with pleading eyes, she did not want to talk to anyone.

CIRCLE OF LOVE

Tiffany, understanding the expression on her mother's face, nodded and stood to answer the phone. She picked up the receiver as the phone was beginning to ring its third time.

"Hello" she said then paused to hear who was calling. "Hi, Joe. No, I am sorry, Mom isn't really up to taking any phone calls. Maybe some other time…I appreciate that and I am sure she would too…Okay, thank you. Bye." Tiffany replaced the receiver on its cradle and turned back towards her mom, "It was Joe, Mom. He wanted to see how you were doing and said that if you needed anything at all to just let him know. He heard about the your loss. He is very sorry. He was very kind, Mom."

Beth sighed and gazed out the window and watched the raindrops hit the glass.

"I am sure he was, sweetheart. But I just can't talk to anyone yet. I am sorry to make you have to do that for me," her saddened eyes looking back to her daughter for forgiveness.

"It's okay. We're going get through this. We all miss him. All of us."

Tiffany lowered herself down and tenderly kissed her mother's cheek, then turned and went upstairs to study. She did not realize that her mother was not alone.

Chapter 21

Joe held the receiver in his right hand for a moment and stared at the counter. He had heard that the man who had won Beth's heart had been killed, but was not told what had happened. He had also heard through mutual friends that she had been devastated by the loss and her family had requested a leave of absence from her firm. It had been many months since he had seen her in the supermarket and he had remembered how her eyes had been filled with such joy and happiness when she said his name was 'Alex'. He had envied the man who caused that love to radiate from her eyes. Joe loved her too and it was an unrealistic dream for him to believe that he could ever see that same light in her eyes when she gazed at him.

Slowly his eyes blinked as he realized that he was still holding the receiver in his hand. Quickly he replaced it on its cradle and turned and walked over to his desk. He pulled the chair from the desk and lowered himself down onto its hard surface. For a moment he just sat and stared into space. "If only I would have just treated her differently, I could have at least been her friend...I could have helped her get through this," he thought. He reached up and put his hands through his thick, dark hair and sighed heavily. "There has to be something I can do...but what?"

As he sat at the cold desk, his mind was flooded with memories of all the horrible and cruel things he had said to her in the past. He had treated her so unkindly because of his own insecurities and fear. She had always tried so hard to win him over and he had only pushed her away. Now, as he sat in his hard chair, he realized that his actions were inexcusable. He would never be able to comfort her because she would never trust him. Strangely, as he sat and recalled his past actions his heart began to get stronger. Its will was no competition for his intellect as it was determined that it would have its chance to love and be loved. He would go to her and apologize for her loss and he would then offer to her his friendship. This time he would not allow his fears or insecurity to keep him from her.

He pushed himself away from the desk and stood up. He turned and headed to his bedroom to retrieve his keys, which he had left on his dresser. He then made a quick surveillance around the room to make sure he hadn't left anything lying out on the floor and headed towards the front door. He felt the numerous butterflies in his stomach as he momentarily questioned what he was doing. He hesitated for a brief second, and then quickly pulled the door shut behind him. He took the front door steps two at a time as he raced towards his vehicle. He knew that if he slowed he might change his mind and he did not want that to happened.

He opened the truck's door and jumped in. He put the key in the ignition and quickly sped out of his parking space. Beth's house was right around the corner and it would only take him five minutes to get there if he took the back roads. Deciding that it was important not to waste any time, he turned down the back road that led into her subdivision. He was not sure what words he would say to her when he saw her. He only knew that he was going to prove to her that he

Dawn Elizabeth

was indeed sorry for her loss and would be there to help to get through her pain if she wanted him to be. As he headed down her street, he could feel his heart pounding faster and faster with anticipation of how she would react when she saw him. He looked ahead and observed that her car was in the driveway and there were lights in the windows. Slowly, he pulled in behind her car. He quickly shifted the truck into park and turned off its engine. Without hesitation, he jumped from the vehicle and closed its door. He took large strides as he approached the house. As he stood on her front porch, he paused for a moment and closed his eyes. "Please help me get through this, Father. Let me help her," he quietly prayed then reached for the doorbell and pushed in its button. After hearing the sound of the bell inside the house, he released the button and stood in front of the door with his hands crossed in front of him as he waited for someone to answer.

Chapter 22

Alex and Michael walked side by side through the dim beam of light. As they reached its end, Alex looked around and realized the beam had brought them into Beth's house. He quickly turned his head from side to side as he recognized her living room and heard the soft sounds of female voices. He looked back at Michael and waited for guidance.

Without making a sound, Michael nodded his head in the direction to which the sound of voices was coming from, indicating that Alex should go and see what was ahead. Understanding the angel's expression, Alex turned and walked in the direction of the open dinning and kitchen areas. As he reached the open rooms he came to an abrupt halt when he saw Beth a few feet in front of him. She was sitting next to the window with her daughter kneeling down in front of her. He watched as Tiffany tenderly wiped the tears that were flowing from her eyes. He closed his own eyes and allowed his soul to become one with Beth's. He felt the intense pain she carried deep in her heart due to his death. He could hear her grieving soul pleading with God as she tried to understand why Alex had been taken from her. Her pain was intoxicating as Alex stood silently and allowed it to consume him. Michael slowly came and stood next to Alex as he, too, observed the woman who was grieving before them. Alex looked at the angel, not understanding what was happening. The angel motioned to him to wait and watch the events that were starting to take place.

Dawn Elizabeth

The angel slowly turned as the phone began to ring. Alex gazed at Beth and felt her fear at having to speak with whomever it was that was calling. He heard her thoughts pleading with God to help her get through this pain. He watched and listened to Tiffany who had now answered the phone.

"Hi, Joe. No I am sorry. Mom isn't really up to taking any phone calls. Maybe some other time...I appreciate that and I am sure she would too...Okay, thank you. Bye."

"Alex, it has begun. There is a reason for everything that happens. Events that take place lead to certain outcome. It is now time for your work to begin. This is where the true love that your souls feel will become intertwined throughout all of eternity. There are two souls that need you and it is time for you to be there for them. Please know she will feel your spirit here, although she will not see you. Guide her to him and help her to allow herself to feel his love."

Puzzled, Alex looked at the angel, not understanding how he could lead his Beth to love another. As he started to approach Beth, he was startled as Tiffany walked through him and headed up the stairs. He felt the warmth of the young girl's soul as it passed through his spirit. Silently he watched as she slowly walked up the stairs and briefly hesitated. She gradually decided that her mother needed the time to herself and felt that she would be fine. She reached the top of the stairs and looked back to see her mother sitting next to the huge window. She felt her own heart break because she too missed the man who had become a member of her home. She lowered her head

CIRCLE OF LOVE

so her mother wouldn't catch her wiping the tears from her eyes and continued on to her room.

"Can I go to her now?" Alex questioned.

"Yes...yes you can go to her side. But remember...she will be able to feel your spirit."

For a brief moment Alex stood silent and stationary and gazed from a distance at the woman sitting next to the window. He closed his eyes and searched her soul to feel her emotions. He felt as if his own heart were bleeding and crying for its missing love. Slowly he opened his eyes and walked over to where she was sitting. As he came within reach of touching her, she quickly turned her head in his direction.

A familiar sensation soared through her body that Beth had experienced whenever Alex was near.

"Alex...?" she quietly whispered. "Alex, are you here?"

Tears rapidly started to pour from her eyes as she stood up. Her eyes tenderly began searching the space in front of her trying to find him. She slowly closed her eyes as the tears continued to stream down her cheeks. She tilted her head back and allowed her thoughts to be clear.

"I feel you, Alex. I feel you here with me."

Once again, Alex turned to Michael to question what he was permitted to do. Michael softly smiled and nodded for Alex to go to her.

Little by little, Alex moved closer to Beth and stopped when he was standing only inches from her. For moments he remained still and silent as he looked down at her beautiful face, which was once filled with happiness and was now stricken with deep grief. He

Dawn Elizabeth

watched as the tears streamed at a steady pace from her eyes and flowed down her soft cheeks.

"Oh, Princess, I am so sorry I had to leave you."

Instinctively, his hand reached up to wipe the tears that flowed down her face. His hand barely touched her cheek when her eyes opened wide as she felt his touch.

"Alex. You *are* here with me. I can feel you..." she whispered.

Once again she closed her eyes, tears flowing endlessly from them. Overcome with emotion, she began to sob, her body shaking as she wept tears that would fill buckets. She leaned down in her chair and cupped her face into her hands as she cried uncontrollably. Tiffany, hearing her mother's sobs, quickly ran down the steps and rushed to comfort her.

"Mom. What's wrong? Mom, it's okay." She said as she snuggly wrapped her arms around her mother's shaking shoulders.

Beth raised her head from her hands and looked into her daughter's face. Her nose was bright red and her eyes almost swollen shut from the heavy crying. As she started to speak the words came out broken and stuttered.

"I-I-I-I f-e-l-l-l-l-t him. He is here. He-e-e-e t-o-u-u-u-u-c-hed my face." she finally said.

Frightened from her mother's behavior Tiffany started to wipe the tears from her face and tried to understand what she was saying.

"Who was here Mom? Who touched your face?" She questioned uncertain as to whether or not she wanted to hear her mother's response. She tightened

CIRCLE OF LOVE

her hold around her mother's trembling body as her mother quietly repeated.

"Alex. He is here. I can feel him." She slowly looked up and turned her head from side to side as she searched the room for a sign that he was indeed in the room with her. Within moments, Beth started sobbing rocking her body back and forth. She reached up and held her cheek where Alex had touched.

In anger, Alex turned back and looked at Michael who remained silent through the entire event. Alex felt as if his soul was being ripped apart piece by piece as he witnessed his love being overwhelmed with grief and knew it was because of him. He backed away from Beth, hoping to allow her soul the freedom from his, and thinking that by doing so it would lesson her pain. In one swift moment he was in front of the angel, his soul filled with rage as he was forced to witness the woman he loved being tormented by his presence.

"What is going on here, Michael? I cannot put her through this! I will not hurt her anymore! She feels me and I feel her. It is ripping both of our souls apart! Can't you see it with your eyes?" he yelled and pointed to where Beth and her daughter were sitting.

The angel reached up and grabbed both of Alex's shoulders and held him still.

"Listen to me! Yes, I do see what is happening to both of you. There is nothing that I can do. As I said there are events that must take place in order for there to be a certain outcome." As he spoke the last words the front doorbell rang as its chimes echoed though the house. The angel released his grip and slowly nodded towards the door.

Dawn Elizabeth

"There is a reason for everything, Alex. Trust me", he said. Then turned back and looked at Beth.

Tiffany was unable to calm her mother and was starting to become frightened when she too heard the doorbell ring. Praying that it might be someone who would be able to calm her mother, she raced to the front door and quickly opened it.

As she flung the door open it took her only a moment to recognize the handsome face of Joseph O'Dea standing on her front doorstep. Relieved that it was a familiar face, she quickly grabbed his arm and yanked him into the house pulling him into the room where her mother was falling apart.

"Tiffany, what's wrong?", he questioned as he allowed the teenage girl to pull him into the house. It took only a few moments for Joe to realize what was going on. As he reached the open dining room he spotted Beth sitting in a chair in front of the bay window crying and rocking back and forth. He quickly ran to her and picked her tiny body up and then sat back down in the chair. He held her body close to his and began to console her.

"Its okay, Beth. You go ahead and cry. Let it all out. I know it hurts. Let it out… I will hold you for as long as you need to be held. It's okay, sweetie, I know how bad it hurts," he tenderly spoke. He searched the room and saw a box of tissue sitting within his reach. He grabbed a couple and began tenderly wiping the tears that covered her face. He held her tightly as she sobbed allowing her to release the grief.

Beth remained in Joseph's arms as she shed the many tears that overwhelmed her soul. They seemed to be without end. She didn't try to push Joe's hand away each time he gently wiped the tears from her eyes. As he held her in his arms, Joe's heart finally escaped the walls that he had built around it for protection. He felt his own soul ache as her body trembled in his arms as she wept for the man she had lost. He wanted desperately to ease her pain and was extremely worried about her. She needed rest and, from her appearance, it was clear that she was close to collapsing from exhaustion. He looked to Tiffany and quietly asked.

"How long has she been like this? Where is your brother?"

"She has been crying on and off since Alex died. But not like this. She was okay just a few minutes ago. Then suddenly she started talking and saying things that scared me. She said Alex was here…that he touched her face. She was hysterical and shaking… I didn't know what to do." Tears started to fill the young girl's eyes as she looked at her mother with concern. "I don't know what to say or do for her, she misses him so much."

Joseph continued holding onto the tiny woman that cried in his arms. He looked at the young girl who stood next to him.

"Tiffany, it's okay, sweetie. Your mom will be okay. We need to allow her the time to cry. She has lost someone she loves very much. It is a very difficult time for her. But she needs rest. How about you help me get her into her bed and we will comfort her and maybe we can convince her to go to sleep," he said softly.

Without speaking, she nodded at the dark haired man who tenderly held her weeping mom. She moved back and gave him room to stand up and followed him

Dawn Elizabeth

as he carried her mother up the stairs to her room. Once they entered Beth's bedroom, she quickly moved to the front of the bed and removed the decorative pillows that were scattered at the head of the bed. She looked around the room and found Big Bear lying on the floor and quickly picked him up. She looked as the dark haired man tried to lower her mother onto the bed. She was surprised when she saw her mother's arms go around the man's neck as she buried her face into his chest and continued weeping.

"It's okay, Beth. I won't leave you. Go ahead and cry. Let it out."

For hours Joseph sat on the bed and held Beth in his arms, allowing her to cry for the man she had lost. He rocked her back and forth and held her tenderly in his arms. Slowly, the tears started to slow until finally she was calm and quiet. He felt her release the hold she had around his neck as she rested her face on is chest. He realized that she had cried herself to sleep so he carefully stood up, still holding her in his arms, then turned and gently laid her on the bed. He smiled when he saw that Tiffany had placed Big Bear on the bed next to her. He knew how much she had loved that stuffed teddy bear and how it had always been with her. He knew the story of how it had been sweetly given to her. He walked over to a chair and retrieved an afghan that was folded over the arm of the chair. He unfolded the blanket and carefully covered Beth's little body. He knew she would want Big Bear close to her so he tucked the bear under the blanket as well. As he turned around to turn on the tiny lamp sitting next to the bed, he spotted a photograph sitting on the table. He quickly turned on the lamp and picked the picture

CIRCLE OF LOVE

up to see what the picture was. It was a picture of Beth and a dark haired gentleman cuddled on the couch in the family room. As he looked at the picture he slowly began to recognize the man holding Beth. Joseph let out a heavy gasp when he realized from where he recognized him. He lowered himself down on the bed next to Beth and continued looking at the picture.

"Oh—my—God," he whispered.

Tiffany had been watching Joseph and was puzzled by his reaction of the picture of her mom and Alex.

"What's wrong, Joe?" she questioned.

Still holding the picture, he looked up at the teenager.

"Tiffany…this man with your mom…is this…is this…Alex?" he asked her.

The young girl moved over to where Joe was sitting on the bed and sat down next to him. She glanced over her shoulder to make sure that her mother was still sleeping and was careful not to wake her.

"Yes…that is Alex." she whispered, "That was their favorite picture. I took it on the first night that he had come to the house for a visit. They looked so sweet together. For some reason I had wanted to capture the moment."

Joseph took in a deep breath, closed his eyes and slowly shook his head.

"What's wrong, Joe"? She once again asked.

Slowly he began to tell the young girl how he recognized the man in the picture. Quietly, not to awaken Beth, he began, "I was coming out of the gas station that day and he was going in. I can still see the way he looked at me, almost as if he could see deep into my soul. There was such warmth around him. I

Dawn Elizabeth

remember it gave me a warm, fuzzy feeling, very peaceful. Suddenly he stumbled and I caught him. After I was sure he had regained his balance, he told me that he was proposing to his special lady that day. He said he didn't think he was worried but must have been because he was feeling a little dizzy. I told him that he was going to be fine and I was sure the special lady would say yes." As Joe spoke these words, he kept his eyes on the picture of the man he had seen at the gas station that day. With his eyes never leaving the man's face in the picture he continued, "I didn't realize that he was your mother's 'Alex'. What happened to him Tiffany? How did he die?"

Tears started to fill the young girl's eyes as she slowly began to answer his question. "He was on his way home. It was right after he left the gas station I think. He was going to propose to Mom that day. Ohhhh, he had this beautiful romantic evening planned. He had gotten Renaissance costumes for all of us. It was so romantic what he had done. He had written a poem for her and had three roses delivered on the hour, each with a paragraph of the poem. Greg and I were to accompany him and I was to carry the last three roses. He was going to be dressed as a knight. The whole thing was beautiful. But he never got the chance to propose. Nine of the roses and part of the poem was delivered and so was her gown. Greg and I were in our costumes and we were waiting for Alex. But something terrible happened. As he was leaving the gas station he dropped the engagement ring and bent down to pick it up and wasn't watching the road. An elderly man had had a heart attack and his truck was out of control."

CIRCLE OF LOVE

As Tiffany struggled to finish the story her tears escaped her eyes and found their way down her little face. With her little hand she reached up and wiped the tears, took a deep breath and continued.

"Greg and I heard mom speed past the neighbor's house where we were waiting. Then we heard the loud sirens, which were at the end of the street. By the time we reached them, it was too late. Alex had died in mom's arms. It was so sad she tried to wipe the blood from his face and kept pulling the glass from his hair."

As more tears flowed from her eyes she quickly used both hands to wipe her face off frightened that her mother would hear her crying and wake up and start to cry again.

Joseph looked at the young girl who too was grieving for the man they had all lost. He leaned over and gave her a gentle hug.

"I am so sorry, Tiffany. I know how painful it is to lose someone you love. If it helps you at all to know…you aren't alone. We have all lost people that we have loved, and it is difficult to get through. But, sweetie, I think one thing that helps people when they have lost someone…is knowing there is someone out there who cares about them. I promise you that if your mom needs me at anytime, no matter if it is day or night…I will be here for her. You won't have to get through this by yourself. I will do all I can to help you and your brother bring your mom back to being her old happy self. I am not going to lie to you though, Tiff…it is going to be a long rough road. She is going to need some special care."

The young girl nodded as she listened to the kind words the man was saying, understanding clearly what

Dawn Elizabeth

he was trying to say to her. He had known her mother for many years and a feeling in her own heart told her that this man would indeed help her mom through the horrible tragedy of losing Alex. At the same time, she knew for some reason that he would never try to take Alex's place in her mom's heart. She looked at her mother who was now cuddled with Big Bear and sleeping peacefully. Careful not to disturb her, she quietly bent down and kissed her on her soft tear stained cheek. For several moments she remained standing at the side of the bed looking tenderly down upon the woman who had brought her into the world. She remembered the many times her mother had held her in her arms and comforted her when she had felt sad. She remembered the numerous times she had played the role of a nurse and mended a tiny scratch that seemed at the time to be the largest cut to Tiffany. Tiffany smiled softly as she realized, that no matter how small and trivial an injury, her mother never made the girl feel as if she was a bother. Her mother was always there for her holding her close and drying her tears. As she remained next to the bed she remembered the many times she had been scared by a storm and her mother would smile and quickly pull her covers back allowing the young girl to jump in bed beside her. Feeling that her mother was now sleeping peacefully, she slowly turned and looked at Joe. She knew this man would watch her as she slept and would not leave her side. Unconscious of her actions, she bent down and gave the dark haired man a tender hug. Then softly whispered "Thanks, Joe." The dark haired man returned a soft hug and nodded as he silently tried to convey everything was going to be okay. She

CIRCLE OF LOVE

slowly stood up and headed towards the door. She paused for a moment before she reached the doorway when she felt an overwhelming warmth rush through her soul. The feeling gave her the oddest sensation. It did not scare her but rather, calmed her. The warm feeling faded and she continued through the doorway toward her own room. She had no idea that the warmth she had felt was radiated from Alex's spirit. She unknowingly had walked through him as he and the angel had also been in the room witnessing and listening to all that was being said.

Alex and Michael both stood quietly at the end of the room and watched as Joseph removed all the items from a rocking chair that was to the side of the bed. After placing the several objects neatly on the floor, out of the way, he slowly sat down and stretched his long legs out in front of him. He affectionately looked over at Beth and watched her as she now lay peacefully sleeping. She was curled up on her side with her arms tightly wrapped around her large, soft teddy bear; its head was tucked under her chin with her arms encircled around his neck. Joe silently smiled to himself as he noticed how tightly she had her arms wrapped around the large stuffed animal. He knew that Big Bear was one of Beth's most cherished possessions. He leaned back in the chair and slowly began to rock, listening to the sound of the soft squeaks of the chair as it moved up and down. He decided the moment that he had seen her crying downstairs that no matter what, he would not leave her side. He would remain for as long as it would take to help her find her way back to her children. He rested his head back and closed his eyes, listening to the

Dawn Elizabeth

hypnotic noise the chair made in its slow motion. Within minutes he, too, had drifted off into a peaceful sleep.

    Beth turned to her other side taking Big Bear with her. She was unaware that sitting in the chair next to her bed was Joseph O'Dea, stretched out dozing. Also standing at the foot of the bed were Alex and Michael watching over her as she slept.

Chapter 23

Alex stood for several moments at the foot of Beth's bed and watched her as she slept. She had rolled over to her right side and had found Big Bear next to her. Instinctively, she grabbed the bear and pulled it closely to her chest and wrapped her arms around the stuffed animal's body. Her blonde hair had fallen from the clip that had held it up on her head and was now fanned out behind her on the pillow with several strains falling down around her face. Her breathing was in a slow, rhythmic pattern as she slowly inhaled then exhaled. Her face was quite pale and it was obvious that sleep had eluded her for a long period of time. As he watched her sleeping he could feel that at this moment she was in a much-needed peaceful state and she would receive the rest that her body hungered for. After feeling her body drift off into a peaceful dream, he felt that it was safe to approach her. Slowly he allowed his hand to run along the brass footboard as he carefully eased his way to the side of the bed. As he came within inches of her, she quickly turned from her right side to her left bringing the large stuffed teddy bear with her. She released a heavy sigh but continued to sleep. Not wanting to take the chance of waking her, Alex lower down to a kneeling position beside her bed then glanced over to where Joseph was sitting to make sure the man was still asleep. He turned to the foot of the bed to where the angel had remained and began to softly speak.

"Michael, look at her. She looks like an angel herself. She *is* dreaming of me. And, for some reason,

Dawn Elizabeth

I do not believe she has been able to dream since my death. But now as she lies there, holding on to Big Bear she is at peace, but it is a peace that is connected with me. Is it because I am here with her... and yet not as a man but as a spirit?" He questioned and looked to the angel for an answer.

The angel turned and walked back away from the bed. For several moments he was silent as he tried to compose the words that he needed to say to Alex, as he knew Alex was looking for his guidance.

"Her soul feels you, Alex. It is her soul that knows that you are with her. For what seemed only minutes to you on your journey to the entrance of Heaven's Gates, has been a month for her. It was a month her soul was abandoned and left alone...without yours to comfort it, to guide it...to more or less complete it. Her mind does not have the ability to understand that you are present with her...but her soul does. Do not be afraid to disturb her, talk to her, Alex...let your souls unite and, in it she shall be at peace." The angel nodded towards Beth, his eyes beaming with sincere kindness as he gave instructions to Alex.

Alex, still feeling a little hesitant, looked down at his beautiful Beth as she slept. His heart ached to draw her to him and feel her breath on his face. He slowly moved towards her until their faces were almost touching. With his left hand he reached up and removed a strand of hair that had fallen across her face, amazed that as a spirit he had the ability to do such a thing. Not questioning this ability, he allowed his hand to caress her head as he let his fingers run through the softness of her hair. As he looked at the woman lying before him, his body was filled with a tormented loss in knowing that he would never be able to comfort her and dry her tears as the man now asleep in the chair had done. He continued to run his fingers through her hair then gradually drew his hand up near her face. As his fingers became close to her cheek, he noticed a single tear had escaped from her eyes and was slowly moving down towards his hand. Quickly, his hand went to where the tear had traveled, and as his hand came in contact with it, the teardrop sparkled, and then vanished. It was as if God had understood his agony and had allowed him the opportunity to dry her tears.

"He knows your pain, Alex. He does not want you to suffer. Let the bond that He blessed the two of you with be joined as she sleeps. No harm will come to her, I promise. It will be fine. Let her soul come to you," he whispered.

For a moment Alex did not comprehend what the angel was saying, but strangely within seconds he knew that during the time in which she slept it was safe for him to talk to her and that her soul would indeed come. Very quietly he began to speak.

"Beth, my princess...I am here. I am with you."

In astonishment Alex watched as Beth's soul lifted up and magically drifted out of her body. It slowly floated to the foot of the bed and gradually began to take form of its humanly body. Her soul turned and smiled at Michael then slowly approached Alex.

"Alex... You've come back. You did not leave me," she whispered.

Puzzled by the spirit-like form before him, and the figure lying on the bed, Alex looked to Michael. Knowing that he was now confused, Michael quickly began to explain the events.

Dawn Elizabeth

"It is her soul, as she sleeps it is allowed the freedom to remove itself from the humanly form in which it resides and come to you. When she awakes she will have no memory of it at all. To her it will be as though she dreamt it. And it will be left at that. Go ahead, Alex…talk to her…she needs you."

Before he could utter a word her soul began to speak.

"Alex…my Alex…you have come back for me…I knew you would…"

"Oh, sweetheart…no I have not come back for you, but I am here to help you. You have a life to live…you mustn't hold on to me because you have so much more ahead of you. You must let go, as painful as it may be, you must let go of me. I will always love you. Death does not take love away…it still remains."

"No, if you are not here with me…I do not want to live. I feel half, not whole…Please take me with you. Don't make me stay in a world where I am left without you. I cannot bear it. Look at me, Alex. Look how I am falling apart." She quickly turned and pointed to the humanly body as it lay on the bed holding onto the stuffed animal. The body did indeed looked worn and withdrawn as if it had lost its will to live.

Alex turned and looked at Beth as she lay sleeping, then he turn back to face her soul. "I will not leave you until I know that you are living without me in your life. I love you, Princess, and I shall always love you. But for now go back and rest and I will remain and watch over you."

Hesitantly, her soul moved back to where her body lay. It lowered itself on top of the body looking back with pleading eyes toward Alex then quickly lay back

CIRCLE OF LOVE

and became one with its humanly body. Once again, a single tear escaped her sleeping eyes and began to travel down her cheek. As Alex moved to wipe the tear from her face his own heart was filled with the cries from Beth's soul.

"Please don't leave me. Please stay with me always."

Upon the moment that his hand reached the tear to wipe it he felt as if his own soul was being ripped apart, as it too wanted to be with its soul mate. He stood back and turned to look at Michael. He sighed and began heavily, "Michael I cannot do this, I love her too much. I feel as torn and empty as she does. I want to remain with her always."

"Yes, you do love her, trust in that love and you will be able to do this. He is watching over you and knows how difficult it is. But remember love exists in letting go. Soon you will see this and you will know what to do."

As Michael started to finish he was interrupted by a loud snore. The angel quickly turned to where the sound was coming from and was amazed that the loud nose came from the man sitting in the chair next to Beth's bed. Alex started to chuckle as he observed the astonished look on his guardian angel's face.

"Now are you still sure that he is the one for my Beth?" He asked.

The angel quickly turned back and flashed Alex a magnificent smile of his own.

"I am sure…as you too will be." He laughed as yet another snore echoed from Joseph O'Dea.

Dawn Elizabeth

The two spirits both turned towards the sleeping man as he continued to snore, some louder than others. Alex just shook his head and laughed.

"She will never tolerate sleeping with someone who snores," he replied.

"Oh we will see, there is more for you to see and learn. Time will show you. In time she will allow this man into her heart. And she will not mind if he snores louder than a train."

Just then Joseph let out the loudest snore as his lips began to quiver. Both Alex and Michael began to laugh as his snores became louder and louder.

Chapter 24

Greg walked into the kitchen and quietly laid his sheet music and drumsticks on the kitchen counter. He had been at drum-line practice, which had lasted for several hours. He had not been enthusiastic about attending the practice and had felt guilty about leaving Tiffany home alone to care for their grief stricken mother. He walked over to the steps and looked down into the family room to see if his sister and mother were there. Although there was a lamp on, the room was empty and quiet. He backed away from the steps and started to head upstairs to the bedrooms, hoping his sister was able to convince his mother to lay down. As he reached the top step, he heard the door to Tiffany's bedroom slowly open and then his sister's worried face peeked around the doorframe. She slowly drew one finger up in front of her lips in an effort to keep him from calling out her name. Once she saw that her brother would remain silent, she motioned for him to come into her room. She backed into the room allowing him space to quietly enter. Once he was completely in the room she moved around him and eased the door shut.

"What's going on, Tiff, where's Mom?"

"You were gone forever! I thought practice was only going to be for an hour, two at the most". She snapped.

"It was supposed to be, but we were all having a hard time with the new piece so we had to keep playing it over and over. I am really sorry. Why…what's up? Is Mom all right? Where is she?"

Dawn Elizabeth

Tiffany crossed her arms over her chest and gave her older brother a look of anger. She shook her head from side to side and clenched her teeth together as she tightened her tiny thin lips. She closed her eyes and took a deep breath to control her anger with her brother's absence before she started to tell him the events that had taken place that evening. She knew that this was not the time to lash out at him because he was taking Alex's death rather hard. He hadn't intended on going to the drum practice because he was neither in the mood to practice nor be around his peers. He was overwhelmed with concern when his mother had drifted into her quiet world after the paramedics had taken Alex's crushed body away. He had witnessed the light slowly fade from her beautiful blues eyes and was frightened that it may never return. Seeing the overwhelming concern on his face, Tiffany's anger vanished and she relaxed her arms. She backed up and slowly sat down on the side of her bed. Greg, seeing that she desperately needed to say something, walked over and sat next to his younger sister. He reached over and gave her a tender little hug around her shoulders then let his arm remain as he rested his hand on her shoulder. As he waited for his sister to speak he glanced around her bedroom and studied the walls decorated with posters of various entertainers and teen idols. In an effort to get her to talk he began.

"What happened, Tiff? Is something wrong with Mom?" he cautiously asked. He was uncertain whether he was ready for her response.

Tiffany once again took a deep breath and finally started to tell him what had happened that evening.

CIRCLE OF LOVE

"Mom is okay now…but she wasn't. Joe calmed her down…"

"Joe calmed her down? Joseph O'Dea?" he interrupted.

"Yes, *Greg*, Joseph O'Dea. Do you know another Joe? Didn't you notice his truck in our driveway?" she said sarcastically.

"Hey, don't get snippy with me. Joe hasn't been around in ages. It just surprises me that he was here…that's all. His truck… I don't remember seeing his truck. Man, am I that out of it?" The teenager quickly stood up and went to the window. He lifted up the blinds and looked out the window to see if there was a truck in the driveway. Sure enough, parked directly behind his mother's car was Joe's teal green pickup truck. He had been so preoccupied that he hadn't even noticed the vehicle in his driveway. He shook his head and returned to the bed and sat down next to his sister.

"Joseph O'Dea is here now? Right now?" he questioned. Go ahead, continue. What happened?"

"Yes. Right now he is here. I'm trying to tell you what happened. Don't interrupt." She ordered. "Mom was sitting and staring out of the window. And she was crying, not sobbing, but the tears were slowly going down her cheeks. I went to her and comforted her the best I could and I thought she had settled down. So I left her and went up to my room. I was up there for five minutes, if it was even that long, when I heard her sobbing. I ran down to check on her and she was crying uncontrollably. She was hysterical. Then she started to scare me because she said Alex was here. She said he touched her face. Greg, it was really scary.

179

Dawn Elizabeth

She really believed Alex was here. Then in the middle of everything the doorbell rang and, thank goodness, it was Joe. He came in and saw the stressed out state she was in and raced to her. You should have seen how he picked her up and cradled her in his arms. For hours he just held her and let her cry on his chest as he rocked her back and forth." Tiffany let out a heavy sigh before she continued.

"We were able to get her into her room but when he went to lay her down on her bed she started sobbing again so he held her and rocked her as she cried. She cried herself to sleep in his arms. Oh, Greg, it was so sad. I was so surprised at the loving way he held her and comforted her. It was like his heart was breaking as he observed her pain and agony. His arms must have been aching at the long time he held her. But he never moved or tried to push her away. He held her almost in the same way Alex used to…and the way he looked at her…It was odd… for a moment I thought that he was in love with her too."

"Joe? Are you serious?"

"Yes…believe it or not…I think Joe loves Mom too." she replied. Anyway let me finish," she snapped.

"Okay, okay…sorry…finish," Greg said.

"After she fell asleep I helped him lay her down on her bed. After we had her all snug with Big Bear by her side he noticed the picture of Mom and Alex on her night table. Remember the one I took the first night Alex was here? The one of them cuddled on the couch? Anyway— You should have seen the look on his face. He turned as white as a sheet then asked me who the man in the picture was. I saw the pain and

CIRCLE OF LOVE

hurt on his face when I told him it was Alex. Greg, he saw Alex right before he died!"

As Tiffany tried to tell her brother what Joe had told her, tears filled her eyes and quickly found their way down her soft cheeks. As she tried to control the tears she started to breathe heavily, and her body began to shake as she desperately tried to stop from crying. Seeing his sister's distress, Greg quickly pulled his sister next to him and tried to sooth her. Pulling his sweatshirt sleeve down over his hand he quickly wiped the tears that were now covering both sides of her face.

"It's okay. You don't have to tell me, Tiff…it's okay…don't cry," he whispered.

Tiffany took a deep breath and shook her head. "I am okay…I want to finish…I'll be okay," she stuttered.

The young man nodded his head and patiently waited for his sister to finish her story.

"Joe said he was coming out of the gas station when Alex was going in. He said Alex stumbled almost as if he was going to faint or pass out. Joe caught him before he fell. He said that Alex said he was feeling a little bit strange but thought maybe it was because he was nervous about proposing to Mom. Joe said that he told him that he was sure whoever the lucky lady was she would say yes and everything would be fine. Joe had no idea that the lucky lady Alex was going to propose to was Mom."

Shocked by what she had just told him, Greg stood up and began to pace in his sister's small room. He reached up and rubbed his forehead with his hand several times trying to somehow to block out the feeling that it was an extraordinary coincidence that

Dawn Elizabeth

the two men just happened to meet on the day that Alex was killed. In fact, their meeting was only moments before Alex's life had been taken.

Noticing the worry on her brother's face, Tiffany stood up and walked over to where her brother was now pacing. In an attempt to stop him, she stood in his pathway making it difficult for him to walk in a line.

"Greg, Mom is okay for the time being. She is sleeping and Joe is asleep in the chair next to her bed. He said he wasn't going to leave her in case she woke up in the middle of the night and started to cry again. Come with me. I will show you." She motioned with her hand for her older brother to follow her to their mother's room.

The two teenagers stood in the doorway and peered into their mother's room. Their mother was sleeping peacefully on her bed with her teddy bear wrapped in her arms. Her breathing was slow and steady indicating that she was sound asleep. In the chair to the left of the bed was the tall dark haired man slouched down in the chair with his long, muscular legs out in front of him. His head was resting on his hand as his elbow was propped up on the arm of the chair. Every so often a snore escaped his mouth. Quietly Tiffany spun around and headed to her room. When she returned she was holding a multicolor pastel afghan her grandmother had made for her. Careful not to wake either of the adults, she crept into the room and gently lowered the blanket over the sleeping man. Once she was sure he was covered, she turned and headed out of the room, motioning for her brother to follow.

"Let's not disturb them. We should just wait and see what happens in the morning. The important thing

CIRCLE OF LOVE

is that Mom is resting," she said as soon as they were a good distance from the room.

"Yes, she is finally sleeping," her brother agreed. "Let's see what happens in the morning. I am tired myself so I am going to turn the lights off downstairs and go to bed."

"Me too. I am exhausted. I will see you in the morning. Night."

Greg had already headed down the stairs but quickly turned back to wish his sister 'goodnight'.

Alex looked up at Michael and smiled. The two spirits had witnessed the whole scene that had taken place between the brother and sister. Michael gave Alex one of his warm smiles and said. "They are going to be fine Alex…don't worry."

Alex smiled as Gregory passed him and headed down the hall toward his own room; the young boy was unaware that Alex was watching him as he entered his bedroom and turned on the light. For several moments Alex remained staring at the closed door as he remembered the male bonding he and Gregory had developed. He knew that Greg was a strong young man and he would be able to help his mother through this rough time. He felt saddened because he also missed the kids deeply. The angel feeling his distress, walked up and gently placed his hand on Alex's shoulder.

"They're all going to be fine. I know it is difficult for you to see all of this. But in time you will understand. I promise."

Alex glanced over his shoulder at the two adults sound asleep in the room. Slowly, he looked at the

Dawn Elizabeth

angel and nodded his head. Something in his soul told him the angel was right.

Chapter 25

Beth turned slightly in her bed when she felt the warmth of the gentle breeze against her face. In her dreamlike state she could hear the birds chirping outside her window as if they were singing a song especially for her. The birds were out on a branch in a tree directly outside of her room and were continually chirping. "Chirp, chirp, chirp" one would say, and then the other would repeat the exact same sound. The cheerful sound of the birds singing to each other pulled her from her sleep and she slowly started to open her eyes. For a moment she just lay there and watched as the breeze from the window blew the curtain back and forth. The curtain swayed in a slow and hypnotic pattern causing her thoughts to drift to the night before. She sighed lightly as she remembered sitting and staring out the dining room window watching as the drops of rain traveled down the pane of glass. She had thought they were symbolic of how she had been feeling; it was like the entire heaven grieved with her at the loss of Alex. Her heart felt utterly numb and empty without him. Leisurely she turned on her back and grabbed Big Bear and pulled him into her arms. She rested her chin on the top of the teddy bear's head and allowed her thoughts to take her back to the last morning that she and Alex had been together.

For some reason he had awakened in such an affectionate mood. The moment he awoke he had immediately turned to her and started to cover her sleeping face with tender little kisses. He kissed her forehead and cheeks and even her nose, stopping

Dawn Elizabeth

between each kiss to see if it had awakened her. The very first kiss on her forehead had, but she was enjoying the display of affection and she wanted to see how long he would persist. It took all of her energy to resist returning the kisses; she lay there motionless as he continued touching his lips to her face. He felt that she was still too deep in sleep to feel his kissing so he began to talk to her in his mind hoping it would wake her.

"I love you, Princess". He said over and over in his thoughts. "I love you so very much. Today you will see just how much I do love you."

As the last words traveled to Beth's mind she quickly opened her eyes and looked directly into his warm handsome face, which was barely an inch away.

"I love you too...my handsome knight," she whispered.

She reached up with her left arm and wrapped it around his neck. Their eyes locked for a moment then he quickly bent down and kissed her, slowly at first, until his passion burned with heated desire and his lips engulfed hers. Beth reached her arms up around his neck and pulled his body as close as was possible to hers. She felt his body quiver as his bare chest touched her exposed breast. As he felt her breast against his skin his body began to perspire at the anticipation of what was to come. Gradually, he pulled his lips from hers and moved to her neck and started kissing it and then began moving in the direction of her ear. He covered her ear with his mouth and slowly allowed his tongue to explore its inside. Tenderly, he took her earlobe into his mouth and gently started to nibble on it as he breathed heavily into her ear. Beth let out a soft

CIRCLE OF LOVE

moan and arched her back as she felt his hand make its way to her exposed waiting breasts. Her eyes closed as she felt his finger touch her nipple as it moved in a circular motion causing it to stand up at his touch. In a swift movement his head moved down taking the firm breast into his mouth as he allowed his tongue to flick the button-like nipple back and forth. As her moans became heavier, he reached down and removed the silk panties she was wearing and let his hand remain and explore her warmness. Gently, he guided her legs apart as he raised himself and removed his own under garment. Beth opened her eyes and looked up at the pure beauty that was in the eyes of the man that's soul was intertwined with her own. She watched as he lowered his body onto hers as his hardness search for the opening that would connect them as one. When she felt him enter her, a small moan escaped her lips as she welcomed his body to be joined with hers. Together they started moving in a slow rhythm, each thrust deeper and deeper into her. She allowed her legs to open wider giving him the ability to thrust farther inside. As their passion was united he quickly reached and took both of her hands in his and their fingers became sweetly locked together. He held on to his fervor until his body started to shudder, pleading to be granted release. She felt his soul on the verge of exploding and surrendered to its request. As he felt her insides quiver he could hold back no longer and exploded with force sending his seed inside of her.

For moments they lay there holding onto each other tightly, neither wanting to let go. Reluctantly, Alex lifted himself off Beth and positioned himself on his side next to her now nude body. Tenderly, he raised

Dawn Elizabeth

his hand and began to caress her cheek. She opened her eyes and began to smile. He smiled back at her and whispered, "I will always love you, Princess."

He then lowered his head down to rest on her exposed breasts, and they both drifted back into sleep.

Beth closed her eyes tightly as she recalled that last morning with Alex. She stretched her arm out to the middle of the bed as it searched the unoccupied space, desperately seeking and longing to touch her lost soul-mate. Her hand gradually touched the barren surface moving in a slow side-to-side motion as it fondly remembered the man who once had occupied its space. A soft sigh escaped her lips as she recalled the smile he had on his face when she had woken the second time that morning. She remembered thinking that he looked like the cat that had swallowed the canary, as there was a mischievous glow around him.

She closed her eyes tightly and shook her head from side to side. "No, I will not think about anymore of the events of that day," she thought to herself.

Quickly she threw the covers off of her body and sat up and gazed out of the bedroom window. The birds were still chirping on the branch outside, one singing sweetly, then the other echoing in reply. The sun was shinning brightly and a gentle breeze was blowing. She could hear the ducks splashing around in the pond below as they welcomed the early morning sun. Her gaze was drawn to white, billowy clouds that seemed suspended in the sky. They were as white as purified cotton. As she stared at the clouds her thoughts were taken back to the dream she had had last night when she slept. The dream was vivid, almost as if it was more a reality than a dream. She saw herself sleeping with her faithful Big Bear in her arms. Mysteriously, she began to feel herself pull apart, almost being torn in half. She felt one of the halves drift to the end of her bed, while the other remained peacefully sleeping. Her soul floated and continued to travel to the end of her bed, then quietly took shape in her human form in front of a man that she had never seen before. She remembered the man having long shoulder length hair that was a radiant color of harvest wheat. It seemed as if there was a constant breeze blowing around him as his hair gently moved off his shoulders as he remained in place and looked at her with a deep kindness. She smiled at the man dressed in the long white gown, and somehow she knew that he was there to help her. She turned from the man and saw Alex standing at the side of her bed. Her heart was filled with deep emotion as she saw the man she loved silently standing and waiting for her to come to him. Suddenly the vision faded and she found herself still staring out the window up at the billowy clouds that filled the sky. She felt a deep sadness as she realized the vision had only been a dream. Once again she closed her eyes and quietly whispered.

"Alex, I am sorry. I love you so much and I am trying to be strong. Really I am. But, honey, I need you. I need you so badly...I feel lost without you...Why did you leave me?"

She did not know that he had not left her, not even for a moment. While she slept, he and Michael had stood silently in the dark room watching over her. He had felt every feeling she had felt and could see every dream she dreamed. His soul could not deny her calls any longer as he quickly moved to the side of her bed.

Dawn Elizabeth

Momentarily, he glanced over his shoulder to seek the guidance of Michael. The angel had only nodded his head in approval and waited and observed as Alex drew closer to Beth.

She felt his spirit around her immediately, just as she had felt his hand touch her cheek the evening before. She opened her eyes and looked at the space next to her bed. Her eyes betrayed her as all she could see was the window and the curtain slowly moving back and forth in the breeze. Somehow she knew her sense of vision was distracting her sixth sense, she quickly closed her eyes. She did not allow herself to be frightened by the feeling of his spirit for fear that he would leave.

"I feel you here with me Alex, just as I felt you touch my cheek last night. I cannot see you...but I know you are there. Please touch me again so I know that you can hear me."

Alex remained silent and still as he listened to the words she spoke. Tenderly he gazed down at her face as she waited for him to touch her. His senses remembered the softness of her lips, the sweet taste of her kisses and the velvet touch of her hands. These were all sensations that he knew he would never again experience. Surprisingly he could still feel her emotions, hear her thoughts and was still intertwined with her soul. Oddly he knew she felt no fear as she patiently waited for some sign from him that he could hear her as she could feel his spirit. He knelt down next to her and in slow motion reached his hand up to touch her hand that was holding onto the teddy bear. At the touch of his hand to hers he felt the warmth of her soul rush as a surge of energy through his spirit.

CIRCLE OF LOVE

She did not open her eyes when his hand came down and rested on hers, but quietly sat and held on to her bear. Rapidly tears swelled up in her eyes as she felt the warmth and familiar sensation that was present when he was near. She felt the missing half of her being joined with his soul; her emptiness faded as she once again felt whole and complete. She lifted her hand slightly and opened her fingers, allowing his to connect with hers. Knowing she felt no fear at his touch, he tenderly wrapped his fingers and locked them with her tiny ones and affectionately squeezed. His eyes slowly filled with tears and one by one his teardrops flowed down his cheek. Not letting go of her hand, he moved closer to her until he was leaning directly over their held hands. A soft sigh escaped her lips as she felt his affectionate squeeze, knowing that he was with her in spirit. He had not left her and somehow he could hear what was in her heart.

Overwhelmed with the deep emotion of love, her tears ran uncontrollably down her cheeks. As he knelt beside her holding on to her hand he too was overwhelmed with emotion and did not notice when a teardrop had traveled down his face and dropped onto their held hands. At the moment his tear came into contact with the surface of her hands, her eyes opened wide as she looked down at her hand that was rested on the teddy bear's body. Careful not to move or to break the connection she had with Alex she bent down to look at her hand. There, on the back of her hand, was a tiny glistening teardrop. She turned her head from side to side as she looked at the tiny drop of water and was bewildered as she gazed upon the way it sparkled on her hand. She knew, without question, the tiny drop of

Dawn Elizabeth

water on her hand was indeed a tear that he had shed for her. Desperately she searched the space directly next to where she sat, knowing his spirit was there. She took in a deep breath as she tried to compose her words. She then quietly began to talk to him.

"Oh, Alex…I feel you here. It's okay. Don't cry for me. My handsome knight, you have not left me. I feel you here as if you had never left. I do not need to see you to know that you are with me now. We have our bond, don't we, Alex? This indescribable bond we share."

As he listened to her words, the pain that had once overwhelmed his heart began to fade. Even in death their bond had not been broken and their love remained. He knew that love did not need to be physical or need to be seen with a naked eye, but rather something that was felt in the deepest emotion of one's heart. True love is not destroyed when someone dies. It would last throughout all time and did not need to be expressed in living. He knew that no matter what man came into her life the love she felt for him would never die, nor would it be given to another. Their love was unique and would never be duplicated. He did know however, that she needed to live her life and to do that she would need to love another.

"I love you, Princess. I will always love you. But you need to go on with your life. There is a reason for everything. And even though I do not understand myself why we were pulled from each other, I know that you need to live…without me. I will not leave you until I know you are loving again. And just because you love another man, it does not mean you no longer love me. I realize that now. I will do

CIRCLE OF LOVE

everything I possibly can to unite you with the man who is worthy of your precious love."

As he spoke his last words he bent down and kissed her hand that remained entangled with his. Reluctantly, he released the grip that held their hands together and withdrew his hand from hers. He looked down at her tear covered face and slowly backed away from the bed. He lowered his head and walked back to where Michael remained watching. The angel tightened his lips and began to slowly nod his head, as he knew that the man that he had watched over from birth was becoming aware of his destiny. He knew the deep love and conviction that this man and woman shared. As an angel his heart, too, was overwhelmed with their undying love. As Alex approached him he opened his arms and he knew it was time to comfort his soul.

Alex turned back to see the tears pouring from Beth's eyes as she realized he was no longer standing near her or holding her hand. Tears flowed uncontrollable from his eyes as he allowed the angel to embrace him. He wept for the love that he felt for his Beth and for the life that they would never share together.

Chapter 26

Joseph picked up the papers that had fallen off his desk and placed them neatly in a stack on the desktop. He walked over to the window and stood and stared out at the beautiful summer day. There was not a single cloud to distract from the beauty of the most magnificent shade of light blue. He watched as a squirrel was scurrying up the big maple tree outside of his window. Its cheeks were apparently full of nuts that the animal was hording as it made its way back to its home. He was amazed as the animal quickly jumped onto another branch not losing its balance, nor the nuts it held in mouth. As he stood by the window watching the wild animal maneuvering its way through the tree, he crossed his arms over his chest and tilted his head to the side. His mind drifted off to the time he had last seen Beth. It had been three weeks since he had held her in his arms while she cried for the man she had lost. She had clung to him and poured her heart to him that night. He recalled how he had tried to lay her down and she had tightened her arms around his neck. After all the years he had known her, that evening was the first night he had actually seen the love she was capable of feeling.

He turned from the window and walked over to his recliner and sat down in its puffy, soft cushions. His hand reached down and searched for the handle on the right side of the chair. He lifted the handle up and the chair reclined back, releasing its footrest. He pushed the back of the chair causing it to recline further. He lifted his arms and crossed them behind his head and

CIRCLE OF LOVE

stared up at the ceiling. He wanted to call Beth and see how she was doing, but decided against it, feeling it was best to let her call him. He remembered how he had walked into her bedroom on that morning and seen her holding her Big Bear quietly crying. She had not been sobbing as she had the night before, but her crying was more as if she had come to accept or realize something. He had stood in the doorway for a few moments before he slowly entered the room. He walked over to her side and sat on the bed next to her. He recalled how she had pulled her hand from him as if she was afraid that he would touch it, almost as if she was guarding something. Then without warning she had quickly wiped her tears and jumped out of bed. She told him that she was fine and thanked him for comforting her the night before. Then politely she had asked him to leave. He had felt crushed, but respected her wishes and had left. He had not phoned her since that day but had not let her out of his thoughts either.

Memories flooded his thoughts, as he remained reclined in his chair with his arms behind his head. He tried to remember every word the man had said to him on that beautiful spring day. The thing that had stood out in his mind most on that day was the way the man's eyes had lit up when he spoke of the lady he was about to propose. He felt as if he was looking at a refection of his own eyes when he looked at the stranger. As he had listened to him speaking about his special lady Joseph couldn't help but think of Beth. A sad and lonely feeling had overcome him as he realized that she was with someone else. He had wished the man luck and walked away. He had never imagined that the man he helped that day had been the man who

Dawn Elizabeth

Beth had fallen in love with. He wondered how he would have felt had he known that he was, in fact, Beth's love. He looked up at the wall and quietly thought to himself.

"I would have thought, I couldn't have chosen a better man for her. That man loved her and would have given her everything that she deserves…things that I could never have given her. It doesn't make sense." He thought as he shook his head. "Alex, I am sorry I never had the opportunity to have formally met you. You would have been so good for her. Damn…it isn't fair."

The dark haired man in the white suit grinned as he glanced over at the angel standing to his side. This man had shown kindness to him when he had stumbled, careful not to let him fall. He had given his best wishes when he was told of his plans to propose to his love. And now, after finding out that the woman the stranger was to propose to was the same woman that had captured his heart, he still remained kind. He had not been bitter or jealous. He had felt broken at the knowledge of knowing that she had loved such a decent man and had lost him. He had not tried to take his place, but only offered his comfort and support. Alex walked over and sat on the couch next to the recliner and observed Joseph, he too looked up at the ceiling searching for answers. His attention was drawn back to the man in the recliner when he heard his name spoken.

"Alex, I am sorry we never met. Tell me what to do…you see…I love her too. And right now I am at a loss. I don't want to take your place…I just want to love her and let her feel my love. She is hurting so badly right now. Tell me what to do, Alex. Please." Joseph shook his head at the last word he spoke then shook his head feeling helpless, as if he was going insane. He was asking for help from someone who couldn't help him. He rubbed his forehead and tried to push the thoughts from his head.

Alex sat up and looked at the man who had spoken to him without knowing he could hear each word he had spoken.

"I will help you, Joseph. There is not a better man for my Beth than you. Don't give up. You will feel her love soon...I promise."

Michael looked at the two dark haired men who both loved the same woman, each loving her in a different way. He looked up into the Heavens and smiled, as he knew it was all falling into place.

Dawn Elizabeth

Chapter 27

Beth picked up the brush that was lying on her bed and walked over to the beautiful pedestal mirror that stood in the corner of her room. Before glancing at her reflection she stood back and looked at the beautiful wooden mirror. It was oval in shape and framed with a beautiful, dark mahogany stain. It had an air of Victorian times as it stood on its sculptured legs. She reached to the side of its base and gently unscrewed its knob so that she could adjust the tilt of the mirror. Once she was satisfied with depth of the reflection, she tightened the tiny knob and stepped back to allow her entire body to be in the mirror's view. Slowly, she looked at the woman who stood inside of the mirror. There before her stood a tiny woman with hair the color of honey wheat which hung loosely around her face in different layers, with the longest extending slightly past her shoulders. Wispy bangs covered her forehead and triangular pieces framed her cheeks, each piece falling a few strains down from the other. Her blue eyes were sunken and sad, missing the sparkle that had once radiated from them. Her completion was clear, yet painfully pale, as the color had been drained from it. She let out a gasp, as she did not recognize her own reflection.

"What has happened to me?" Beth thought as she slowly started to brush her soft hair. "Alex would never want to see me looking like this. It would crush him. Somehow I need to find some strength to allow the woman he loved to return. My children have lost

CIRCLE OF LOVE

their mother. I have loved and I have lost. But I still have my kids and they need me!"

She took a deep breath and then looked intently at her reflection. She stepped closer to the mirror and quietly began to talk to herself.

"Okay, Beth Hanson. You are hurt and grieving over your loss. And it hurts... it will always hurt. But this is no way to love Alex. He wouldn't want you to be like this. He was here and you felt him. He will always be here with you. Let him see that your love for him is strong. Pick up the pieces and go on with your life." As she spoke the last words to herself she nodded at her reflection as if she was making a promise to herself. As she backed away from the mirror she felt the slightest tingle rush through her body. She turned her head from side to side and then closed her eyes and began to focus on the man who possessed her heart and soul.

"I know you're here, Alex. I will be strong. I will find my way back.," she whispered to the man she now felt in the room with her.

She turned from the mirror and headed towards her closet, determined to find an outfit that would brighten her up and add color to her now drab appearance. It was a hot and humid summer day, she wanted something that would be light and comfortable. She moved the hangers down the rod until she spotted a soft yellow flowery sundress. She withdrew the dress from its hanger and walked over to the mirror and held it in front of her. Yes, she thought, this dress always made me feel young and pretty. She could curl her hair and give it some bounce and apply a touch of make-up to her bare pale face. Perhaps she would surprise the

Dawn Elizabeth

kids by taking them out for a nice dinner as well. Pleased with her choice of clothing she spun around to lay the sundress on bed intending on taking a shower. Suddenly, she became dizzy and caught herself before she stumbled against the footboard of the bed.

"Goodness, I must have turned too quickly." While she held onto the brass frame of her bed she edged her way to side of the bed then lowered herself in a sitting position. She took in a few slow deep breaths until the dizziness left her. Once she felt completely back to normal she stood up and headed to her dresser to retrieve clean undergarments. She opened a drawer and spotted a beautiful beige bra with matching panties. She withdrew the two items then headed for the bathroom. She quickly removed the baggy t-shirt and shorts she was wearing and grabbed a large bath towel from the linen closet. She moved the shower curtain slightly to the left in order to reach the faucet and adjust the water. Content with the warm temperature she pulled the nozzle down under the faucet directing the water to flow from the showerhead above. She removed her panties and stepped into the tub allowing the water to splash her nude body. Once completely in the tub she pulled the shower curtain back to make sure no water would escape onto the bathroom floor.

For moments she stood with her back to the shower of water and allowed the water to hit her back. She was amazed at how relaxed this made her feel. She backed up a little until her head was directly under the spout and allowed the water to cover her head. Once her hair was completely saturated she reached for the shampoo and poured a small amount onto her hand. She rubbed her hands together causing the shampoo to lather then

CIRCLE OF LOVE

placed the suds onto her head. In circular motions she covered her hair with the scented shampoo then playfully started to make various sculptures with the thick lathered hair. She giggled to herself as she pulled her hair together and shaped it in a point that extended upward remembering it was a silly trick her mother used to do with her as a child. Feeling childish she backed into the water allowing her hair to be rinsed from its suds. She next applied the conditioner and then started to soap up her body while she allowed the conditioner to seep into her hair. After she shaved her legs and bathed herself, she rinsed the conditioner out of her hair then rinsed the remaining soap from her body. Content that she was now clean from head to toe, she turned off the water and pulled the shower curtain back. She bent down and picked up the bath towel, which she had set on the floor by the tub. She towel dried her hair then continued to dry off her body and stepped out of the tub.

Her mind drifted back to the first night that she and Alex had spent alone. She walked over to the mirror that once again had been fogged up from the steam of the shower. She let out a soft sigh then leaned towards the mirror above the vanity. Slowly in large letters she wrote:

"I WILL ALWAYS LOVE YOU ALEX", then enclosed the words with an enormous heart. She then bends forward and tenderly kissed the mirror then backed away to observe what she had written. As she looked at the heart and large letters that were now on her mirror, she smiled. She didn't feel hurt, nor did she feel empty. The words that were beginning to fade were words that she knew would forever remain true.

Dawn Elizabeth

Even though they disappeared from the mirror, they would never disappear from her heart.

Greg and Tiffany were sitting on the bar stools that were in front of the counter, each teenager reviewing his and her music that they had been given at band practice. Tiffany was the first to notice their mother descend the stairs. Not wanting to alarm her brother, but wanting to get his attention, she gently nudged his leg with hers. Greg looked up from his music then quickly spun around as he too noticed his mother coming down the stairs. His heart began to pound as he recognized a familiar face that he had feared had been forever lost.

"Mom!" he exclaimed as he bounced from his stool and ran towards her. "Mom, you look beautiful, absolutely beautiful." He said, as he stopped directly in front of her.

His mother was wearing a beautiful yellow sundress that had straps that went over her shoulders. It appeared to have a solid pale yellow satin slip with a sheer flowered overlay. The dress hung loosely around her waist and had a full skirt that hung directly above her knees. On her feet she wore beige colored sandals with each of her toenails painted a summery shade of pink. The nails on her fingers were the same color as her toes and were all perfectly shaped. Her face was no longer pale but had a touch of make-up and a light color of lipstick. Her beautiful hair had all been curled and each layer bounced. The light that had seemed to vanish from her eyes was now glowing with hope of the future. Greg's heart was overwhelmed with the sight of the mother he thought he had lost. Unable to

CIRCLE OF LOVE

contain his emotions, he reached for his mom and gave her a tight hug.

"Mom, you look so beautiful. I was so afraid we had lost you forever." Beth tenderly kissed her son's cheek and hugged him back.

"You and Tiffany haven't lost me Greg. I just needed to find my way back; I love Alex, and will always love Alex. But he wouldn't have wanted me to stop living. So the love I have for him will get me through this. And I can start being your mom again."

As Tiffany listened to the words her mom was saying her own heart felt warm, as she knew the strength it had taken for her mom to come back to her and her brother. She sprung to her feet and ran to where her mother and brother stood. She encircled her own arms around the two and squeezed. Slowly she withdrew her hold and looked serious at her parent.

"Mom, welcome back. We have missed you."

Beth reached for her teenage daughter and pulled her into her arms.

"I have missed you too, Munchkin. I promise I will never leave you again."

The young girl smiled then nodded at her mom knowing she meant every word that she had spoken. Somehow her mom had found her back out of her world of silence. She knew that things could never go back to the way it had been. But it was a start perhaps to some happy times in the future. Alex would always remain in their hearts and memories.

Chapter 28

Alex paced back and forth in the small living room which belonged to Joseph O'Dea. Michael stood near the large picture window and occasionally glanced out at the beautiful spring day. He had remained with Alex and would remain until the dark haired spirit had accomplished his task of bringing Joseph and Beth together. During his time since his return as a spirit he had tried to keep away from Beth, it still tore at his heart to see her. As their bond still tied them together, he could feel that she still grieved deeply over his death. On the outside she was trying desperately to act if she were happy and back to her normal self. But her soul still cried out to him that she was lost. On the days he would choose to go "visit" her, no matter at what distance he was from her, she always felt him there. He had decided that he would only go to her home on days that she was surrounded by others in hopes that the commotion would distract her from their bond.

At the moment, Alex was frustrated. It had been a month since Joseph had made any contact with Beth and he was unsure as to how to get the man to move faster. He was pivoting around to start his walk back when Joe entered the small room. He was dressed in jeans and a pale yellow oxford shirt. He had a shadow of a beard beginning on his face and his dark hair was growing out as well. He walked over to the coffee table and picked up a sports magazine then quickly sat down and started to read an article about a football player who had decided to retire. He re-read the first line over

CIRCLE OF LOVE

and over then, out of frustration tossed, the magazine back on the table. Alex stopped pacing and watched as the dark-haired man became anxious.

Joseph leaned forward and put his elbow on one of his knees and began rubbing his face with hand. His eyes surveyed the room, as it was apparent that he was desperately thinking about something. Alex glanced at Michael who only grinned and then turned to look out the window at the birds that were sitting on the electrical wire. Alex walked over to a chair that was near Joseph and sat down. Joseph removed his hand from his face and sat quietly on the sofa staring into space. He had worried about Beth during the past month and had wanted to phone her to say hello, but did not want to bother her. As he sat, his thoughts were filled with memories of the times he and Beth had been together. He smiled as he remembered one occasion he had walked into her home and was so taken at the way she was dressed that he wasn't watching where he was walking and tripped over one of the kid's shoes. Beth had seen him stumble and had rushed to try to catch him before he fell. Rather than falling they had ended up in each other's arms. He could remember the way her hands had held the small of his back. Her hair had smelled heavenly as it bounced off her shoulders when she had quickly ran to help him. For moments they had remained standing holding on to one another looking for what seemed an eternity into each other's eyes. It was at that moment he knew he had loved her with his whole heart and soul. Oddly, it was also at that moment that he had decided that he wasn't worthy of her love and had built the wall around his heart protecting himself from loving her. Joseph threw the magazine back onto the coffee table and stood up. He walked over to the window where Michael stood and stopped by the angel's side. The angel did not move but did look down at the face of the man who now stood next to him. As Michael silently watched the dark-haired man his long hair slowly started to lift off of his shoulders as if it was being blown by a gentle breeze. With great concern the angel studied the face of the man standing next to him. Quickly, he turned and called to Alex.

"Alex, he is hurting. He is worried about Beth, yet he is unsure as to how to approach her."

Alex jumped up from the place he had been sitting and joined the angel and Joseph by the window. He looked at the man who now stood and stared aimlessly out the window. He looked at the lines that had formed on Joe's forehead and the way his lips were drawn tightly closed. The bond that he shared with Beth did not exist with Joseph and he was not able to go into his soul and feel his emotions. As he looked at Joseph he knew a bond was not necessary to feel what this man was now feeling. It was quite obvious that this man was hurting and grieving also. Unlike Beth, who was grieving for the love that she had lost, this man grieved for the love that he had never experienced. He had kept the love he had for Beth locked deeply inside of his heart, denying it a chance to be given. Now his heart was aching as the love desperately wanted to escape the walls that bound it and kept it prisoner deep inside. Alex crossed his arms over his chest and looked back at Michael.

"Why does he torment himself like this? It's obvious how much he loves her. Why doesn't he just

CIRCLE OF LOVE

go over there and see her? What is keeping him from telling her how much he loves her?" Alex asked with deep sympathy in his voice.

"He has been hurt deeply in the past. When he loves, he loves deeply and with great devotion. But sadly, the people in his past to whom he had given his love to have either hurt him or abandoned him. He is afraid that if he shows her or tells her how much he loves her, she too will abandon him. So he denies himself of the feeling in a way to protect him from being hurt. You cannot feel what he is feeling. You do not know what he is thinking about as he stares out this window. He does not see the beauty in the way the sun is shining brightly. He does not hear the sound of the birds as they sing sweetly. As he stands there staring, looking, sadly he sees nothing. He is such a good soul, Alex. Trust me in the words I say. This man deserves happiness and love. He would not have let you fall as another would have. He would have been kind and caring. He would give everything he owns to someone who had nothing. He deserves all the riches that Heaven offers."

"Then why, Michael, why was he so cruel to Beth? She told me so many stories about how much she had loved him. But he would never give her or them a chance. He would use her, then leave. I don't think he ever knew how many tears she cried for him. It was strange though, because whenever she spoke of him, I was never jealous. And jealousy was something I always felt with other women should they bring up a former lover. But when she talked of him, I felt her love. I guess it was because of our bond. I knew the love she possessed for him was real, it wasn't a passing

Dawn Elizabeth

fling, it was as strong as the love she felt towards me..."

"You felt her true love. The love she will forever feel towards you and the love she feels for him. He has spent too many years alone, not receiving love. He needs love, Alex. Beth is the one woman who can give to him what he so richly deserves."

As the angel spoke to Alex, he walked to the opposite side of Joseph who continued to stare aimlessly out the window. The angel lifted his hands in front of himself with his palms facing up as he tried to instruct the soul that he had guided throughout his life on Earth.

"Alex, you must go to her. She still feels you. Find a way to bring her to him. As long as she holds onto you she will not allow herself to remember the love she once felt for this man. Their love is beautiful...just as the love, the tie that connects your soul to hers is...she needs him right now...just as he needs her. The only thing that is keeping them apart is her love for you. The love she has for you will never die. It is as I told you when you first saw me, your love is a circle...it has no beginning and it has no end. It will last throughout eternity. It does not need to feel the physical touch of being human. It is a part of your soul. But as long as she holds onto you, her love for you, she will not give her love to another."

Alex listened to each word the angel spoke. He was not angry. He was not jealous. He knew the angel spoke the truth. He looked at the dark-haired man who stood motionlessly staring out the window at the beautiful summer day knowing the man did not see the same beauty that he could see. He knew the man was tormented with pain caused by a love he felt for a woman, the same woman who he had loved, and would love throughout eternity. He knew he was not capable of expressing his love to her any longer in a humanly form, yet somehow he knew he could still give his love to her as a spirit. He knew that they would be connected forever and ever.

As he watched the man stare out the window, he knew that this man was meant to be with his Beth. He knew that he would love her and give to her the things that he would never be able to give. This dark haired man, who knew Beth before he had, was the man with whom she was meant to live her life on Earth. He would protect and share his dreams with her. The two of them would laugh and cry. Their hair would turn gray, then white as they spent many years together. The one question that remained unanswered was how? How would he bring the two of them together? He knew all the angels in Heaven and even "He" anxiously watched, as it was only Alex who would be the one to bring these two together. Alex knew that in order for him walk through the Gates of Heaven, he would have to figure out how to bring Beth and Joseph together.

As he now looked at the man who was meant to be with his Beth, his heart felt heavy, as it did not know if he would ever fulfill his destiny.

Chapter 29

Beth felt chilled by the morning air and swiftly reached for her white robe. It was Saturday and the kids were with their father this weekend. She hadn't felt very well that morning and felt incredibly tired and extremely sick to her stomach. Greg had just gotten over the flu and she knew that she had caught the nasty bug herself. She had taken her temperature but according to the thermometer she didn't have a fever. Nevertheless, she still felt cold and miserable.

She wrapped the thick soft robe around herself and quickly tied the belt. She walked around her room looking for her warm fuzzy slippers to put on her feet. She found one under her bed and slid her foot into it. She looked for its match under the bed, but it was nowhere to be found. She rubbed her stomach gently as she felt it turning inside her. Quickly she turned wasting no time and headed for the bathroom. She flung the bathroom door open and did not flinch when it made a loud noise as it hit the inner wall with strong force. Her thoughts were overwhelmed with panic as she felt the vomit rise in her throat. She ran to the toilet and lifted its lid, reaching its opening in time. She knelt down and heaved with a strong force. She felt her stomach muscles contract as it violently tried to rid her body of the contents that were not sitting well within it. Finally, feeling that she had no more to heave, she reached for a washcloth and wiped her mouth. She stood up and walked over to the sink and turned on the cold water and began rinsing her mouth. She then opened the drawer in the vanity and withdrew a small bottle of mouthwash. She poured a cap full of the mint-flavored solution into a paper cup and then began rinsing her mouth. After she no longer could taste the bitter trace of the vomit she wiped her mouth off again and threw the paper cup away. For several moments she stared at her reflection in the mirror. Her face was very pale and her eyes had watered.

It was times like this she missed Alex the most. Whenever she wasn't feeling well he had always tenderly taken care of her. She smiled to herself as she was unsure if he had done it out of love or, because since he felt everything she did, he didn't like the upset feeling either and knew the quicker she was feeling better so would he.

She closed her eyes and felt the warmth of tears forming in her eyes. It had been a month since she had thought she had felt his hand touch her cheek and she had broken down. Every now and then she would swear she could feel him around her. She would close her eyes and try to focus on the feelings but once she would begin, strangely, the feeling would fade. The feelings were strongest when there were others around, but she would be distracted and she would never get the opportunity to focus. She reached up and wiped a tear that had escaped from her eye and was traveling down her cheek. She missed him so much. It had been two months since his death and she had tried so hard to be cheerful and happy. But on the weekends when she was alone she didn't have to pretend to be happy for the sake of the kids. She turned and headed back to her bed and removed the one slipper on her right foot. She was still chilled so she did not remove her robe. She

Dawn Elizabeth

pulled the covers back and reached for Big Bear then climbed back into the warmth of her bed.

She pulled the covers up around her chest and tucked Big Bear under the covers with her. She closed her eyes and allowed her thoughts to focus on Alex. Her heart cried out for her soul mate as she lay silently on her bed. Slowly, her body started to tingle as the familiar sensation started to travel deep into her soul.

He stood at the foot of her bed as she lay there calling out to him. He had been with her from the moment she had wrapped the robe around her chilled body. He had wanted to wrap his arms around her to warm her like he had done so many times in the past. He had grinned when she recalled how he had always taken care of her when she had felt under the weather. He had even laughed when she had wondered whether it had been out of love or because he didn't like the ill feeling he experienced as well. There were a few times that it was because of the later, but the majority of the time was because he loved her and hated to see her suffer.

As he stood and watched her lying under the blankets and comforter, he yearned to take care of her as he had before. She was so beautiful, almost like an angel, and yet more beautiful. He knew he couldn't take care of her, but he knew someone who could, a man who would relish the opportunity. He closed his eyes and allowed himself to drift into her thoughts.

"Beth, remember how Joe took care of you when you cried? You never thanked him. Call him, Beth. Call him, Princess," he whispered.

CIRCLE OF LOVE

Beth's eyes opened as he heard the soft whisper of Alex in her mind. She lifted herself up and looked around the room.

"Alex?" she said softly.

Cautiously, Alex backed away because he did not want to upset her with his presence. She felt his concern as he pulled away and quickly called out to him. "No, Alex, don't leave. I am not afraid. You were here that day... that day with Joe. Look, I will lay back and close my eyes. Talk to me, *Alex*. I will listen."

Beth once again pulled the covers around her and lay back onto the pillows then she closed her eyes. As she had told Alex, she was not afraid and knew he was trying to tell her something. Even though he was not physically with her, she still trusted him and knew that he would not do or say anything that would hurt her. Patiently, she waited to hear him whisper to her again.

Alex remembered what Michael had told him about going to Beth. The angel was not with him now and had chosen to remain with Joseph. He had sent Alex to Beth and he would join him shortly. The guardian angel had convinced Alex that there was nothing he could do that would cause either Beth or Joe harm and that the spirit should trust in himself. Unsure whether he was doing the right thing he slowly started to walk towards where she was lying. As he reached the side of her bed she slowly moved over in the bed allowing him room to sit on its edge. He lowered himself down on the space and tenderly leaned down over her and gazed at the beauty of her face.

He sighed as he saw the glisten of a tear escape her eye. He reached down and gently wiped the tear. Just as before as his fingers touched the teardrop it had sparkled, then quickly vanished.

"Oh, Princess...I love you so." He whispered.

A smiled formed on Beth's thins lips then tenderly she responded.

"I know you do, my handsome knight. I love you too. I knew you would never leave me. Even though I cannot see you, I feel you...I hear you. Even though I don't understand... I do know I will love you forever...throughout time."

"Yes our love will exist throughout time. It will go on forever...but right now...in this time...*you* have to live. You have to go on without me physically in your life...why haven't you called Joe? He took care of you when you were hurting. I watched him as he gave his whole heart to take care of you. He was tender and he was kind...why won't you let him take care of you now?"

As Beth listened to Alex speak, she remained still taking in slow tiny breaths. She did not want anything to distract her from the soft sound of his voice. She knew he was waiting for a response to his question but was unsure as to how to answer.

"Oh...I know he was here. But I also know he was just being nice. That's Joe. He is nice to everyone..."

Alex leaned back and quickly interrupted before she could continue. "Beth, he wasn't just being nice. He cares about you. Give him a chance."

Angered and caught off guard by his interjection, Beth bolted up in a sitting position and opened her eyes.

"What! Alex you want me to give *him* a chance! You want me to give Joseph O'Dea a chance? Have

CIRCLE OF LOVE

you somehow forgotten all of cruel things he said to me? Don't you remember all the stories I told you about him? No! Absolutely not! I will never give him a chance! Alexander, how could you of all people even ask me to do such a thing?"

The feeling of nausea began to return. Beth threw the covers back and darted once again for the bathroom. She paused for a moment when she felt the warmth rush through her body as she passed through Alex's spirit. Reaching the toilet in time she knelt down and once again started heaving.

Alex had followed her to the bathroom and remained behind her as she heaved over and over. This was one feeling he had not missed feeling. He knew that she was feeling miserable and that her stomach was tender from the muscle contractions but he could not feel the physical pain.

She reached for the washcloth and once again wiped her mouth. She knew Alex had remained with her the whole time she threw up. She slowly stood up and flushed the toilet then headed back to her bedroom. She stopped for a moment when she once again felt her body pass through his spirit.

"Does that hurt when I do that?"

Alex was puzzled by her question. "Does *what* hurt?"

Beth put her hands into the pockets of her robe and titled her head to one side. She bit down on her lower lip and was hesitant to respond. Alex, knowing that she could hear him and feel him but that she just was not capable of seeing him, walked and stood directly in front of her and again asked.

"Does what hurt?"

Dawn Elizabeth

Beth removed her hands from her pockets and started fidgeting with her belt.

"Does it hurt when I walk through you? I have done it twice now. Once when I ran to the bathroom to throw up and again when I headed back to my room. I feel your spirit and I walk right through it."

Alex let out a little chuckle and looked at the serious expression Beth now had on her face.

"No, Princess, it does not hurt. What does it feel like to you?" he replied.

"Hmmm...what does it feel like to me? Well, it feels warm... incredibly warm and light. Kind of like a warm fuzzy. Like a tender jolt of electricity...if electricity can be tender," she laughed.

Suddenly, Beth started to feel dizzy and the room began to spin. Alex, seeing her face beginning to pale, quickly reached for her not realizing what he was doing. He lifted her up and carried her over to her bed and gently laid her down as her body became limp as a rag doll in his arms. He felt her spirit go into an unconscious darkness as it lay still on her bed. He did not hear Michael enter the room and come up behind him.

"She is okay," he quickly told his companion. "She fainted."

Alex turned to see Michael standing behind him looking over his shoulders. Worried, the dark-haired spirit quickly started to question the angel.

"Fainted? But she wasn't afraid——"

Michael leaned around Alex and walked over and sat down next to Beth who had drifted into a sleep. He gently reached down and rested his hand on her face, then removed it. He stood up and walked to the foot of

CIRCLE OF LOVE

the bed and observed, as Alex remained watching Beth still worried.

"Alex, she did not faint because of you. Well...actually in a way she did. But not in the way that you are thinking," Michael replied. His face was suddenly glowing as he smiled at Alex.

Confused by the angel's comments, Alex got up and walked over to stand next to the angel.

"Michael, I do not understand what you are saying. You said she did not faint because of me...then actually in a way she did. Could you possibly explain that comment to me?" Alex asked.

The angel looked at Beth, who was now peacefully sleeping on the bed, with her arms hugging the big stuffed teddy bear that had been her bed companion for many years. He then looked back at Alex who was patiently waiting for an answer to his question. He did not feel that Alex was ready for the true answer, and because he was an angel he could not lie so he carefully chose his words before he spoke them.

"Your souls are still connected. Although her soul is not afraid of hearing your voice so clearly her humanly being is confused. With the mixture of the two beings so to speak it became overwhelming for her and her soul shut her body down for a brief period so it would not frighten her. That's all. She will be fine. I promise." He grinned then suddenly turned away so Alex could not see the way his eyes were sparkling with what he had not told him.

Michael walked over to the window next to Beth's bed and drew the curtain back so that he could watch the beautiful early fall colored leafs. They slowly floated through the air dancing back and forth and

Dawn Elizabeth

twirling as one by one they made their way to the ground where they would rest for the remainder of the season until time would take them back into the Earth from which they originally had begun. The angel knew that soon the trees would be bare, almost in a naked state, as they would gradually fall into a deep, peaceful sleep until the spring sun would warm and awaken them. He smiled knowing that a circle was involved in many of His creations. Some of those circles were more obvious than others. Some were seen with the eyes, others felt within the heart.

He had not experienced the feeling of cold or hot temperatures so he did not know the difference in that aspect of the seasons changing. He felt the change through the magnificent colors. Each season's colors were always extremely vivid and magical. It was the color that radiated the music almost as beautiful as the choir of angels that sang in Heaven. He sighed quietly as he missed the beautiful voices of the choir as they sang their joyous songs. He anxiously looked forward to the day that he would once again hear them singing, as he would walk with Alex through Heaven's Gates. There were still so many events that had to take place before that glorious day. He nodded his head as he heard His voice softly assure him that Alex's destiny was unfolding as it had been intended to do.

The angel turned from the window and looked down at Beth. She indeed was a beautiful creation. He could see deep into her soul and could feel its goodness. She had loved deeply, without conditions or rules. She gave rather than took. She forgave without any regrets. Her tears overflowed buckets in Heaven. Tears she shed not for herself, but tears she cried for others. The love she felt for Alex was the most beautiful of all He had created. Alex and Beth were like two puzzle pieces, each fitting perfectly with the other. Their love would go on forever even until the end of time. Their love would bring love into the lives of others. They would never feel jealousy towards the other, no matter where each soul resided. Each had enough love to give to another soul should they need it to be given. At this moment in time it was Beth's love that was needed by someone special. It would be Alex who would guide her to the man who so desperately needed her love.

Michael stood silently at the back of the room and watched Alex tenderly gaze at Beth as she held her stuffed bear and slept peacefully. The angel knew, when the right moment presented itself, Alex would know what to do and Beth would listen. Now it was time for her to rest and dream. Her world was about to change and she would have an angel, her soul mate, and the love of a wonderful man to help guide her through it.

Chapter 30

It was a miserable, dreary fall day. The rain was pouring down and rapidly beating against the windows. Tap, tap, tap was the sound as the raindrops steadily hit the glass. Although it was early in the afternoon, the sky was dark and gloomy. The storm clouds had swallowed the beautiful sunlight and replaced it with a damp darkness. Beth was alone in the house and was busy trying to distract herself by cleaning the kitchen. The kids were late getting home from marching band practice and she was beginning to get worried. She turned to get a dishrag to wipe off the counter when the loud roar of thunder startled her causing her to jump. Suddenly, she heard the sound of the front door open and slam shut as her two teenagers came running frantically into the house.

With the damp dishcloth still in her hand she hurriedly headed towards the living room to see what was causing all the commotion. She stopped abruptly when she saw both of her kids standing on the plastic runner on the living room carpet. Both Greg and Tiffany were completely soaked by the downpour and were deeply upset and distraught about something. For a brief moment she felt an odd sensation that once again something tragic had happened. She held her breath and waited for one of them to speak.

"Mom, there's been an accident..." the teenage boy quickly began. Water was dripping from her son's face. He reached up and wiped the water that was running from his rain-drenched hair, and then quickly

CIRCLE OF LOVE

continued, "Mom, it's Joe, he's been in a serious accident."

Beth felt the room spin as the words her son had spoken began to sink in and register in her brain. Unexpectedly, she felt Alex next to her as he tried to calm her and keep her alert to what her son was trying to say. She felt the warmth of his soul as he tenderly stood behind her and rested his hands on her shoulders. The spinning stopped and she was able to focus on her children who stood in front of her. She noticed tears were beginning to form in Tiffany's eyes. She walked over to her teenage daughter and enclosed her arms around her daughter and wiped the water that also covered her face. Somehow, she found a deep strength within herself as she encouraged her son to explain what had happened.

"What kind of accident has Joe been in and how do you know it was Joe?" she began with deep concern and worry in her voice.

"When we were coming home from practice there were a couple of police cars directing and blocking traffic. There was only one lane open and they would only let a few cars go through at a time. When it was finally our turn to go and we got close to the crash scene, the paramedics were getting ready to take him away. The police stopped us so the ambulance could leave and I looked ahead to see what had happened. Mom...his truck...it was crashed into a tree. There were these long dark black tire marks on the road where it looked like he had tried to stop and swerve to avoid hitting something. It looks really bad. I pulled over and told one of the officers that I was a friend of

Dawn Elizabeth

the driver and wanted to know where they were taking him…"

"What hospital, Gregory? Do you know what hospital?" Beth questioned as the feeling of panic began to overwhelm her.

Greg had barely got the name of the hospital out when Beth ran for her raincoat, purse, and car keys. She tried to convince the kids that she should go to the hospital by herself but neither teenager would agree to being left alone and so all three ran out to the car and headed to the hospital.

As she drove down the road to the hospital where they had taken Joseph O'Dea, she did not feel Alex with her. She knew he had been with her when the kids had told her about the accident but had silently backed away when she decided to go to see Joe. She knew he was not angered by her going, she felt that it was something he wanted her to do. He had rested his hands on her shoulders when the room had begun to spin as if he knew she needed to be calmed and needed to be able to hear what the kids were saying.

The rain had slowed and now it was sprinkling as she and the kids pulled into the emergency parking lot at the hospital. She didn't bother locking her car doors and hurriedly ran to the emergency room outer doors. The doors quickly opened, as she and the kids was within a foot of them each door parting open to the side. The trio ran to the attendant at the front desk who was busy reading a report on her clipboard.

Out of breath Beth began, "Excuse me, we believe a friend of ours was brought here earlier. Could you tell me where we might find him…and find out what his status is?"

CIRCLE OF LOVE

The attendant gave Beth a look of question and then glanced at the two teenagers that stood close to the worried woman's side. It was obvious to the attendant that the trio was deeply concerned about their friend and she wanted to do her best to put the three of them at ease.

"I can help you," she began. "What is your friend's name?"

"Oh, I am sorry, his name is Joseph O'Dea."

Beth began to feel overwhelmed with emotion and started to ramble on about his appearance. "He is a tall, dark-haired man. He is very handsome. He has hazel eyes and …oh he has a distinctive large mole on his face. Umm, it's on his lower right cheek."

The attendant realized by the broken speech and rambling of this woman that this man must be someone very dear to her. Quickly, she looked down at her clipboard searching for the gentleman's name. She flipped to the second page and found his name was on her list. It indicated that he had been in a serious car accident and was still being attended to in trauma. She drew in a deep breath and carefully began to relay the information to the concerned small group.

"Yes, I am afraid your friend is here. It seems he has been in a very serious car accident. Right now he is in our trauma unit. I am sorry but while he is in there, no one is allowed with him. If you would like, I can show you to the emergency waiting area and as soon as I hear something I will let you know."

Beth felt her heart drop as she heard the words "trauma and serious". "Not Joe", she thought. Tiffany, knowing her mother's heart was once again breaking at the thought of losing someone else who was a part of her life, tenderly reached for her hand and held it in her own. With her other hand she slowly began rubbing her mom's hand, which had begun to tremble.

Gregory was the first one to break the silence. "Yes, please show us to the waiting area. I think my mom should sit down."

The attendant quickly motioned for the group to follow her down the corridor of the hospital. She stopped in front of a room that was dimly lit and had various hard, uncomfortable looking chairs in it. The three slowly entered the room and reluctantly sat down in the chairs. In the corners of the rooms were small tables with scattered magazines on them. At the end of the room on the wall was a clock, its face large and easy to read.

The attendant offered to get them something to drink. They graciously thanked her but declined her offer. After once again assuring them that she would keep them informed of Mr. O'Dea's progress and status, she turned and left them alone.

For several hours they all waited. Occasionally, Beth would get up and pace back and forth, all the while looking at the entrance, waiting for the attendant to come back with some news regarding Joe. She had decided that having a clock in a waiting room was a very insensitive idea. No matter how many times she looked at its face, it seemed it took forever for its hands to move. She looked at her kids who both looked extremely tired and exhausted. She hated seeing them go through this. They were so young and had already been through so much with Alex's death. She started

CIRCLE OF LOVE

to go back to sit down when the attendant appeared in the doorway with her clipboard still in her hands.

"Mr. O'Dea is out of trauma," she began.

Normally, there was a waiting period before patients were allowed visitors when they are initially taken to a room, but for some reason the woman felt it was important that the petite woman who stood before her, with deep concern covering her face, should be taken to this man as quickly as possible. As if a strange force was guiding her, the attendant put her clipboard down on the counter outside the door and turned to the blonde woman with the boy and girl.

"He has been taken upstairs. Come with me and I will take you to him." She smiled, and extended her hand as she pointed in the direction of the elevators.

Beth and the kids quickly followed the young woman to the elevators and remained quiet until the doors opened on the third floor. The young woman stepped out and turned to the left and headed down a long corridor with doorways all on the left side. As she reached the end of the hall, she stopped and turned towards Beth.

"Okay. This is his room. You can go in, but I am going to take the kids to the waiting room that is just at the end of the hall on the right. It is just before the elevators. He hasn't had any visitors so you stay as long as you would like. If you need me my name is Trisha."

The young woman smiled then turned and headed the kids down the hall towards the waiting room. As she walked with the kids she was telling them something, but Beth could not hear or make out the words that she was saying. She watched as Tiffany

Dawn Elizabeth

turned back and smiled, assuring her mom that they were fine.

Beth paused in front of the large hospital room door, afraid of what she would see when she entered through it. The attendant had not given her any information about Joe's condition so she did not know what to expect. Slowly, she reached for its handle and pulled it down. The door opened and she carefully pushed it in, trying not to make any noise in case he was sleeping. As she entered the room, she noticed that it was dimly lit and that the room held two beds. The bed that was closest to the door was quite high and empty. There was a pale yellow blanket neatly covering the mattress that lay perfectly flat. Beneath the blanket was a stark white sheet that had been neatly folded down and hung over the railings on either side. A large, puffy pillow with a matching starched white pillowcase lay at the head of the bed. The name of the hospital was stamped on the edge of the pillowcase and on the top border of the sheet. It was obvious that this bed had no occupant. A pale yellow curtain with soft pastel squares hung from the ceiling and stopped a few feet from the floor. It was now pulled between the two beds and slightly drawn around the bed that was closest to the window.

Little by little, she walked passed the first bed. She took a deep breath and bit down on her lower lip. She let out a little gasp as she reached the end of the curtain and looked up and saw the man lying on the bed. Large tears began to fill her eyes as she walked up the side of the bed and looked down at the man she had known for many years. His head was bandaged and his face was bruised and swollen, with numerous tiny cuts.

CIRCLE OF LOVE

His left arm was in a cast from the hand up to his elbow, his fingertips barely showing. Both of his arms were covered with scratches and deep, large bruises. An IV was inserted in the back of his right hand and it lay motionlessly on his abdomen. An IV pole stood next to his bed with a large and small bag hanging from it, the contents slowly dripping into a long tube that was connected to his hand. His legs appeared to both be completely bandaged and were both covered by an identical white sheet and pale yellow blanket matching the other bed.

Beth wiped the tears that had run down her cheeks and walked to the head of the bed. Joe's eyes were closed and his breathing was slow and steady. Every now and then he would let out a soft, painful moan. As she approached the head of the bed she reached down and softy touched his hand that held the IV. Careful not to touch the needle that was inserted into his hand, she gently stroked his long fingers. Upon her touch, his fingers slowly began to move and his hand reached for hers. When she saw his fingers open, she sweetly grasped them in hers and gave them a tender squeeze.

She looked up so see Joe slowly opening his eyes. It was apparent that he was heavily sedated and was trying to flight the drug to open his eyes to her. She tried to smile as she watched the effort that he making in order to acknowledge he was aware of her presence. She leaned down over the bed and began to softly speak to the injured man.

"Hey, you. What are you doing here? Don't you know you aren't supposed to get into fights with trees…they are bigger and they usually win," She stuttered, desperately trying to keep composed.

Dawn Elizabeth

Joseph tightened his fingers around Beth's and let out a little sigh as he tried to laugh at her comment about fighting with trees.

"I guess it is my turn to take care of you, huh? My shoulders aren't as big as yours, but I am strong for being a little lady. You get some rest and I will stay with you all night just like you did for me when I needed someone. I won't leave you, Joe. Close your eyes now and get some rest. When you wake up I will be right here. I promise."

Joe's eyes flickered open and closed as he desperately tried to fight the drugs that he had been given for the pain. His head was pounding as the blood throbbed at the laceration he had received when he hit the windshield. His arm felt numb and a cast now surrounded it, keeping it stationary. His swollen face ached from the bruises that covered it. Through his pain he felt the warmth of Beth's fingers locked with his, and he tried to hold on to them for fear that he was dreaming. The warmth he felt from her fingers was proof that she was indeed standing next him. When he couldn't fight the medication any longer, his eyelids slowly closed and he drifted off into a dreamlike state.

Chapter 31

Beth sat in a rocking chair next to Joe's bed. Once she was sure he was sleeping peacefully, she had walked down to the waiting room and talked to the kids. Both teenagers were deeply concerned about Joe's condition and were sad that he had been injured, but were also relieved that his condition was not critical. A nurse had noticed Beth coming out of the man's room and had approached her to see if Beth was a family member. She had told Beth that he had been brought into emergency in the early part of the afternoon and had not had a single visitor. She said he had been unconscious throughout the whole ordeal and was surprised when Beth told her that he had squeezed her hand. She said that no one seemed to know exactly what had happened to cause the man to swerve on the road and slam into the tree. Beth had gotten chills when the nurse told her how his truck had been wrapped around the tree but that his injuries were minor compared to what they should have been. Tears had swelled in her eyes when the nurse had told her, "His guardian angel was definitely watching over him today. It is a miracle he survived that crash."

As the nurse spoke to Beth and her children they all became intensely quiet as they all remembered the few months ago that Alex had not survived his car accident. As the nurse stated the extent of Joe's injuries, Tiffany began to cry and Greg lowered his head and put his hands in his pockets. The nurse's words cut deeply into Beth's heart as she, too, remembered the day that Alex had been taken from her. Now, just a short distance down the hall, there was another man whom Beth had loved who also had been injured in a car accident, but had survived. She told the nurse that she was not a family member but was a friend of Joe's and had promised him that she would be there when he woke up.

The nurse could see the importance of the promise that this woman had made to her patient and did not make her leave. She told her that the love of someone is sometimes the best medicine and told Beth she was welcome to stay with Joe as long as she wished. The nurse then told Beth that if there was anything she needed she was just to ring his call button that was next to his bed and she would be right in. The nurse then left Beth and the kids and quickly found a comfortable rocking chair that was in one of the vacant rooms and took it to Joe's room so that Beth would have a nice chair to sit in. She also found a pillow and blanket and placed them in the chair so that Beth would be warm while she sat with the dark-haired man.

Beth told the kids that she was going to stay with Joseph all night and instructed the kids to go home and get some rest because it was getting rather late. She gave Greg the car keys and told him she would call him in an hour to make sure they made it home safely. Tiffany was hesitant to leave her mother alone because she wasn't sure what kind of effect the situation would have on her. With constant assurance, the kids finally agreed to go home and each hugged and kissed their tired mother. The trio walked to the elevator and Beth remained until the elevator doors closed taking her children down to the main floor of the hospital.

As she walked back to Joseph's room, her thoughts were filled of the day that Alex had been killed. She hadn't been given the opportunity to sit with him in a cold hospital room and hold his hand while he slept. She hadn't heard the soft moans of pain that had escaped his lips. The only thing she was able to do was cradle him in her lap and remove the glass fragments from his hair and face. His beautiful face had been covered with blood from the many cuts he had sustained. She could hear the sound of his voice as he whispered his last words to her with his dying breath. "I will always love you, Princess," he had said. Then he had closed his eyes and left her.

As she entered Joseph's room her heart felt as it had been ripped repeatedly over and over. She walked over to the rocking chair and lifted the blanket and pillow and sat down. For several moments she stared into space as the tears once again swelled in her eyes. Rapidly, the tears streamed down her face as the vision of that horrible day played over and over in her mind. The sound of Joseph's moans drew her back to the present situation and she quickly jumped from the chair and went to his side.

She noticed that his hand was slowly moving next to his side as if he were searching for something in his dreams. She reached down and gently took hold of his hand and tenderly gave it a soft squeeze. She looked back and felt her heart ache as she looked at bruises and cuts that covered his face. His lower lip had stitches in it and there was dried blood in the corner of his mouth, a mouth that she had often seen grinning in the past. Her heart felt heavy as she remembered the many times she had seen those lips smile at her. The dark brown eyes that were now swollen closed beneath the lids always had radiated such warmth, even when he had been cruel to her.

She remembered the way he had looked at her when they had ran into each other in the supermarket. He had seemed happy, and yet, also sad, when he had seen her. She remembered it was at that moment that she realized that he had shaven his moustache off.

Without being aware of what she was doing, she leaned down and softly kissed his battered lips. She lifted herself up slightly and continued to look at his face that was now black and blue with tiny cuts scattered around his eyes and cheeks. She could not see the darkness of his hair because a thick wrapping of gauze and bandages now covered it.

As he lay on his hospital bed, the man whom Beth had known for nearly nine years looked small and helpless. His tall, muscular body now was badly beaten and shattered. This man who now lay sleeping had come to her during a time when she was overwhelmed with grief and pain. He had lifted her into his arms and held her for hours knowing that the tears she cried were for a man she had lost. The kindness that he had kept guarded in his heart had somehow found it's way to her when it was needed the most. It was now her turn to allow her kindness to pour out on him.

She looked down to make sure that the sheet and blanket covered him and that he looked as comfortable as he could under the conditions. She rested her arms on the guardrails on his bed and tilted her head to the side biting her lower lip. Silently, she remained standing at his side watching his chest move up and

CIRCLE OF LOVE

down as he inhaled then slowly exhaled. She lowered her tiny hand down and once again started to caress his hand in which the IV was placed. She looked back at him and softly whispered, "Don't worry, Joe, I will take care of you. Maybe somehow we will find our strength in each other. Who knows why things happen? I am sorry I never said thank you for comforting me. I will say it to you when you awake. Sweet dreams, Joseph O'Dea." Beth released her hand from his and backed into the rocking chair. She put the pillow behind her head and unfolded the blanket and covered her body. She leaned her head back into the pillow and closed her eyes. Her thoughts were empty as she drifted into sleep. She was unaware that Michael and Alex were in the room with her and Joe.

Alex looked at the angel who stood at his side. He grinned with pride as he said, "That's my girl. It isn't hard to see why I love her so much, is it?"

The angel smiled broadly and replied, "As I have said before, she is a very beautiful, loving creature, one of His most special. We all love her, Alex. We are part of the circle too."

Light sparkled from the angel's eyes as he stood silently watching over the injured man and the woman who sat at his side. He remembered the way the man had swerved out of his way in order to prevent the small girl from being hit by his truck. He recalled the way the man had sacrificed himself rather then hitting the child. He pictured the look on the man's face when he had spotted the child. He knew all of these things because he had been the illusion that Joe had seen that day. Michael had been the little girl who somehow was lost in the rain and couldn't find her way home.

Dawn Elizabeth

Michael slowly nodded his head as he thought, "Certain events must take place for there to be certain outcome." Joseph O'Dea's accident had been such an event.

The angel smiled as he thought of the secret that was yet to be revealed to all of the souls in the hospital room, the circle of love that was growing each day.

Chapter 32

Beth held on to the cold metal railings on the hospital bed. She stood silently and looked down at the battered man who was finally resting peacefully. The darkness of the night had seemed never-ending and heartless as she stayed and watched over him The stars had even hidden from her behind the clouds, offering no solace to her heavy heart. She had tried to sleep in the chair that the nurse had provided for her but the sounds of Joe's moans had kept her from drifting into a deep, peaceful dream. She would close her eyes and slowly start to fall asleep but was quickly awakened by the sounds of his painful moans. She would jump up from her chair and go to his side and try to comfort him in whatever way she could. She would stand and softly caress his hand, careful not to disrupt the IV or the connecting tubes. She would lean down over the railings and softly whisper to him, assuring him that she had not left.

His moans would ease and she could see his body physically relax. His breathing would slow and become steady, rather than deep and in gasps. As long as she was at his side he would remain peaceful and content. Moments after she would return to her chair, the moans would start again and his breathing would become deep and sporadic, as if all of his air had been removed from his lungs with her absence.

Now, as she stood and looked down at him, her heart felt empty and lost. Her thoughts were confused and jumbled as one question after another ran through her mind. She had experienced the devastating loss of

Dawn Elizabeth

a man that was part of her soul. He had also been involved in an automobile accident. The day of his accident had been beautiful with the sun shining brightly. It was a clear day with no clouds in sight. His vehicle had been running perfectly to her knowledge and he had not operated it in any wrong fashion. There were no inclement elements to cause him any obstacles, to obstruct his vision. He had been excited in anticipation of the joyous event he had carefully planned for her. He had secretly gone to a costume shop and chosen an authentic Renaissance chain-mail suit that would be perfect for any knight. He had lovingly involved her two children to take part in the occasion and had not selfishly kept it to himself. They, too, had been taken to the costume shop and were fitted for costumes as well. He had chosen the beautiful gown and headpiece for her to wear. It was a beautiful gown ivory in color, with tiny gold flowers covering the dress. The skirt of the dress was full with the bodice tight and the sleeves full and puffy at the shoulder and then becoming fitted at the elbow. Tiny gold buttons and eyelets traveled down the bottom of the sleeves causing the sleeve to fit snuggly around the forearm and wrist. The neckline of the dress scooped in a u-shape, purposely meant to accentuate the firmness of breasts that it held within its fabric, revealing a deep cleavage. There was a beautiful brown satin ribbon that joined the bodice to the flowing skirt and gold braiding trimmed the skirt's edge.

The matching headpiece was in the same ivory material with the gold flowers. It had a half moon shaped cap covered with an assortment of ivory beads that was meant to sit towards the back of the head. Connected to the cap was a long flowing piece of opaque material that would hang down covering the back of the hair and rest on the shoulders.

She recalled the wonderful feelings she had experienced that day when she was presented with the historical gown. It had fit her perfectly, as if the seamstress had made it especially for her. She remembered how she had stood in front of her pedestal mirror and swayed from side to side and spun in circles as she gazed at her reflection. She had felt as though she had magically been transported into a different time period and was waiting for her knight to beckon her to his kingdom.

Her heart hardened as she remembered how the beautiful gown had turned into a nightmare as she had become entangled in its yards of fabric when she tripped as she raced to reach Alex in time. In the end, it was the beautiful gown that had won the agonizing battle with all its yards of material.

She sadly relived the last moments of that day, as time seemed to stand still when she desperately tried to reach Alex in time. She remembered how extraordinarily heavy the dress had felt as she lifted it above her knees to allow her legs the freedom to run to him. When she had finally reached him, she had used the skirt of the gown to wipe the blood from his face.

The dress had been badly stained and torn during the horrible ordeal. The owner of the costume shop had known about the romantic proposal that Alex had planned and had been heartsick about the tragic accident. She had told Beth's family that she was to keep the gown and the knight's costumes and did not charge her for them.

Both costumes had been carefully placed in garment bags and were being stored in the attic of Beth's parent's home. She had not allowed the gown to be cleaned or repaired. The beautiful gown remained torn and soiled with Alex's blood as it hung side by side the costume of the knight that had never been worn or taken out of its original bag.

The sounds of Joe's heavy breathing snapped Beth back to the cold, unfeeling hospital room. She gently reached down and once again began caressing his hand.

She sighed softly as she gently touched his hand. As her fingers came into contact with his, his long fingers opened to hers as if they were asking to be held. Understanding his gesture, she slid her hand under his allowing his fingers to intertwine with hers. Tears began to swell in her eyes as she felt the slight squeeze he gave to her once their fingers were united.

Her thoughts were suddenly flooded with numerous memories that had spanned eight years of her life regarding her involvement with Joseph O'Dea. She recalled the first night he had come to her house and the events that had taken place. If she had said "no" on that evening, would things be different now? Would she have ever met Alex, or would she be married to Joe? She shook her head as she tried to push the thoughts from her mind. Now was not the time to think about the "what if's". What had happened had happened, and it couldn't be changed. She had met Alex and she had loved him with every part of her being. It seemed so ironic that the man she had loved

CIRCLE OF LOVE

so deeply had been taken from her and, that this man whom she had also loved lay broken and battered in a hospital bed. Unlike Alex, Joseph had never allowed Beth to love him. She had pleaded and begged for him to give her one chance and he had angrily denied her each time. It was only upon meeting Alex that she had given up and walked away from Joe. Alex had given her the love and devotion she deserved. Theirs was a magical love, one that included a very special bond.

The love that she felt for the two men was completely different. Each had a passion, but only one had the feeling of a perfect fit. It was extremely difficult to consider whether or not she and Joseph would have a feeling of a "perfect fit" because they were never involved completely in the same way that she and Alex had been. They had never spent any time with each other doing different outside activities. They had never cuddled and watched a movie on the couch and shared a huge bowl of buttered popcorn. They had never gone to a sporting event and yelled and cheered their favorite team to victory. They had never strolled the malls and window-shopped. So many wonderful things they could have done with each other, but he would never allow it. To him she was just a quick roll in the hay then he would quickly push her away, never really seeing what kind of woman lived within the body he so passionately used.

Anger began to build within her heart as she silently compared the two men she had loved. Impulsively, she pulled her hand from Joe's and backed away from the bed. She felt as if she was a traitor to Alex. "No," she whispered in panic, "no, I cannot do this." Tears suddenly began to pour from her

Dawn Elizabeth

eyes and travel down her cheeks. She turned to the window and began wiping the tears from her face. No matter how quickly she wiped them there was a constant stream flowing from the corners of her eyes. Her body started to tremble as her heartache crept into her soul and began to engulf her. Unable to control herself from weeping, she allowed the sorrow to the surface. The tears she cried were not for the man she had loved and lost, but rather for the battered man who now lay a few feet from her; the man she had also loved but had never been allowed the opportunity to express her love. He had come to her when she had been torn inside and out due to her grief over Alex's death. He had comforted her and held her while she had wept for hours. He had finally opened his heart to her and she had turned him away. He had given her a chance and she rejected it. She was confused and bewildered. It had only been a short time since Alex had died. For her to allow herself to take care of this man would be a disgrace to Alex's memory. She could not do that to Alex, but she did not want to leave Joe alone either.

She briskly began wiping the tears from her face. Her efforts were all in vain as teardrops continually escaped her now swollen eyes. She looked around the room searching for a box of tissue. A small box was lying on the nightstand on the opposite side of the hospital bed. As she started to make her way around the foot of the bed a young nurse entered the room and looked at her sympathetically.

"Are you okay?" the young nurse questioned. "Is there something I can help you with?"

CIRCLE OF LOVE

Beth reached for a tissue and started to wipe the tears from her face. She took a deep breath then looked up at the nurse who was now standing at her side.

"Yes, I am okay. I guess I am just a little tired."

The nurse put her hand on Beth's shoulders and looked at her with deep concern. It was apparent to her that the woman had been crying for a long period of time. The petite woman looked extremely exhausted and distraught. The nurse was used to seeing the worried faces of family members but this woman was emotionally drained beyond mere concern. The woman's face was pale and her eyes were deeply bloodshot and swollen. Her nose was red and running. She gently took Beth by the hand and escorted her over to the chair that sat by the window.

"I don't mean to pry, but you look drained and exhausted. Maybe I should have a doctor come and see you. Perhaps he could give you something to help you relax. You can't help Mr. O'Dea in this condition."

Beth knew the young woman was right. All of a sudden, the tears began to swell in her eyes again and her body started to tremble. She lowered her head and cupped her face in her hands. She felt as though her heart was being ripped from her chest in its conflict of staying with Joseph or leaving out of respect for Alex. In a soft whisper she heard Alex's voice. She kept her eyes closed and allowed his comforting voice to enter her thoughts.

"Beth, you are not a traitor. I know your love for me remains in your heart, Princess. This man needs you. He needs your love. Please do not punish yourself for not being able to care for me. Care for this man. He

Dawn Elizabeth

is giving you the chance that you have always wanted. Do this for me. Our love will never die."

As she sat in her chair, even though she could not see him, she knew that Alex was knelt in front of her. She heard the concern in his voice as he softly spoke to her in her mind. She felt as his strong yet gentle hand reached up and wiped the tears from her face. She did not see, however, how each tear sparkled and then vanished at his touch.

Michael stood at the side of Joseph's hospital bed and watched as Alex had calmed Beth. He smiled as he saw the tears sparkle as Alex had wiped them from the tormented woman's face. His own heart began to feel light and warm, he knew the secret that he had kept from Alex was about to be revealed. He turned and looked back at Joseph's bruised and lacerated face. He quietly leaned down over the sleeping man and gently blew his breath onto the man's face. A beautiful ray of magnificent colors began to twirl and dance over Joe's face then slowly came down to rest on his many injuries. As if a magic wand had touched his face, the bruises gradually disappeared leaving only the laceration on his lip. His breathing became more steady and calm and his painful moans stopped completely. Michael reached his hand up to the bandage that had been wrapped around his head and allowed it to remain for several moments. At his touch the same beautiful colors began to seep into the bandage as they traveled deep to the laceration that he had sustained in the accident. The long, deep cut slowly started to mend itself and close. The sutures disappeared as the wound was healed, as if it had never existed.

CIRCLE OF LOVE

The angel stood up and looked down upon the sleeping man and softly began to speak, "Joseph, you will not remember any of the events leading up to your accident. It will all be forgotten. You have injuries still remaining, which must be present in order for her heart to be softened. Soon she will need your help as well. Trust your heart and allow its feelings to be free."

As the angel spoke the words, Alex remained kneeling by Beth and was not aware that Michael was in the room with him. He had not observed the angel touch the injured man, nor had he heard the words he had spoken. As he remained knelt in front of Beth he felt Michael's hand upon his shoulder. He glanced up to see a beautiful light surrounding the angel's face as he looked down at Alex. Gradually, Alex arose and stood by the angel's side somehow knowing that another "certain event" was about to take place.

Dawn Elizabeth

Chapter 33

Beth had not noticed that the young nurse had left her to go find a doctor. The moment she had heard Alex start to speak she had blocked out all outside noises so she could hear his voice clearly. She knew that Alex had remained in the room with her, but for some reason he had moved away from her. As she opened her eyes she saw the young nurse was entering the room with a doctor by her side.

The doctor was a middle-aged man who was balding and wore glasses. He was a short, stout man. He was wearing dark dress pants, a white dress shirt and tie, and a long white doctor's jacket with his name, "Dr. Mark Jones" embroidered on the pocket. Around his neck was a black stethoscope with its earpieces circling around the back of his neck. The bottom piece of the instrument hung loosely down the center of his chest and bobbed up and down as he walked. Beneath his spectacles were bright blue eyes. The glasses rested on the bridge of a wide, short nose. His lips were long and thick and there was a deep cleft in his chin. The doctor dashed over to Beth and sat down on the edge of the bed in front of her.

"Hello, my name is Dr. Jones. The nurse seems to be very concerned about you and asked that I come in to see if you are okay."

A single tear had escaped Beth's eye and was slowly making its way down her cheek. She looked up at the doctor who now sat across from her, waiting for her response. She tried to muster up some energy to stand up and convey to the doctor that she was okay,

CIRCLE OF LOVE

perhaps a little tired, but as she started to rise, the room suddenly began to spin. She felt as though she was on a playground merry-go-round and someone was turning the toy faster and faster. The noises around her all seemed to blend together and sound muffled. She turned her head to the side trying to bring her surroundings into focus. As if a black cloud was floating around her darkness, slowly began to engulf her, taking with it all light. She felt her body collapse as the doctor quickly caught her before she fell.

In an instant the nurse was helping the doctor move the now unconscious Beth to the unoccupied hospital bed in the room. The two adults carefully placed Beth on the bed and the doctor broke open a smelling salts capsule and placed it under Beth's nose. Beth quickly turned her head away from the capsule unaware of what had just happened.

She lay on the bed and stared up at the white ceiling tiles. She felt a little light-headed, but oddly, she also felt she had somehow received a burst of energy. She had no knowledge of where she was or how she had gotten there. She did not know what day it was, nor what time of day it was, whether it was morning, noon, or night.

Looking down at her was a bald, middle-aged doctor with a young nurse at his side.

"How are you feeling, Miss? You scared us there for a bit," the doctor softy said.

Beth looked up at the doctor, puzzled about what had happened. She looked around the room and slowly remembered where she was. She was at the hospital. Joseph had been involved in a serious car accident. She remembered coming up to the hospital

Dawn Elizabeth

and knew she had stayed the night. She closed her eyes and tried to focus on Alex. Hopefully, he would be able to help her to remember what had happened.

The doctor looked at Beth and knew that she was confused and slowly he began to explain what had happened.

"Your friend was in an automobile accident and you have been here staying with him. You have not left his side. But I think the stress is taking its toll on you because you fainted. You have been crying for some time and the nurse was worried. She came and found me. When I came in to see and check on you, you collapsed. I think maybe we should check you out to make sure everything is okay. Would you allow us to take you down to emergency and run a few tests?" the doctor cautiously asked.

Beth opened her eyes widely and looked at the doctor, confused and puzzled. She did feel a little bit strange, actually very strange, and quite dizzy. Maybe it would be a good idea to be examined. She nodded her head and slowly sat up. With the doctor and nurse at her side slowly they eased her up until she was finally standing. She felt a little weak as she stood between the two medical personnel. Her burst of energy had vanished and suddenly she felt completely exhausted and drained.

Realizing she was breaking her promise to Joseph, she stopped and looked at the doctor.

"Wait, I need to tell Joe that I will be back. I promised him that I wouldn't leave him," she slowly began. As she spoke the words, her voice began to quiver. She had been torn between staying with him and leaving earlier. But now she didn't want to leave his side, frightened that something would happen to him during her absence. She had felt that he truly wanted her to remain with him through the night. If he awoke while she was off having tests done he would never know that she had stayed by his side and held his hand. He would feel that she didn't care and had left him alone.

She walked over to his bedside and gazed down at this bruised face. His eyes were closed and his breathing was slow and steady. Careful not to bump his IV she tenderly reached for his hand and slowly began caressing his long fingers with her own. To her surprise, his hand raised and affectionately began to return the gentle caresses to her tiny fingers. She turned back to see his eyes opened and gazing at her. He closed his eyes as he drew in a deep breath and let out a little moan from the pain he was experiencing throughout his battered body. He stopped caressing Beth's fingers and took her hand in his.

In a hoarse voice he began, "Beth, you look so tired. You stayed here all night didn't you?"

Beth allowed him to tightly hold her hand as she moved to the head of his bed. With sweet sincerity she looked down at his battered face and answered his question.

"Yes, I stayed here with you all night. You had a rough night I'm afraid. That tree gave you quite a beating. But you gave a gallant fight."

Joseph looked up at Beth as his vision slowly began to get clearer. He studied her face and could see that her eyes were puffy and bloodshot and her face was painfully pale. His heart ached, realizing that his accident had caused her to worry about him. She was

Dawn Elizabeth

slowly starting to come back from her silent world of grieving over Alex and now he was concerned that his accident might send her back to her world of silence. He did not remember exactly what had happened to cause the accident. He knew it had been raining and he was coming home from the store. Out of nowhere was a small child who ran out in front of him. He had pushed on the brakes as he tried to stop his vehicle but they were too wet and the truck would not halt. He remembered swerving the wheel to avoid hitting the little girl and had hit a tree. Mysteriously, he remembered the look on the child's face moments before his impact. She did not appear to be frightened at all by the on-coming truck. It seemed strange to Joe as he recalled that the child had seemed to nod her head only moments before he slammed into the huge, old oak tree.

Joe jerked his head as he remembered the girl's sweet, little face. It had been the most angelic face he had ever seen. Her hair was a sandy brown and her eyes were a beautiful shade of blue. A strange light seemed to have sparkled from them.

"The little girl", he began, "Is she okay? I missed her didn't I?" he asked quickly.

"Little girl, Joe? There was no one else there. The police found you alone. No one else was hurt," Beth replied. Tears began to swell in her eyes once more as she continued.

The doctor, noticing that the tears were once again streaming down the woman's face, stepped forward and rested his hand on her shoulder. Careful not to alarm the injured man, he interrupted the conversation.

CIRCLE OF LOVE

"Beth, since Mr. O'Dea is awake why don't we let the nurse check him over and we will go find his doctor and allow him the chance to examine him." The doctor gave Beth a sympathetic look; he wanted to get her down to emergency so she too could be examined.

Beth, understanding what the doctor was trying to do, nodded her head and agreed with the doctor that Joe should be looked at by his own doctor. She did not want to scare Joe so she carefully chose her words agreeing with the doctor.

"The doctor is right, Joe. I will step out and let the nurse get your doctor. I am sure that he will want to give you a thorough examination now that you are awake. The kids are at home waiting to hear how you are doing. I will go call them and let them know you are awake. Then maybe I will go downstairs and get something to eat. I will be back though…I promise."

Joseph looked up at Beth and signed heavily as he saw how tired and drained she looked. He felt a little ashamed of himself for being selfish in wanting her to stay with him. He was terrified that if she left, she might not return and he would lose her forever. He had loved her for so many years and had been so horrible to her. By some means, his heart had become stronger as it fought desperately to be allowed to display its true love for this woman. He wanted to take away every ounce of hurt that he had caused her to feel. He wanted to hold her and comfort her. He wanted to dry her tears. For some reason God had spared his life last night. God had given him a chance to make things right with Beth. He was terrified that if she walked out that door she may not come back.

Dawn Elizabeth

Beth recognized the concern on Joe's face. She knew he was worried that she may not return. She turned to the doctor and nodded that she would be there in a moment, then bent down over Joe's hospital bed. She drew her hand up and gently caressed his cheek. She then lowered her face down so that she could look directly into his eyes. Through the tears a light sparkled from her blue eyes as she gazed into his.

"I promise you, I will be back, Joe. Let the doctor examine you and before you know it I will be right back here at your side. I am going to go check on the kids." She then gently kissed his lip, careful not to put too much pressure on his stitches.

She stood up, turned, and started to walk out of the room but stopped and turned back to look at Joseph. She touched her fingertips to her lips, kissed them, then lovingly blew him a kiss. She then quickly turned and left the room. The doctor was waiting directly outside of Joe's room with a wheelchair and nodded for her to take a seat in it. Beth sighed and did as the doctor instructed. As she lowered herself into the seat of the chair her thoughts cried out to Alex. She was scared and knew that if he was near he would be able to calm her. As the doctor wheeled her down the hall towards the elevator she kept her head down with her eyes closed.

"Where are you, Alex? I am scared. Please talk to me."

As the elevator doors closed, Beth felt strangely alone. She knew Alex had been with her in Joe's hospital room, but now he was not. She would face the tests by herself. What was wrong with her? Why did she faint and why did she feel so dizzy lately? Her

CIRCLE OF LOVE

heart began to pound rapidly as the elevator doors opened and the doctor pushed her into one of the unoccupied rooms.

Alex, confused, looked at his guardian angel. He had not left Beth during any of the time. He had tried to respond to her when she begged for him to talk to her. For some reason she had not heard his voice responding. Anger began to overwhelm him.

"What's going on, Michael? What's wrong with Beth? And why couldn't she hear me when I was answering her?" Alex shouted.

"Alex, she did not hear you because her heart is slowly starting to open up to Joseph. It is happening, Alex. The circle of love is continuing. Remember all that I have told you. Your love is never-ending. It will last throughout eternity. Be patient as the events are now taking place."

Alex's heart felt heavy as he listened to the angel speak. He felt as if he was losing Beth and there was nothing he could do to prevent it. He lowered his head and walked away from the angel. He headed back towards Joseph's room. He knew that this man would be the one to share his love with Beth and he wanted to make sure that he would, indeed, recover from his accident. As he approached the injured man's room he felt a soft light cover his face. It was a warmth like he had never known. For some reason he knew that something very special was about to take place. He spun around quickly to see Michael standing a few feet behind him. His hair was blowing off of his shoulders and a bright light was encircling him.

Dawn Elizabeth

The angel looked at Alex and smiled. Softly he said, "The circle of love continues, Alex. The circle of love continues."

Chapter 34

Beth sat on the cold hospital bed and tried to pull the thin hospital sheet up across her chest. The nurse had asked her to remove her clothing and put on one of the hospital gowns so she could be examined. The gown was made out of the same cotton material as the hospital sheets. It was white and had tiny blue squares covering it. Two strings tied around her back, closing the gown, one at her neck and one at the middle of her back. She shivered as she sat on the stiff, cold hospital bed. The mattress was very uncomfortable and was covered with some sort of waterproof material, which protected the mattress from being damaged. She was sitting on one of the creases from the bed being positioned in a sitting, angular fashion. She tried to shift her weight to one side to find a smooth place on the mattress, but her effort was useless. As long as the bed was in that position there would be that crease, she decided she would just have to deal with it.

She rested her head back against the stiff hospital pillow and looked up at the tiles on the ceiling. Her eyes searched the specks of gray in the tiles as she tried to calm herself from worrying about what the doctor had found from his examination. He had taken her blood pressure and said it was slightly elevated. He also indicated that she was running a low-grade fever. He asked her if she had experienced any type of stomach problems such as pain or nausea. She told him that she hadn't had any pain, but had felt sick to her stomach and a little dizzy. This comment resulted in the doctor calling a nurse in to take a blood sample.

Dawn Elizabeth

She turned her arm over and looked at the bandage that was now in the crease of her arm. She let out a soft sigh as she remembered how skillfully the nurse had taken the blood without her feeling the slightest prick. Normally, Beth was a baby when it came to needles. She hated shots and heaven-forbid she needed to have a blood test taken. She always tried to be brave and let the nurses poke the needles into her arm without flinching, but she would always end up saying, "Ouch". This time however, it hadn't hurt in the slightest bit. The nurse had poked her, drew the blood, and bandaged her arm all in a matter of seconds.

She felt a shiver run through her body and quickly started to rub her arms to get warm. She wondered how Greg and Tiffany were and felt irresponsible for not calling them earlier and advising them of Joe's condition. She knew that they were probably worried and concerned since she hadn't called. She scolded herself in her mind and decided as soon as she was finished talking with the doctor about her own condition she would call the kids. As she lay in the bed her, thoughts drifted to Alex. She knew he had been with her in Joe's room but wondered why, after she had fainted, he had not answered her when she called. As she closed her eyes and began to call out to him in her mind, the large wide door to her room opened and Dr. Jones walked in with her chart in his hands. She pushed herself up so she was sitting up straight and waited to hear what results were found from the tests.

The doctor sat the clipboard down on the table next to her bed and walked over to her bedside.

CIRCLE OF LOVE

"Well, the tests definitely explain why you have felt dizzy and fainted," he began. The doctor raised his arms and crossed them over his chest.

"Ms. Hanson, the reason that you have all of these symptoms is because you are pregnant."

Beth's eyes opened widely in disbelief at what the doctor had just said. Tears filled her eyes and rapidly began to stream down her cheeks. The doctor misunderstood the tears, believing that the pregnancy was deeply unwanted. He reached for a box of tissue next to her bed and quickly handed them to her.

"I take it this is an unwanted pregnancy," he started.

As the tears flowed down her face, she looked up at the doctor. A smile slowly began to form on her lips as she remembered the last morning that she and Alex had shared. Their beautiful love-making had created a child…Alex's child. Her right hand immediately went to her lower stomach and she gently started to move it in small circles knowing that deep inside of her womb a baby was growing.

"Unwanted pregnancy…" she smiled. "Oh, Dr. Jones…this is the best news that I could have received. This baby is very much wanted. How far along am I?" she asked, already knowing what the doctor's answer would be.

The doctor, relieved at his patient's joy, gave her a broad grin. "Well, that I can't really say without examining you. The blood test only tells us that you are pregnant. If you would like I could have a nurse come in so that I can examine you. Or if you would rather, you can make an appointment to see your own

Dawn Elizabeth

doctor. It is your decision and I respect it, whatever it is."

Beth, feeling as though she was given the most precious gift, looked back at the doctor, her hand remaining on her belly. "I think I will make an appointment to see my own doctor. Unless you feel there is a need to worry and I should be examined now."

The doctor smiled and reached down and patted Beth's hand that was lying at her side. "No, I don't think there is a need to worry. As long as you promise me that you will make an appointment as soon as possible to see your own doctor. I will have to insist though that you get some rest. You are both physically and emotionally drained. Your baby needs you to get rest. I know you are concerned about Mr. O'Dea, but I am going to order you to go home and get some sleep. I am sure he will understand."

Beth had forgotten all about Joe in the midst of her news. She knew that the doctor was right and she indeed did need some sleep. She would explain to Joe that she would go home to get some rest and be back to see him tomorrow. She did not want to do anything to jeopardize the life of her unborn child, Alex's child.

The doctor gave Beth a few instructions and once he was sure that she would go home and get some rest he left her alone.

Beth was overwhelmed with joy as she removed her gown. She looked down at her belly to see whether or not it had started to show that she was pregnant. During her grieving for Alex she had not paid attention to her body and had not noticed that there was a roundness beginning to form to her once flat stomach. She had been so lost that she had not seen the changes that her body was going through. Her breasts were becoming larger as they were getting ready for the child that was now a part of her. For a moment she stood in the cold room and let her hands survey her belly knowing that a part of Alex was growing in her. God had taken Alex, but had not taken him completely.

She looked up towards the heavens and whispered. "Thank you, Father...for leaving a part of him with me."

She laid the gown on the bed and began to get dressed. She was tired and knew that she needed to get some sleep. She would go up and check on Joe then go home and take a much- needed nap. She decided that she would not mention the pregnancy to Joe nor the kids. She wanted to wait until after she had seen her own doctor to make sure everything was fine with both her and the baby. She was unsure as to what Joe's reaction would be when he learned that she was expecting. For some reason she felt that they were becoming closer and she did not want to hurt him by telling him she was carrying another man's child. The thought that he would be discouraged at the news lasted for only a moment as something told her that he would be the one to help her though the next months. She walked towards the door and paused for a moment and closed her eyes.

"Alex...Alex, can you hear me? Oh, Sweetheart, I am going to have your baby." she thought. Although she could not see or hear him, she felt that he was near her and she could feel his happiness flow deep in her soul.

Dawn Elizabeth

As Beth left the room, Alex turned and looked at his guardian angel. The angel walked towards Alex, his eyes shining brightly. He could feel the happiness beaming from the soul of the man he had guided. The angel also felt deep happiness, as he knew that God had blessed Beth with Alex's child. He knew that the woman would grieve deeply for the loss of her love and God did not want to leave her without a part of Alex. He knew that in taking the life of Alex it would bring love into the life of another man who desperately needed and deserved love. He also knew that this man would love the child as if it were his own. There were still many things that Michael knew were to take place, and in time, Alex would also learn of these things. Some things would be painful for Alex to see, but in time he would understand. The angel smiled as Alex began to speak to him.

"Michael, Beth is having our baby...my baby?"

The angel chuckled as he saw the happiness in the dark-haired man's eyes. "Yes, Alex. Your baby grows inside of Beth. It is as I said, the circle of love continues. It is never-ending. The love that you and Beth share will go on through all of time."

"But, Michael, when she called to me, and I answered she couldn't hear me. Why?"

The angel knew that the words he was about to say would hurt the man who stood before him. The tall angel looked down and then looked back directly in the dark eyes of Alex. "Alex, she will be able to feel you near her. But she will no longer be able to hear you. Her heart is starting to soften towards Joseph. As long as she thinks that you are here and she can talk to you, she will never give him a chance. Remember, you were sent back here to bring them together. It is your destiny. Just because she can no longer hear you does not mean her love for you has died. Your child is growing within her. That child will be a constant reminder to her of the love the two of you share."

Sadness filled Alex's heart as he listened to the words the angel spoke. Beth was pregnant with their baby and he would not be able to tell her how happy he was. He would hear her talk to him and would not be able to respond. For a brief time the grief that they shared had been eased by the bond that still remained between them, even after his death.

He lowered his head then raised his face towards the ceiling. "I do not understand", he whispered.

The angel rested his hand on Alex's shoulder. "You will, Alexander. You will," the angel assured.

The angel and spirit then slowly left the room in which Beth had been given her joyous news and headed towards Joseph O'Dea's room.

Dawn Elizabeth

Chapter 35

Joe sat in the rocking chair that the nurse had moved next to the window for him. She wrapped a blanket around his shoulders to keep him warm from the chill that was in the air. Beth had kept her promise to him and visited him every day. He had been in the hospital for several weeks and would remain there a bit longer. The doctors were surprised at how quickly the laceration on his head had healed. The thick bandaged had been removed exposing his thick, wavy hair.

He had a faint recollection of the accident and did not remember having any injury to his head. The numerous cuts he had sustained on his face and hands were slowly starting to heal, leaving minimal scars. The stitches on his lip had been removed several days after the accident, but his lip remained numb. There was a deep purple bruise completely covering his chest due to the impact of hitting the steering wheel in the crash. Both of his legs remained bruised and swollen. Although his legs were not broken, they were covered with deep lacerations and the wounds were still very painful. One laceration extended down the majority of his left leg. It took all of his energy to use his walker while being accompanied by a nurse or sometimes Beth.

As he looked out the window he felt drowsy from the pain medicine the nurse had given him. He knew that Beth wasn't expected for another hour or so. He tilted his head back and allowed the pain medicine to take effect. Little by little, his body became relaxed and he drifted off into a dream.

CIRCLE OF LOVE

His dream took him back to his childhood. He was eight years old and was walking with his father. He saw the happiness and admiration on his young face as he listened intently to each word his father was saying. To the young Joseph, this man was a hero. The young boy watched as his father coached the teenaged boys of his neighborhood in different sporting events. All of the kids loved him. He was always encouraging, no matter what the outcome of their game. He would never yell at them if they missed a ball or failed in a play he had called. He would pat them on their backs or their helmets and tell them it was okay and they would do it next time. School officials always commended him on his coaching ability and the incredible way he related to kids.

Joseph always looked up to his father with great admiration and deep respect. He had made a promise to himself that when he grew up he would be just like his dad. His father had always made time for him, no matter how busy and hectic his schedule was.

As he drifted deeper into his dream the scene changed to a year later. He saw his father lying in a hospital bed, all color drained from his face. His mother stood next to his bed crying. He saw himself holding tightly onto his father's hand screaming and crying as the child witnessed the life vanished from his father due to disease that had no cure. The young boy had watched his father fight for his life for over a year and cried hysterically when his father had finally lost the battle. He felt the emptiness and sadness from his heart being broken over losing this man he loved dearly.

Dawn Elizabeth

The dream then jumped to Joe as a teenager. His heart had hardened after the loss of his father, afraid to allow himself to love for fear of losing someone. He felt as a child that he had done something wrong and that was the reason that his father had died. He would not allow anyone the chance to get close to his heart and kept it constantly guarded.

As he grew into a teenager he had become a handsome young man. He had thick, dark brown hair with soft, hazel eyes. He had reached the height slightly over six feet and was very athletic with a strong, muscular build. Whenever he walked in the halls of his high school many teenage girls would stop to watch him pass by them, each secretly hoping he would look their way. He was the star quarterback of the varsity football team and everyone idolized him. He watched as his teenage self flirted with one of the cheerleaders then observed tears fill the young girl's eyes when he rudely walked away from her. He felt the longing the young man had for the cheerleader, but once the young girl started to melt his heart he would become cold and quickly leave her crying or confused as to why he had become so mean. Later in the evening, when he was studying, or lying in his bed, he would feel guilty about being cruel to the young girl. In his mind he felt he didn't deserve to have someone love him and would not allow it, no matter how sweet or pretty the girl was.

Joe's body jerked as he drifted deeper and deeper into his dream. He saw himself on the day he first met Beth. He remembered how his heart had softened at the sight of her. He had not heard her speak but he had made slight eye contact with her. He thought she was

CIRCLE OF LOVE

the most beautiful creature he had ever seen. Oddly, that night he had dreamed of his father and he was saddened at the many years without him. The dream had caused him to tell himself to stay away from her because like his father had left him, she would too.

The soft sound of Beth's voice pulled him from his dream and he opened his eyes to see her standing in front of him smiling. "Hey there. You were dreaming. Are you okay?" she asked.

Joe reached up and wiped some sleep from his eyes and looked at Beth. She looked glowing. She had her hair pinned up at the back of her head with pieces of hair fanning out above the clip. She was dressed in loose-fitting overall jeans with a pale yellow turtleneck. On her feet were brown, slip-on loafers with chunky heels. She looked much younger than her actual age.

Beth could feel Joe looking at her up and down and was nervous he would notice the roundness of her belly. Quickly, she walked over and set her purse down on the bed table.

Joe, noticing her quick movement, wondered what had caused her action. "Hey… are you okay?"

Feeling very uncomfortable, she walked back and sat down on the bed in front of Joe's chair. She leaned over and took one of his hands in her own trying to hide her uneasiness.

"Of course I am okay. How are you? Have you had your walk today? How are the stitches in your leg feeling today? Are they still pretty sore… Oh the kids said to tell you 'Hello'."

Joe chuckled at her questions, and began to answer her. "I am doing okay. The doctor says I have to stay

Dawn Elizabeth

here for another week. As for my walk, yes, the nurse was here earlier. The stitches seem to pull a little when I walk, but I manage…Be sure to tell the kids I said 'hello'. How are you Beth? You look cute today in your overalls. I don't think I have ever seen you in them before. You seem to be glowing."

"Really? Hmmm, actually I am doing okay. Glowing, huh? Is that good?" she asked.

"Yes, glowing is good. Usually when a woman is glowing in the way you are, she is expecting…" he began.

Caught off guard by his comment, she swiftly got up and went to the window.

"Isn't it a beautiful day, Joe? Just look at the way the sun is shining. And it is actually warm for this time of year."

Joe, recognizing that she had hurriedly changed the subject, turned to look at Beth who now stood next to his chair looking out the window.

"Beth…are you…," he stuttered.

Beth bit her lower lip and closed her eyes. In her mind she called out to Alex.

"Alex, how do I answer his question without hurting him?" she thought.

"Beth?"

Little by little Beth turned around and knelt down in front of Joe. She held both his large hands in hers. She took in a deep breath and began.

"Joe, the morning after your accident I fainted. The nurse had been concerned about me because I had cried all night after they brought you in. Shortly after you woke up, the doctor took me downstairs and ran some tests. I guess during my mourning over Alex I

CIRCLE OF LOVE

wasn't really paying attention to the symptoms. The morning sickness, the constant running to the bathroom…," she looked directly into Joe's eyes and continued. "Yes, Joe, I'm going to have a baby. I haven't told the kids. And I wasn't sure how I was going to tell you."

Joe held Beth's tiny hand in his and gave it a gentle squeeze.

"Awwwe, Beth, I am happy for you. You shouldn't have worried about me. Listen to me. I can't pretend Alex never existed. You two had a very special love. Remember I saw you when you were involved with him at the grocery store. I don't think I've seen you more happy. Your eyes sparkled whenever you said his name. And he was so excited about proposing to you…"

"What…what do you mean he was excited about proposing to me?"

Joe, realizing what he had said, closed his eyes and held his breath. This was not how he had wanted to tell her about his seeing Alex shortly before his accident. Beth pulled her hands from Joe's and stood up and backed away.

"Joe, what are you talking about?"

Slowly, he opened his eyes and let out a heavy sigh.

"Beth, I didn't realize the man at the gas station was your Alex. I had never seen him before. I knew that you were in love with a gentleman named 'Alex' but that is all I knew. I had stopped to get gas that day. I had just paid for my gas when he was walking in. He stumbled, almost passed out in front of me. I grabbed hold of him before he fell. After I saw that he was

Dawn Elizabeth

steady, he told me that he was planning on proposing to his special lady. He never said your name, just that he was a little nervous. I remember thinking he was such a lucky man. The sparkle that shone in his eyes was the same sparkle that I had seen in yours. I am sorry, Beth. I really did not know he was your Alex. I discovered it myself on that night I came to your house when you were crying. When I laid you down, I noticed the picture of the two of you on the table by your bed. Tiffany told me that the man in the picture was Alex and she also told me what had happened…It bothered me because I had seen him what was probably only moments before the accident happened."

Beth covered her mouth in disbelief. Suddenly, she felt sick to her stomach. She ran to the bathroom located in his room and began to vomit. Once she was finished, she rinsed her mouth out with cold water and dried it with a paper towel from the dispenser hanging next to the sink. She thought it was a strange coincidence that Joe had seen Alex on that day he had been taken from her.

Chapter 36

Alex stood in the corner of Joe's room and noticed the sad expression which appeared on his face when Beth had made her dash to the bathroom. He leaned back against the wall, crossed one of his legs in front of the other, and then crossed his arms over his chest. As he watched the injured man sitting in the chair with the blanket around his shoulders, he knew that the pain this man felt in his heart was more painful than injuries he had sustained when he had crashed into the tree. Alex quietly watched as Joe lowered his head and listened to Beth getting sick in his bathroom. It was apparent to Alex that this man did not feel jealousy, but rather sympathy for the long road he knew Beth had ahead of her. Alex had been an observer in his dreams and saw how Joe had lost his father at a young age. He knew that as a child he had tried to protect himself from feeling another person's love. He wouldn't allow himself the opportunity of getting too close to someone, frightened that should he love a person, he or she would leave him too. He had needed his mother after his father had died. But rather than reaching out to her son, his mother had withdrew into herself and had forgotten about her child who desperately needed her comfort. In essence, Joseph had grown up desperately needing someone to love but had been abandoned by the one person he had needed the most.

Alex shook his head in confusion as to why these certain events had to take place. He knew that Joseph was a good man, and he did deserve to be loved. He also knew that Joe's heart was crying out. He also knew that Beth would shower Joseph with love... if the man would only ask. She had been to the hospital every day since his accident, offering her kindness and love to him. Alex knew that Beth had felt guilty at first, but he also knew that another man could never replace the love she felt for him. Theirs was a special love that few people experience. It was a love that lasted without conditions or rules. It did not feel jealousy or mistrust. It was having faith in the other person's decisions, knowing without doubt or hesitation that he or she would do what was right. As the dark-haired spirit stood and watched the man who had caught him when he stumbled, he knew that this was the man he wanted Beth to love. He wanted this man to experience the joy and happiness that was taken from him when he was such a young boy when his father had died and his mother had abandoned him.

He glanced up as he saw Beth come out of the bathroom. He agreed with Joseph, she was absolutely glowing. Her cheeks were no longer pale but rather a healthy, rose color. Her eyes glistened and sparkled at the happiness that consumed her, knowing his child was growing inside of her. The quick onset of nausea did not seem to bother her in the least as she walked over and once again sat on the bed in front of Joseph. Alex smiled as he watched the way she would unconsciously rest her hand on the roundness of her belly and gently begin to make tiny circles, as if she was tenderly caressing or soothing her unborn child. The sound of Joseph's voice caused Alex to look back up to listen to what the man was saying.

"Beth, are you okay?"

CIRCLE OF LOVE

Beth smiled at Joe and leaned forward so she could carefully push a piece of hair that had fallen down on his forehead. He remained still and allowed her to move the hair. His eyes followed hers until finally she paused, stopping to look directly into his eyes. She felt tiny goose bumps raise on her arms and legs as she realized that one of her prayers had been answered. During all of their years together, she had never observed such warmth in his eyes. During all the years that they had known each other he had never let his eyes linger, looking into hers, for more than a second before he would quickly turn his face away, or close his eyes. During their nights of passion, he would always have the lights dimmed or candles burning. This way he would be able to hide his true feelings in the darkness. As he sat in his chair all battered and bruised, he had somehow gained the strength and courage not to hide the feelings that he had kept locked deep in his heart. Slowly, he reached his hand up and cupped it around Beth's soft cheek. When she started to look away he softly whispered, "No, Beth, don't look away. Look into my eyes and tell me what you see."

Eagerly she turned her eyes back towards him and smiled at the warmth that beamed from his hazel eyes. A feeling of understanding transcended through her soul as she gazed into the eyes that had once been cold and distant towards her. These were not the eyes of a man who could not feel love as she had once thought. No, these were the eyes of a man who felt love deeply and had hidden it deep in his soul. She realized that all the cruel words that he had spoken to her were not

Dawn Elizabeth

words truly meant to hurt her, but rather somehow they were intended to protect her.

Beth lowered herself off the bed and knelt down in front of Joe's chair. She reached up and took his hand from her cheek and tenderly kissed it. She felt her hands tremble as she remembered the many tears she had cried because she did not understand why he always pushed her away. Her thoughts were flooded with memories of the many nights she had lain on her bed crying holding Big Bear and praying to God to please give her some answers.

Alex, feeling the confusion that Beth was experiencing, quickly walked over and knelt down next to her. He knew she could not hear him but he desperately wanted to ease her pain. He felt helpless as he watched her tiny hands tremble in Joe's. He felt her soul being torn apart as she realized that God had heard every prayer she had made. He looked over his shoulder and waited to see what Michael would say. The angel only nodded. Alex knew that it was another one of the "events" that had to take place. He sighed heavily, wondering if he would ever be able to fulfill his destiny.

As the angel read his thoughts he answered him by saying, "Yes, you will, Alex, yes, you will."

Chapter 37

Beth had felt bewildered during her visit with Joseph. She had been puzzled when he mentioned that he had seen Alex on the day of his tragic accident, the accident that had taken him from her. She had also been confused when she had seen the warmth that glowed from Joseph's eyes when he looked at her. She knew in her heart that she should have remained with him and talked to him, but she did not feel ready. So many things had happened to her during the past several months and she was still mourning Alex. Joseph had seemed to understand the confusion in her face and did not push her, nor beg her to stay. He had told her that he was tired himself and it might be better if they talked tomorrow. She had promised him that she would be back in the morning and would be the one to help him with his walk. As she left him sitting alone in his room her heart felt as if it were being torn in two. It loved two men deeply, each in a different way.

As she drove over to her parents' home, she called out to Alex in her thoughts. "Alex, I need you. Why did you leave me? I am so confused. I know I heard you speak to me before…why won't you talk to me now?"

Over and over in her thoughts, she repeated the same questions. Although she tried to feel his presence, it was not there. As she pulled into her parents' driveway, she felt anxious and a bit frightened. She had not been to their home since Alex's death but hoped she would find the inner peace

Dawn Elizabeth

she desperately needed in their attic. She had phoned her mother from the hospital so that she would expect the visit. As she got out of the car she looked up and noticed her mother was standing at the top of the porch steps. Her eyes were filled with deep concern for her daughter. She had witnessed her daughter fall into a world of silence when Alex had died, as if he had taken a part of her with him in his death. During the past few weeks, she had caught a glimpse of her daughter trying to find her way back to them. The older woman smiled as her daughter walked up the stairs of the gray porch. She opened her arms and embraced her once she was in reach.

Beth held onto her mother and allowed her to tenderly pat her back. She knew her mother was concerned and she wanted to put her mind at ease. Without breaking the embrace, she pulled her head back so that she could see the older woman's face.

"I am doing okay, Mom. I know that you're worried. Please, don't be. I have put this off for too long already."

"Sweetie, are you sure? Those things aren't going anywhere. You have plenty of time," the woman began.

"No, Mom, I don't have plenty of time. Let's sit down for a bit. There is something I need to tell you."

Beth's mom tilted her head to the side as she listened to her daughter. She slowly removed her arms from around her daughter and walked over to one of the wicker chairs sitting on the enormous country porch. She watched as her daughter repositioned the cushion on a nearby wicker chair then sat down.

CIRCLE OF LOVE

"I am not sure how to say this. And I pray that you will understand...but the reason that I don't have plenty of time is because I'm going to have a baby to take care of soon."

Beth's mom's mouth opened slightly and was caught off guard by her daughter's news. "A baby?"

"Yes, Mom, I am expecting Alex's baby. I haven't told the kids yet. I just haven't found the right time." Beth continued her voice quivering as she held back her tears. "I need to accept and face the fact that Alex isn't coming back. He was with me for a brief time and I loved him as I will never love again. But his child is growing in me and he or she needs me to be healthy, and so do Greg and Tiffany. I need to remember that day. I can't block it out anymore. Please understand."

The older woman looked at her daughter and knew she was right, especially with the new baby on the way. Secretly, she had prayed to God that somehow Beth would be pregnant. If only she had something of Alex's, perhaps it would comfort her through the years ahead. She went to her daughter and took her cheeks in her hands and held her face still.

"That child is going to need you...and Gregory and Tiffany need you now. If going up there will help you find your peace, your strength, then I am behind you, Elizabeth Hanson."

Beth gave her mother a quick smile then wrapped her arms around her and squeezed. She had never worried that the pregnancy would anger her mother because her mother had always been supportive of her no matter what her true feelings were. The two women held on to each other for several moments, each giving

Dawn Elizabeth

the other support and comfort. It was Beth's mom who pulled away from the hug first.

"Well, I suppose you shouldn't put this off any longer. I will let you go up there. If you need me…just call me and I will be right there."

Beth smiled at her mother and walked towards the front door. Her heart began to beat rapidly as her emotions started to spin around within her. She took a deep breath, grabbed the doorknob and pulled open the screen door. As she stepped inside the foyer of the old house, she looked at the steep staircase directly in front of her. She knew that at the top of the stairs, behind the huge door were memories that she had blocked out of her heart and mind. Some of those memories were happy and joyous. It was not those memories that scared her. It was the memory that filled her heart with pain and sorrow that she had tried to run from. As she began to ascend the wooden stairs, she felt her hands tremble on the banister. She held her head high and did not allow the fear to capture her and scare her away. It was time that she face the memory of that day with courage and strength. It would not matter if she cried because her tears would only cleanse the scar that had been left behind.

As she reached the top step, she closed her eyes and called out to Alex once more.

"Please, Alex, be with me. Help me to get through this."

A familiar tingling sensation overwhelmed her soul as she called out. Although she could not see him, she knew he was there. She opened her eyes and headed for the door leading to the attic. At her side, the dark haired spirit walked with her. Following them was the guardian angel who would watch over them both.

Chapter 38

The attic was filled with boxes, old furniture and large old framed pictures. The floor was wooden, the floorboard creaking as she walked across it. There was a round window at the end of the room, which allowed in the beautiful rays of sunlight. A light bulb hung in the center of the ceiling with a long string hanging from it. As she approached the center, she moved the string out of her way. The window gave the attic a beautiful natural light and artificial illumination wasn't needed. She took in a deep breath as she turned and walked towards the thick plastic clothing bag that was hanging in the far corner of the room. As she got nearer and nearer to it, she felt her heart beating rapidly because she knew there were many memories held inside. She paused for a moment a foot away from the bag and closed her eyes. In her mind, she began to plea for Alex to be with her. She felt his hand gently squeeze her shoulders, indicating to her that he was indeed there. Even though she could not see him, she felt his spirit with her and was calmed knowing that he would help her to see and accept the tragic events of that day. He removed his hands from her shoulders and walked around to stand in front of her. She remained standing, with her eyes closed, focusing her thoughts on Alex.

"Alex…help me to remember what happened that day. Help me to be strong enough to face my pain. Please…"

Alex looked at the pain that covered her face. He felt the sorrow and grief that surrounded her heart. He

CIRCLE OF LOVE

felt her fear connected with his soul as she tried to recall the memories of that day. He knew that it would be painful for her to remember or see the events leading up to his death. It was his destiny to help and show her what had happened on that day in order for her to let go, and continue on with her life. Helping her do this would mean she would, in essence, be letting go of Alex. He felt as if his very soul was being torn apart bit by bit. He knew that he would be sacrificing his time on Earth with her, watching her smile, hearing her voice, as an observer who was not allowed to respond or participate. He had grown accustomed to watching over her as she slept, sometimes peeking in on her dreams. He had grown fond of the man who had been a part of her life long before he had met her. Even when he was alive he could not bring himself to hate Joseph O'Dea and now, as a spirit, he understood why. He had seen the goodness in Joe's heart and soul. He knew the pain the man had carried with him throughout the majority of his life. As a spirit, he watched as the man worried over and tried to care for *his* Beth. He never asked for anything from her, only trying to help her through her rough and difficult agonizing time. Alex knew Joseph related to how painful it was to lose someone you loved so deeply. As a very young boy he had loved and painfully lost his father. He was left alone to suffer his pain and sorrow, never having someone to help him through the mourning and heart wrenching loss.

As Alex stood in front of Beth and looked at her standing silently with her eyes closed, he searched his own soul. He did not want her to suffer any more pain

Dawn Elizabeth

than she already had. He wanted her to be happy again. He wanted her to be silly with her kids like she used to be. He wanted her to giggle, laugh, and sing. He wanted her tears to stop and her heart to heal. Their child was growing in her each day, and he or she would need his or her mom. This child would deserve the same kind of mother that Gregory and Tiffany had. It would be unfair for this child not to have the same loving mother like his or her siblings. There were so many things that Beth could instill in her children, both the son and daughter that she had raised into responsible teenagers and the baby she would deliver in a short time. She could teach them about love, true love, the way God had intended it to be. She could not do this as long as she held onto him, even in his spirit form.

Alex turned and walked towards the bag that held the beautiful gown stained with his blood. The chain mail knight's costume that he had never gotten the opportunity to wear was hanging, as if standing guard to all his memories. His heart held an intense pain that surpassed the physical pain he had experienced on that day when his body had been shredded by the shattered jagged pieces of glass from the windshield, when he was thrown like a rocket through it onto the concrete hardness of the ground. His love for Beth was endless and would go on forever. He could not bear to spend eternity watching her tormented and pulled apart any longer. There was a man who was alive who loved her deeply, a man who deserved to feel her love, a man who was meant to share her hopes and her dreams. This man would protect and love her child, Alex's child, as if that child were his own.

CIRCLE OF LOVE

There was a reason that they had been brought together, just as there was a reason that they had been torn apart. They both experienced a very special bond that very few people had the opportunity to feel. They had been chosen as His very special souls that would be united forever; even if their human forms died, their love would always remain. Alex looked up towards the heavens, as he finally understood the meaning of all the events. Slowly, he nodded his head and stepped forward, touching Beth's hand. He looked at his guardian angel and smiled. He remembered when Michael and he had first met on the beautiful rays of colors just outside of Heaven's gates. He recalled the words Michael had spoken on that day, "Love exists in letting go." He knew that the love that would exist would be the love of Joseph O'Dea and Beth Hanson, the love that would be allowed to exist once two souls finally let go.

Beth felt the beautiful tingling sensation travel from her fingertips deep into her soul. She had felt his hand upon hers as he led her towards the costumes. It was not necessary to keep her eyes closed because his presence was now stronger than she had ever felt before. His strong, large hand held her tiny one tightly as he guided her to remember that day. As she approached the garment bag, she felt his spirit walk around and stand at her side. She was not afraid of the memories and knew he would be there in support as she faced them. She slowly reached up and pulled the long zipper down, allowing an opening to its contents. She withdrew the bloodstained gown from its hanger and held it tightly in her arms. She looked at the many stains of blood that covered the once beautiful gown he

Dawn Elizabeth

had chosen for her. The blood that had been shed from his torn body on at day that was meant to be cherished, not mourned. As she held the dress in her arms, she felt Alex's spirit tell her to look at the knight's costume that remained hanging in the bag. She quickly unzipped the bag holding the silver costume and felt her heart lighten as she saw the way the sword's blade sparkled as the light caught it. She smiled as she imagined how magnificent Alex would have looked in the authentic-looking Renaissance costume. His beautiful dark hair would appear darker on the silvery chain mail. The definition of his muscles would be displayed in the dark leather shirt worn beneath it. She let her fingers run up and down the roughness of the silver mesh tunic, as she imagined how handsome he would have looked in this knight's costume. As she looked at the garment, she noticed a piece of paper that had been neatly folded and placed in the bottom of the bag. Quickly, she withdrew it and felt her heart race as she recognized Alex's handwriting on the paper. She took a deep breath and unfolded the worn piece of paper. Tears began to fill her eyes as she read what he had written.

> *If ever asked "Have I known love?*
> *My answer would be honest and true.*
> *I would answer that I fell in love,*
> *on the day that I met you.*
>
> *I would tell them how right it felt,*
> *when your arms were holding me,*
> *And how if I had my choice,*
> *there would be no other place,*
> *I would rather be.*

I would tell them how complete I felt,
Each time you stood by my side.
And how my heart was filled with joy
on the day I asked you to be my bride.

The question I ask today comes from my heart,
Knowing our love was meant to be,
Will you answer the question "Yes,"
And say you'll marry me?

She lowered herself and sat down on the wooden floor of the attic, holding the paper with his beautiful words written on it close to her heart. Her teardrops fell on the paper and smeared some of the words he had written. He had planned such a romantic way to propose to her and he had never had his chance to fulfill it. Her tears streamed down her cheeks as the bitterness in her heart escaped its prison. She felt him sit down on the floor next to her as his fingertips tried to dry her heartbroken tears.

"Alex, you know that I would have said yes," she began, each word quivering as she spoke. "It was a beautiful poem. It was such a sentimental gesture for you to go to such an elaborate plan because you wanted that day to be special for me. I know how deeply you love me. And even if I can't see you, or hear your deep wonderful voice...I know you are here with me. Death will never take you from me. Love never dies, Alex. I need to know what happened to you on that day. Please show me what happened. Show me the moments prior to the accident. Please...Alex. Let me see what you did. Let me feel

Dawn Elizabeth

what you felt." The tears now flowed down her cheeks in a steady stream as she cried out to her soul mate. Patiently, she remained sitting on the hard floor and waited for Alex's response.

Alex looked back at Michael as he listened to the request of the woman he loved. The angel closed his eyes and nodded. Alex knew, at that moment, the time was nearing for Beth to let go. He slowly raised his hand and touched her forehead taking her back to the day he had died.

Chapter 39

Beth felt her head swirl and spin as her soul was being guided back in time to the events that lead up to Alex's death. She knew that she was only an observer and would not be allowed to participate or change anything that she would see. It was only meant for her to understand what had happened on that day. She watched as she saw the excitement in Alex's eyes when he picked up the beautiful tear-shaped diamond engagement ring he had specially commissioned for her. The band of the ring was braided with both white and yellow gold. The diamond itself was a carat and, ironically, in the shape of a tear. The wedding band that matched it was in the matching braided pattern of white and yellow gold. The two rings lay in a small black velvet box that Alex had placed in his shirt pocket. Beth silently watched as he hummed along with a song on the radio and then noticed that his gas gauge was indicating he was low on fuel. She bit down on her lower lip as she observed the dizziness that had overwhelmed him when he tried to exit the vehicle. She felt a strangeness come over her when she looked and recognized the teal green truck that was parked at one of the other islands at the gas station. She continued to watch as Alex approached the door of the gas station. He had become overwhelmed with dizziness when Joseph O'Dea had exited the door. The lightheadedness had caused him to stumble, almost falling on the hard pavement. Her heart filled with a sense of pride as she watched Joseph help him before he collapsed. Her heart was flooded with a

Dawn Elizabeth

deep, compassionate love as she witnessed the two men communicate with each other, neither of them realizing that they had a special love for the same woman. Something in her heart told her that even if they did know they would not feel bitterness or hatred for the other.

The tears escaped her eyes at a rapid pace as she continued to watch Alex, driving and humming to a song on the radio, holding the velvet box in his hand. In slow motion, she watched it fall on the floor of his vehicle when he hit a bump in the road. She bit down hard on her lower lip when she saw him release his seat belt in order to reach the tiny box. She began to weep and sob uncontrollably as she saw Alex sat back up in his seat only to see the oncoming truck too late. As if in slow motion, his body was thrown through the windshield and hit the hard pavement. As if his body were a stone, it turned and bounced violently, shattering his bones and ripping his flesh, until finally he came to rest on the shoulder of the road, many yards from his crushed truck. She felt his sorrow as he lay on the side of the road, motionless, knowing he was dying. She listened as he prayed.

"Father, please don't take me until I have said goodbye to her," he began as the tears swelled in his eyes. "Please, Lord…my death is going to break her heart…I don't want her to suffer. I know that you will watch over her and take care of her when I am gone…but please don't let her be lonely. Don't let her live without love in her life. She has so much love to give, let there be someone who will cherish her as I do…allow her heart to love again…"

CIRCLE OF LOVE

She listened as he continued to pray, not for his life, but for hers. She felt her own heart ache when she understood that the pain that tortured him was not physical at all, but because he was worried about her continuing to live without him. Over and over, he pleaded with God to allow her to love again and never to feel the loneliness she had felt before they met.

Beth's body rocked back and forth as she felt the intoxicating love that he had felt for her on that day. She saw herself hold his head in her lap as she carefully tried to wipe the blood from his face. Her body began to tremble as she heard the last words he had said to her, "I will always love you, Princess." As his last words echoed through her mind she felt her soul slowly returning to the light in the attic. She lay down on the floor and curled up in a ball, never letting go of the costumes he had gotten for them. The tears of sorrow continued to flow down her face, and the droplets dripped onto the floor. She remained there for several hours, as she remembered and heard all the prayers Alex had made before he died. They were not prayers to spare his life, but rather pleas to God to watch over and take care of Beth.

"Oh, Alex", she sobbed, "I will not let your prayers be in vain. I will be the happy mother that our child deserves. I will teach this baby to love like we loved. He or she will always know what a wonderful man his or her father was and, how in our love for each other he or she was created. I will not feel sorry for myself any longer...I will cherish every minute of every day that we spent together, no matter how brief our time was. Love cannot be measured in hours or days or weeks. It is a feeling that lasts without boundaries of time. I will always love you, Alexander Fuentas. I will love you enough to let go."

Alex felt his heart being torn from his chest, as he realized that this was the last time Beth would feel his presence around her. He tried to hold onto her soul for as long as possible. He lowered himself down on the floor next to her and tenderly kissed her lips. He wiped the tears that were cried for him and held the teardrops in his hand. Tears swelled up in his eyes and ran down his face. A single tear made its way down and dropped onto Beth's cheek. The spirit's tear slowly moved to an area below her right eye. It remained leaving a pale white teardrop impression that would linger as a sign of his deep love for her throughout the remainder of her life. He felt her slowly being pulled from him, as if their souls were drifting apart. His own body began to tremble as he realized that, in her love for him, she was finally letting go. He sensed his soul lift up above her weeping body as he looked down upon her.

He looked back at Michael, who stood silently next to the window with his hands crossed in front of him. The angel knew that the love this man felt for this woman would fill the Kingdom of Heaven throughout all of time. Alex had made a sacrifice out of love, not selfishness. He had loved Beth and not wanted her to be lonely without him. He had grown fond of the man who would raise his child and love *his* Beth. He had not been jealous or bitter. He had allowed his own heart to be torn apart in order for his soul mate to go on living, giving her love to a man who had deserved it and needed it desperately.

CIRCLE OF LOVE

Michael walked over and embraced the soul that he had guided through life. He gradually released his arms and held his hand out towards a ray of light that illuminated the entire attic. The spectrum of colors danced on the ceiling and the angel and the dark haired spirit walked into it. The long white robe the angel was wearing began to sway back and forth as a magnificent white light encircled him. As Alex watched in amazement, spectacular large, white wings appeared on Michael's back. The angel bowed his head towards the light, as the sound of angels singing filled the room. Michael's wings expanded up and out behind his back, as he looked down and smiled at Alex. It was time for Alex to walk through the Gates of Heaven.

Chapter 40

It was a beautiful, crisp winter day. The trees were bare and had lost their leaves in the previous months as they slowly drifted off into a silent slumber until the beautiful sunlight of spring would awaken them. The sun was now hidden behind voluminous snow clouds as if it, too, were sleeping during the season. The squirrels and chipmunks had all hidden safely in their homes and the ducks that had grown happily in the pond behind Beth's house had gradually flown south for the winter. The familiar neighborhood seemed abnormally quiet and empty.

Beth was warm in her black leggings and long, white, baggy, hooded sweatshirt as she and Joe walked along the sidewalk. They routinely did their daily afternoon walk through the quiet subdivision to give them both the exercise they needed. Beth's belly had become huge as her baby grew rapidly in her womb. As she slowly walked, she leaned slightly back and felt as if she was a duck waddling from side-to-side in order to keep her balance, rather than walking in straight steady strides as Joseph was doing. She felt an inner warmth and affection as she walked with the man who had become her dear friend and companion during the last few months. She smiled to herself, thinking he looked very handsome in his nicely fitted blues jeans and hooded sweatshirt. He had allowed his facial hair to grow and now had a very nicely groomed beard. The dark beard covered some of the scars that he had sustained in his serious accident. He had also allowed his hair to grow out and it was now thick and wavy. A hint of gray hair interspersed through the dark hairs on his temples giving his appearance more character. His hazel eyes that once seemed extremely cold, were now full of warmth and love as he glanced over at Beth to make sure the walk was not too tiring for her.

As the two companions walked, they laughed and talked about scenes in a movie that they had watched together the night before. Since Joseph's accident, the two had remained together and grown exceptionally close. Beth had become Joe's personal nurse and took care of him when he was discharged from the hospital. She gave him encouragement and support when his physical pain became almost overwhelming. Her presence in his life was the perfect medicine and he healed very quickly both physically and emotionally.

As they turned to head down the block close to Beth's house they both heard a loud "pop", similar to the sound a large balloon would make if it were popped with a pin. Beth, caught off guard, came to an abrupt halt and looked down as the water gushed from between her legs. For a moment Joe stood and stared, amazed at the amount of water that soaked her pants.

Beth was the first to speak, "Oh goodness…Joseph…I think I we had better get back to the house!" She remained standing perfectly still, looking down at her now wet clothing. Her heart was filled with excitement as she realized that her child would be born soon and she would finally be able to hold him or her in her arms.

Joe didn't waste anytime. He wrapped his arm around Beth's now expanded waist and guided her back to the house. Luckily, they were not far at all and were finishing the last leg of the walk.

Dawn Elizabeth

"How are you feeling...any pain...any contractions...tell me if we are going too fast."

As they reached the front porch he quickly started to yell for both Greg and Tiffany.

"Greg! Tiffany...it's time to go! Get your mother's things! Greg, call the doctor...the number is by the phone...let him know we're on our way to the hospital! Kids..."

The two teenagers came running up the stairs from the family room when they heard Joseph shouting.

Tiffany had helped her mother pack her suitcase a few days before, in anticipation of the birth of her little brother or sister. She quickly ran to her mother's room to get it. Greg ran to the phone to call the doctor. He then grabbed the keys to his mother's car and dashed out the door to start it.

"Mom, how are you doing...everything okay...are you having any contractions?" the teenage boy asked with concern.

"Yeah, honey, I am okay...a bit nervous...and no...no contractions yet...my water just broke...did you get a hold of the doctor?"

"Yep, I sure did. He knows we're on our way. Tiff's getting your things. This is pretty exciting huh, Joe?"

"It sure is. It won't be long now and you will have a little brother or sister...I'm pretty excited about it too."

Beth smiled as Joe and Greg helped her in the car. She continually rubbed her stomach, waiting for the contractions to begin. Tiffany raced down the front steps with the suitcase in her hand and put it in the trunk.

CIRCLE OF LOVE

"Oh…wait a minute. There is something else I need to get for Mom. Be right back."

Beth looked up and began to laugh as she watched her teenage daughter coming out of the door with "Big Bear". As Tiffany jumped in the back seat and closed her door she leaned up in the seat behind her mother.

"Hey, this baby has to get to know "Big Bear" too. You take him everywhere. I thought you might like him with you now."

Beth grabbed the large teddy bear from her daughter and smiled.

"Thanks, honey. You're right I do take him everywhere."

Beth started to laugh, delighted with her daughter's gesture. Suddenly, she felt a strong contraction. She looked over at Joe, as she felt the intense pain increase in her lower back. "Joe, I think we better hurry. This baby is getting pretty anxious to come out into the world and meet us."

Tiffany tried to coach her mother through the contraction telling her to focus and breathe. "Come on, Mom…, find your focal point…that's it…let's breathe together…you're doing great.".

Gregory felt his stomach in knots, knowing that his mother was experiencing severe pain as her labor began. He remained quiet in the backseat and felt a strong sense of pride as he observed his younger sister remaining calm and collected as she acted as a coach to their mother. His job had been to notify her doctor at the first sign or indication that it was time. He had immediately called the doctor when he heard Joe's calls advising his mother's water had broken and knew the doctor would be waiting for them at the hospital.

Dawn Elizabeth

Joe smiled and winked at the young girl to let her know she was doing a good job as a coach. Quickly, he backed out of the driveway.

Joe remained calm as he drove to the hospital, happily thinking of the last several months with Beth. He had remained in her life after being released from the hospital and a love had grown between the two of them. He had not forced her into a romantic relationship and had only offered his friendship. They had decided that while she was pregnant they would not be intimate and would use the time to get to know each other. They did hold hands and hugged and shared kisses, but never took it beyond that point. Joseph had felt bad for the many years he had used Beth's body and wanted to make up for all the time they had lost. He had taken her to football games and basketball games. They had rented classic movie videos and cuddled on the couch eating buttery popcorn. He had sat by her side as Greg and Tiffany performed in band concerts at the school. He had taken her to her doctor's appointments and was with her during all the ultra-sounds. Unfortunately, the baby was always in the wrong position, so they were never able to see what its sex was. Beth had told Joe she didn't want to know anyway. She wanted to be surprised.

After many years of being afraid to love someone, Joseph O'Dea had opened his heart to Beth. He was no longer worried that he was not deserving of her love. On the contrary, his heart was flooded with joy beyond words as he observed the special light in her eyes whenever she looked into his. He knew that the sparkling came from the joy he had given to her. She

CIRCLE OF LOVE

had taken care of him after his accident, never leaving his side or complaining. She was the answer to his prayers. Oddly, it was on this day that he had decided to ask for her hand in marriage. He had found the most amazing ring and felt the small velvet box tucked safely inside the pocket of his hooded sweatshirt. He was planning on proposing to her that evening when he took her out for a candle lit dinner. For some reason, he had been overwhelmed with this strange feeling that told him he should bring the ring with him when they went for their walk, rather than leaving it at his home. Now, he wasn't sure if it would be an appropriate day to propose to her considering the baby was on its way. He decided he would wait and ask her in a couple of weeks, once everything settled down a bit.

Once the foursome arrived at the hospital, Beth was helped into a wheelchair and a nurse took them to the second floor for delivery. The teenagers were asked to remain in the waiting room and Joseph and Beth were taken to a private labor room. The nurses helped Beth into a gown and within minutes the doctor was in checking the progress of her labor. He told her that it would be a little while and that they would hook Beth and the baby up to the monitors to keep track of the baby's heart rate during the labor. He estimated that it would be a couple of hours before the baby would be born.

After the nurse had inserted her dreaded IV and she was lying as comfortable as possible on the bed anxiously waiting for the next contraction, Beth motioned for Joe to sit beside her on the bed. She knew that he had been preoccupied with something all day and had an idea what was distracting him.

Dawn Elizabeth

"Joe, you have been preoccupied with something all day, is there something you wanted to ask me?" she began.

"Ah…my question can wait," he began feeling overwhelmed with nervousness as he felt the velvet box tap against his abdomen when he sat down on the hospital bed.

"No, Joseph O'Dea, your question cannot wait! And if you aren't going to ask me, well, I am going to ask you." She said in a matter-of-fact tone. She quickly shifted to the right, allowing him more space to sit next to her. Her eyes sparkled with an amazing glow of happiness, as she patiently waited for his response.

Joseph looked down at her in the hospital bed as she remained looking at him waiting for his response.

"You are, are you?"

"Yes, I am…I would really be happy if you did the asking, but…if you won't I will…"

Joe's eyes shined brightly as he gazed at the woman who had captured his heart. Even as she lay on the cold hospital bed, going through the painful labor of childbirth, she reminded him of a beautiful angel. He tenderly picked up her hand and kissed it. Her tiny fingers were so silky soft and her fingernails beautiful manicured. Suddenly, he became incredibly anxious as he realized she was staring at him and waiting for him to ask his question. He reached into the large front pocket of his hooded shirt and pulled out a tiny black velvet box. He looked back at Beth as he saw her spot the tiny box that held a very special item that he hoped she would always love and cherish.

CIRCLE OF LOVE

"Well", he softly spoke, "I wanted to ask you a *very* special and *very* important question. But I wasn't sure if today would be appropriate or not..." He reached over and tenderly began to caress her soft cheek. For several moments he looked into her eyes and observed the tiny tears that had began to grow in them. He took in a deep breath then continued. "But since you said you would ask if I didn't...I think I had better go ahead." Joe felt the butterflies fluttering inside of his very nervous stomach. He knew that he was about to ask her a question that he had been waiting all his lifetime to ask. He wanted the words to be expressed beautifully and heartfelt, with the same strong deep emotion that now lived inside of his heart. He looked into her beautiful, blue eyes as she patiently waited for his question. He quietly took in a deep breath and began, "Beth, I have loved you for many years. I truly believe I fell in love with you on that very first day I saw you sitting at that desk in the office. I can still remember the way my heart raced the first time our eyes met. The feeling was incredibly strong and in some ways bittersweet. I was afraid of loving someone and I doubted myself. Yet...I wanted you in my life...somehow. But the awful position that I put you in was wrong and I deeply hurt you... for that I will always be sorry. Somehow though, I found the courage to follow my heart and it led me straight to you. By some wonderful miracle I was given a second chance...I found my inner strength. Beth, I can't imagine my life without you. I realize that no one knows how long he will live, or how long he will be granted the blessing of sharing his life with that one special person he loves... but I do know for as long or

Dawn Elizabeth

brief a time that I may have on this Earth, I want to spend the remainder of my life taking care of you, Gregory, Tiffany, and the precious baby that is about to come into this world. I know how deeply you loved, and will always love, the father of your baby and I would never attempt to take his place in your heart. Alexander was a wonderful man and he deserves your love for all eternity. But I have a feeling that he would be happy with the question I am about to ask. I feel deep in my soul that he is watching over you…us from Heaven and he is pleased because he knows I will give you the love that you so richly deserve. He knows that I will always take care of you. I think he also knows that I will love your child as if he or she were my own. Sweetheart, my precious Beth, what I am trying to say is I love you with the complete depths of my heart and soul. You have given my life and my heart back to me. You have helped me see that I do deserve to love and I am worthy of receiving it in return. You have become my best friend, my companion…you were my lover…would you do me the honor of also being my wife…Elizabeth Hanson, will you marry me?"

Beth looked up at Joseph from her bed, her eyes sparking with joy. She had waited a long time to hear those words and it sounded like angels were singing in the background when they were finally spoken.

"Oh, Joe…yes…yes, I will marry you. I have waited and hoped to hear those words…and I will always cherish this day because it not only is the day my child will come into this world…but it is also the day that his or her father's last wish and prayer for me was answered. I love you so much…and never stopped hoping that you would find your way to me."

CIRCLE OF LOVE

As she spoke her words, tiny sparkling tears of joy ran down her face. Joseph reached up and tenderly wiped them away.

Joseph then opened the tiny, black velvet box and withdrew the tiny ring. Beth's heart skipped a beat when she saw the tear-shaped diamond ring with the braided band of white and yellow gold. Joseph noticed the surprised look in her eyes when she saw the ring.

"Beth, I'm sorry, is something wrong?"

Beth smiled and replied, "No, nothing is wrong. It is a beautiful ring, Joseph, I will cherish it forever."

Joseph gently placed the ring on Beth's ring finger. He grinned when he saw the joy on her face as she stared down at her beautiful ring. Suddenly, an expression of deep physical pain appeared on her face as another contraction began.

He remained by her side and helped her with the breathing exercises that they had been taught in their birthing classes. He wiped the sweat from her brow as the pain and contractions increased. He felt an overwhelming feeling of warmth in his heart, as he knew that very soon there would be a precious baby that the two of them would love.

Chapter 41

Beth sat alone in her hospital bed with the tiny, warm bundle in her arms. She looked down upon the sleeping face of her precious newborn son. It was simply amazing how much he resembled his father, even as an infant. His head was covered with the same dark brown hair; his facial features soft and fine, his tiny mouth in the exact miniature shape of Alex's. His skin was the beautiful shade of light brown of his Hispanic ancestors. As she cradled him in her arms he slept peacefully, content and warm near his mother's heart.

Careful not to disturb him as he slept, Beth bent down and kissed his tiny forehead. Her soul was filled with happiness as she gazed lovingly at the child she and Alex had created. This was a child who was created out of the love and passion as two souls became united as one. Slowly, she started rocking from side to side as her thoughts drifted to the last time she had felt Alex's presence. He had been at her side when she went into the attic of her parent's home to face the memories she had tried to block from her heart. He had taken her back to the day of his accident, allowing her to hear his final prayers as he lay dying. She had lain on the floor of the attic and allowed the floodgates of her heart to be opened, as she felt the abundance of his undying love for her. Her heart had painfully ached, as she made a promise to him to go on living. She knew that it was at that moment that she would no longer be able to feel his spirit with her, although his love remained in her heart.

CIRCLE OF LOVE

She knew she was not alone in her despair, as she lay holding onto the gown covered with his blood. She had been given a miracle, as she felt his teardrop on her face. Each day, as she looked in her mirror, she would see the tiny pale scar that was white in color and in the shape of a single teardrop forever engraved below the outside corner of her right eye. The scar was a symbol of the pain he also felt as their souls were sent down different paths. She never told anyone how she received the tiny scar on her face; she felt it was a secret that she should keep inside her. "If only he could have stayed until his son was born," she thought sadly.

Suddenly, the familiar tingling sensation ran through her soul, the feeling incredibly intense and overwhelming. As she looked up, her room was filled with an array of magnificent colored beams of light, each beam radiating a beauty she had never seen or imagined before. Her heart began to pound as she recognized the face of the man dressed in white who was walking toward her. She felt her body shiver and tears rapidly swelled in her eyes as she gazed into the warm brown eyes of her newborn baby's father.

"Hello, Princess," he softly whispered, then tenderly reached down and caught a tear that had escaped from her eyes.

"Hello, my handsome knight. I had hoped that you would be able to see your son. I think he looks just like his handsome father. His name is Alexander Joseph," Beth said, each word quivering as she spoke.

"Yes, he does, for now… but as he grows he will be a combination of us both. He is a wonderful creation of us. You have given our son a very

Dawn Elizabeth

wonderful name, Beth. He is named after two very special men, both who deeply love his mother."

As Alex spoke to Beth, the tears continued to stream down her face. Moments earlier, she was remembering how she had felt his presence with her but had never been able to see him. Now, standing next to her bed drying her tears, she was able to see the man whose soul was connected with hers. He felt the love in her heart as strong as it had been when he was alive. It had not diminished after his death; perhaps it had grown stronger. He also felt the love she had for Joseph O'Dea and it overwhelmed his heart with an indescribable joy. He had fulfilled his destiny. Beth would live the rest of her life never feeling lonely or lost. Her prayers had been listened to and answered. She had the love of a man who would grow old and gray with her; who would share her hopes and dreams, a man who would protect and care for her.

Alex looked down at her hand and smiled as the tear shaped diamond twinkled in the rays of light.

"That ring was meant to be worn on your finger. It is a symbol of the circle of love we all share. He has no idea that it was the ring I had specially made for you. A certain very special guardian angel guided him to it…a very special angel who has watched over us all. Joseph O'Dea is a remarkable man with a soul made of gold. He will be a wonderful husband to you and a good father to my son."

As Alex remained standing next to Beth he felt her soul join with his for a brief moment. Her tears were rapidly flowing from her eyes as their bond allowed her to feel the reason she was finally able to see his spirit.

CIRCLE OF LOVE

"Princess, you and I will never say goodbye. Our bond continues through our son. I will be there when he speaks his first word and takes his first step. I will be sitting with him when he learns how to drive. I will feel his pain when he gets his heart broken for the first time. I will watch over him as he sleeps and sometimes I will be with him in his dreams. I will never leave his side. You see...I am his guardian angel. He will never be alone."

As she listened to the words he spoke to her, a smile appeared on her lips. She knew that even though his father would not be alive to hug him or hold him, he would always be there. Even though the young boy would not see him, he would know he was there.

"I will also be able to see you and Joe and the happiness the two of you will share. Don't feel guilty or that you are wrong in loving him, Beth. You were meant to love him. Our souls are unique in that we have a deep everlasting love for each other. It will go on throughout all of time. Our souls are filled with an enormous amount of love that is meant to be given to others. It is your time to give it someone who deserves and needs it. The angels in Heaven are smiling on you. Alexander Joseph is very special and he, too, was given a very special gift. In time, you will see it. Remember the words I spoke to you with my dying breath...I will always love you, Princess."

The man dressed in white then bent down and, for the last time, kissed the lips of his beautiful Beth, as she cradled their son in her arms. The tears continued to flow from her eyes, as she watched him walk back towards a ray of light that outshined the others. He stopped in the ray and looked lovingly back at the

Dawn Elizabeth

woman whose soul would forever be joined with his. Softly, he whispered,

"Remember, Princess, I am his guardian angel and I will remain with him for the rest of his life."

Beth felt as though the joy in her heart was going to explode when as she saw Alex grin and then lower his head. She could not contain her joyous laugh as the beautiful, large, white-feathered wings rose from his back, and she realized that her handsome Alex was now a beautiful guardian angel.

About the Author

Dawn Elizabeth began writing her first novel, *Circle of Love,* in 1998. She lives in Southeast Michigan with her husband and children, and is currently busy working on her next novel.

Printed in the United States
1234200001B/74